NORTH

NORTH

A Novel

BRAD KESSLER

THE OVERLOOK PRESS, NEW YORK

This edition first published in hardcover in 2021 by
The Overlook Press, an imprint of ABRAMS
195 Broadway, 9th floor
New York, NY 10007
www.overlookpress.com

Abrams books are available at special discounts when purchased in quantity
for premiums and promotions as well as fundraising or educational use.
Special editions can also be created to specification. For details,
contact specialsales@abramsbooks.com or the address above.

Library of Congress Control Number: 2021934972

Printed and bound in the United States
1 3 5 7 9 10 8 6 4 2

ISBN: 978-1-4197-5042-7
eISBN: 978-1-64700-108-7

ABRAMS The Art of Books
195 Broadway, New York, NY 10007
abramsbooks.com

FOR FARUDSA

AND

MOHAMMED

And we made the son of Mary and his mother a sign; and sheltered them on a high peaceful hill, watered by many springs.

The Qur'an, Surah 23

I

1

May 2017

Christopher Gathreaux shut his computer and pulled on boots. The blizzard wasn't due until evening, but already the skies outside looked ominous and slate blue. A foot of snow lay in the forecast. Ice accumulations. Whiteout conditions. The monastery would probably lose power. A nor'easter on the mountain in early May was not unheard of—but its timing could be disastrous. Especially to the apples in the monastery's orchard. A sudden drop in temperature could freeze the tender tips on the apple branches and kill the blossoms before they even bloomed. The whole crop would be ruined—if Christopher did nothing.

He climbed into a wool sweater and watch cap. Out the window the clouds lowered over Blue Mountain. The sky was turning a darker shade of denim each minute. It was only one in the afternoon but looked like twilight. He couldn't wait much longer. He'd miss the monks' midafternoon prayers—Nones—but hopefully return in time for Vespers. On his way out of the abbot's quarters, he switched off the lamp on his desk and hurried into the hall.

Outside, wind nearly knocked him over. The unleafed woods bent and roared. Bare oaks broomed the sky. Christopher hunched into the gale, hauling a roll of white row cover over one shoulder, a ladder over the other. When he reached the rise into the orchard, his wire-rim glasses were completely fogged, his face numb. Saplings shook in the squall. Ida

Reds and Gravensteins. McIntoshes and Northern Spies, their branches already ornate with buds. There were over two hundred apple trees in Blue Mountain Monastery's orchard. Christopher would only be able to cover a few. The monks made cider and apple butter as a way to feed themselves *by the labor of their own hands.* Yet cultivating anything on Blue Mountain was becoming harder each year, the winters growing too warm, the springs too cold, the weather unpredictable. The monks were aging too, growing too frail for the work. Few new vocations arrived to fill their empty seats. No one wanted to be a monk anymore in the twenty-first century. The long-hoped-for "monastic revival" the Order envisioned never materialized. Even Father Christopher had to admit: their way of life was dying.

He dropped the roll of row cover on the ground and stood before a Northern Spy sapling. He leaned the ladder into the branches, then shouldered the roll and started to climb. Wind caught the loose end of the cloth and kited it skyward, and Christopher had to reel it in. Then he carefully unwound the fabric clockwise around the tree's crown—as best he could—making a messy cocoon of its upper limbs.

By the time he'd used up all the cloth, he'd managed to cover only a dozen saplings. He climbed off the ladder and stood in the row to survey his work. The saplings looked mummified, or partly injured, with white cloth flapping around their crowns. His efforts might not amount to much but at least he'd tried.

The first snow stung his face. He warmed his hands with his breath, then had the sudden unnerving sense of being watched. When he turned, a towering moose was staring at him from the row. Christopher froze; the hairs rose on the back of his neck. The tall moose wobbled on thin legs a few yards away; she looked skeletal, sick, her bones jutting out beneath a ravaged hide. The moose were dying all over Blue Mountain that year, plagued by ticks kept alive by the warming winters. Christopher had seen their ruined carcasses crawling with ticks along the monastery roads. The calves and older cows succumbed first; this one looked ancient. She could barely stand.

She stared at Christopher in the incipient snow as if asking an unanswerable question. He crossed himself and stepped back. He'd leave the moose in peace in the orchard. Perhaps she'd make it through the storm. He'd pray for her that evening at Vespers, as he prayed each night for all of Creation. It seemed the only thing left for the monks to do: watch the world change . . . and pray.

2

Sahro Abdi Muse waited by the window at the Starbucks on Astor Place. The evening rush was over, the café thinning out, the streetlights burning orange in the dusk. She sat in a corner by a window with a blue knapsack by her feet and scanned the room for a sign. A nod. A knowing look. A cue someone had come to meet her—but no one looked back. Her driver was already thirty minutes late.

Outside on Astor Place pedestrians scurried past the window. Sahro caught her reflection in the glass—and almost didn't recognize herself: the bulky down coat, the red baseball cap, the new pair of jeans. Gone was her elegant hijab, her olive scarf, the long dirac, replaced with clothes she'd hoped would let her fit in. Yet who was she fooling, she wondered, sitting beside the window for all the world to see? Surely someone would notice she didn't belong. The *Alien*, the *Undocumented*. The names she'd recently learned: *Asylee. Terrorist. Haji*. Didn't she wear her unbelonging in her eyes? In her narrow face, her walnut skin? In her accent and overstuffed bag? She'd positioned her knapsack in front of her feet to hide the most incriminating thing of all. The bulge beneath her right pant leg: an ankle monitor she'd been forced to wear since leaving detention.

She eyed the others inside the café. Mostly young. Mostly White. A few Brown or Black. They looked like college students, staring intently into screens or talking loudly on phones. Sahro searched her own coat pockets before remembering she'd scrubbed her messages and e-mails earlier, erased her contacts, removed the battery and SIM card, and packed her phone away. That was the plan. Hide everything. Carry nothing north. Leave no trace behind. Arrive on time inside the Starbucks café at Astor Place and await the driver—a White woman, an American, whose name she didn't know but who'd be wearing, the woman texted, a "yellow-colored coat." Their drive would take eight hours, depending on traffic and weather. They'd reach Canada before dawn, and sometime the next day—inshallah—Sahro would find herself in Toronto, at Fartumo and Ahmed's friend's apartment on Dixon Road.

She'd memorized all the names and numbers (it was safer not to write anything down). The sanctuary people had coached her on the phone. She'd texted everyone earlier that afternoon. All was arranged. So why did she feel so anxious, so full of nameless dread? Hadn't she crossed more dangerous borders in harder countries, without the benefit of an escort and private driver? The sanctuary people were her safest option—everyone agreed. Most made it into Canada without a hitch.

—

A teen with spiked purple hair pushed through the café doors. A White girl in a pink tracksuit. A wave of nausea washed through Sahro. She checked the clock by the counter. She had to call the ICE parole officer in two hours as she had each night for the past few months. What if she missed her check-in and was still waiting without a workable phone? What if the driver wasn't coming at all?

She mouthed the words beneath her breath: *Allah, lighten the journey, make the distance easy. You are my Companion on the road.* She knew the dua by heart from saying it so often . . . *I seek refuge in You from this journey and hardship and from the wicked sights in store.* She watched the glass doors at the front of the café, the figures outside passing through the plaza. It was all still new to Sahro, the city and subway and crowds. Ever since she'd left detention in New Jersey the previous fall, she'd felt at sea. She'd been locked inside the warehouse for nearly two years and never saw sky the whole time and then had to adjust overnight to winter in New York City, the grayscape and concrete, the cold and leaden skies. She hid inside her American sponsor's apartment on 108th and Amsterdam, afraid to leave the one-room apartment on the first floor, afraid of the electronic monitor she'd been forced to wear, that others might see the device around her leg or hear its alarm go off. The city felt forbidding and cold. Even in the well-heated apartment Sahro wore every article of clothing she owned. She felt safer enclosed by four walls, inside the sunless apartment, huddled close to the hissing radiator with its wonderful heat. Angela Simms, her African American sponsor, was never around. The woman taught literature at a college in the city but was teaching that semester out of town. She'd generously offered Sahro keys to her apartment and the run of the place—her TV and books, the couch and bedroom and computer. Sahro was overwhelmed with gratitude—but lonely nonetheless. She had no family or friends in New York City, her phone the only lifeline to the outside world, to Aunt Waardo in Mogadishu and Uncle Cabdi Rashid and the cousins. To Fartumo and Ahmed in Ohio and the extended family network overseas. She'd spend hours on WhatsApp or messaging with friends on Facebook, and when she grew bored, she thumbed through books on her sponsor's shelves, reading what she could, writing down English words in her notebook, looking new ones up online. Making lists each day. New nouns. New verbs. She was waiting for her asylum hearing to be set, the date to be announced. For a phone call from her lawyer. Waiting for her life to begin, to be able to finally move to Columbus in Ohio, into Fartumo and Ahmed's house. Five times a day she washed in the tiled bathtub and performed *wudu*, then cleared a corner by the wall near the couch and set a sarong on the floor. She never missed her prayers, even when her sponsor was there; it was the only time in the course of those days when Sahro felt fleetingly grounded, a connection between herself and her God.

One weekend when Angela Simms was in town, she asked Sahro to join her for a walk in Central Park. Sahro was hesitant at first. She was still a little shy around Angela Simms—they'd hardly spent any time together—but Sahro said sure. It was early March and cold. Angela wore leather pants and hoop earrings, her hair in an uptwist; Sahro, her hijab and dumpy down coat. They walked together in frigid sunshine, past people jogging in the park. Sahro still felt self-conscious, unused to the stares from passing men, the comments they made, and Angela's sometimes casual—often cutting—replies.

They stopped at a street vendor's table on 125th Street, a display of baseball caps on wire racks. Angela Simms insisted on buying Sahro a baseball cap. Sahro protested at first, then found herself dizzily trying on caps while the Korean saleswoman held a hand mirror and announced the ball teams' names.

"*Mets. Cubs. Pirates . . .*"

Angela suggested the Dodgers, but Sahro chose a blue and scarlet cap with a large letter "A" on its front.

The saleswoman lifted two gloved thumbs.

"Los Angeles Angels," she said. "*Very good team!*"

Angela Simms made a face.

"You sure about that?" she asked.

Sahro said yes: "A" for her cousin Ayaan.

"It's your head." Angela shrugged.

Now inside the Starbucks Sahro wondered if Angela was right. The red cap felt too stiff, too bright, too new, her scalp heating up beneath its fabric. Her face felt suddenly flushed. Two White men in matching blue suits stepped through the door, then a Black teen carrying a cello case. What if Sahro was in the wrong café? What if the driver wasn't coming? A small gray-haired woman in a mustard coat appeared just then at her side. Round glasses perched on a ruddy face. Sahro hadn't seen her enter the café. The woman gave her a meaningful nod and stepped close.

"Sahro?" she whispered.

Sahro studied the gray-haired woman. She was older than Sahro expected. Pale face, cherry lipstick, close-cropped hair. A canvas tote hung over one shoulder.

"I'm Jane." The woman smiled. "Your driver."

—

Over the past two years on the road Sahro had learned to trust her intuition. Her grandparents were nomads, she often reminded herself, capable of moving through hostile environments inhabited by predators. Strangers, she learned, came in only two forms: those who'd help and those who'd harm—but mostly came the latter. The key was knowing the difference, discerning something deeper than their words, a sensation or feel. The way a person moved or looked, a concealment in their eyes. Allah would always help if Sahro was paying attention. That's what her grandmother said. *Watch. Hyenas are everywhere.* You learned quick in the Hawd—the scrublands—with the sheep and the goats. Angels came from light, djinns from fire. Americans, White people—the *gaalo*—were often hard to read. Sometimes they said one thing but meant another. Even their kindness was barbed—their need to be liked. And though Sahro's English helped, the language itself could deceive. It was best to trust no one. She learned that in Mexico. *No confiar en nadie.*

A crowd of schoolkids burst through the café doors. The barista was calling someone's name. The small gray-haired woman's smile had transformed into a downturned slash of lipstick.

"Are you okay, dear?" the woman asked.

She looked at Sahro with sympathy. Then two policemen stepped into the café and stood in line. Sahro's heart sank. She lifted her knapsack off the floor and nodded. Then she and the woman walked out of the café without saying another word.

—

Her plans had solidified only in the last few days. After months of awaiting her asylum hearing, the date had finally been set. The pro bono lawyer had phoned Sahro with the news—first the good (she was finally getting a hearing), then the bad (the judge assigned her case was a bastard). They called him "the two-percent judge." "Two-percent" because, out of the hundreds of cases he heard each month, he granted asylum to less than two percent. The chance of Sahro gaining asylum in the United States, in other words, was next to nothing.

She'd phoned Aunt Waardo in tears, waking her in the middle of the night in Mogadishu. After everything Sahro had been through—Mexico and Central America, her months in detention—surely she deserved a chance. Hadn't she been tested over and over? Hadn't she played by the rules, done all the right things, honestly asked for asylum? Why would they deny her now?

Waardo listened and waited, then spoke slowly over the phone: "We will fight," she said, "as we always have. We'll not give up now, *wallahi*. We will find a way."

Which is precisely what Aunt Waardo did. She phoned everyone in the family, in the extended nomadic network. Everyone she knew in Xamar. Fartumo and Ahmed in Ohio. Her nephews in Nairobi. Calls raced from Mogadishu to Oslo, Toronto to Medina, Addis to Dubai. Everyone voiced an opinion. Advice and warnings. Everyone on edge since the American election—everyone's plans thrown into doubt since talk of a *Muslim Ban*. Was it better for Sahro to go through a sham hearing in New York City, only to be put on a plane back to Somalia? After all the time and money, the anguish and pain? With only a two-percent outcome, wasn't it best to just pick up and walk away and disappear? Do what the ancestors always did? Find another pasture, another place farther north? Fartumo and Ahmed knew some Americans who might help. A sanctuary group that sheltered asylees and ferried them across the border to Canada. Yes, it was illegal (the lawyer couldn't know a thing, and neither should Sahro's American sponsor). But all the family agreed: Canada was now Sahro's best option. Go with the *gaalo*, the sanctuary people, they said. It was safer to be accompanied there. What other option was left?

—

The streets felt colder now in Lower Manhattan, the wind more cutting. The sidewalks smelled of spring rain. Sahro shivered in her down coat and pulled her knapsack tight to her shoulders. She followed the small gray-haired woman across a busy intersection. Shop grates shook in the wind. Buses braked; a siren wailed. She hadn't gotten used to the city's strange weather—warm one minute, freezing the next, the season they called "spring," the month named "May." The words themselves confused her. "May" was a noun that was also a verb (the present tense of "might") that itself could mean a separate thing ("power"). *Spring. May. Might.* English had so many double meanings; its words could be a key or a door, a camouflage or a veil. A language as unpredictable as the weather.

They hurried along a side street and entered an empty park. Leaves hissed under streetlamps. A lone figure stood under a lit arch. The gray-haired woman strode ahead. On the far side of the park she unlocked the doors of a Honda and they both climbed in. Sahro placed her knapsack in the back and sat in front. The driver started the engine and turned to Sahro in the dark.

"How are you feeling?" she asked.

"Okay," Sahro said, but her teeth were chattering now—from the chill or her nerves, she couldn't tell which.

The woman let out an empathetic sigh, then reached under her seat and produced a plastic bag, looked around, and pulled out a flip phone and passed it to Sahro.

The woman said the phone had been loaded with everything she needed. Phone numbers and apps. She should add her own contacts right away.

She reached under the seat again and handed Sahro a tool she called a "tin snips"; it looked like a heavy pair of scissors with cross-beaked blades. Sahro squeezed its plastic grips and looked at the driver.

"Here?" she asked.

"Yes, dear." The woman nodded.

"It's better before we leave."

Sahro bit her bottom lip and looked away.

—

Earlier that afternoon, she'd called Aunt Waardo for the last time. Her aunt set them on speakerphone, and Uncle Cabdi Rashid and all the cousins shouted good luck. Sahro put on a brave voice. She told them all she'd be fine, that she'd see them soon, maybe as early as next year, once she was settled in Canada. Maybe she could even come home to visit (though everyone knew she couldn't). Then Waardo got back on the phone and said she and the whole family were praying for her. May she have success, inshallah.

Afterward, Sahro took apart her phone and packed what little clothing she owned, her notebooks and pens. Cosmetics and coconut oil. Scarves and hijab. Underwear. Her bottle of black seed oil. Motrin. Then she left a note for Angela Simms in the apartment's kitchen on 108th and Amsterdam. She thanked her sponsor for her kindness and help, for letting her stay, and told her not to worry. She had to leave, she wrote, because "*the water is safer than the land*"—a reference to a poem that Angela Simms had once shared.

Sahro knew Angela would understand its meaning.

Before she left the apartment, she performed her prayers for the last time, unsure when she'd have a chance again. She unlatched the three locks on the door and let herself out, locked the door again, then stuffed the keys beneath the doorcrack—they almost didn't fit. She'd likely never see Angela Simms again. Just as she'd never see any of the women she'd lived with in detention: Shirin Kishani or Elena Ortiz or Inogenest from Abuja. Those she'd met who helped her on her way. Where had they all gone? Some sent back to their home countries, forced into marriage or jail, others trafficked overseas or maybe dead (like Dalmar and Ayaan), killed in a jungle or drowned somewhere in the sea. "Diaspora" was the English word for the Somali *qurba joog*: the scattering over the earth, a *dispersal of people*. Sahro had looked up the word in an English dictionary in detention. "Diaspora" meant "exile" but it also referred to a mineral, a greenish rock called diaspore, whose elements, when heated, vaporized into air. Wasn't that happening to all of them? Wasn't it happening to Sahro this very moment? A little heat, a little pressure. A small uptick in the earth's temperature, and they were all vaporizing into air, becoming ghosts?

—

The gray-haired woman was waiting in the driver's seat, the engine on. Sahro wondered who she really was and why she'd agreed to help; what was *she* getting out of the arrangement? She squeezed the snips in her hand again, then nervously looked through the windshield at the park. The lampposts, the pools of light. The tree trunks and path. Before the woman could stop her, Sahro pushed open the door and said she'd be right back, then stepped into the night.

She didn't wait to hear the woman's reply. She needed to be alone, to have a moment to herself. She hastened under the lampposts, gripping the snips tight in one hand—a weapon—her pocketknife in the other. She was shivering all over now, her forehead laved in sweat. She was getting sick; she was sure of it. Was it any wonder, after all the drama of the previous week? The all-night texts, the lack of sleep. The tense conversations with Waardo. The freezing apartment at 108th and Amsterdam, where the wonderful radiators had stopped working since the start of May.

She looked around and sat on an unlit bench beneath a tree. A different siren wailed somewhere in the night. A bass beat thumped from a passing vehicle on the perimeter of the park. She lifted the hem of her jeans and touched the cold plastic cylinder around her ankle. They'd let her out of the warehouse under the condition that she wear the thing until her hearing. For the privilege, the family had to pay six hundred dollars a week and she couldn't travel beyond the borough, and she had to report each evening to an ICE agent. All of which she'd dutifully done for months, the shackle a constant reminder her life was still on hold, that someone might be listening or watching wherever she went, while the GPS sent signals into space and someone read them on a screen, her exact coordinates, down to the degree and second, pinpointing her in place, the same technology the American forces used, Angela Simms once told her, to target bombs.

A car horn blared in the street. She looked around again to make sure no one was near. She'd learned long ago how to pray in public without anyone knowing, as she did now on the bench, without washing or finding the qibla. God would forgive her. Allah was All Merciful, especially to the traveler. She recited a shortened salat, two rakats, no prostrations. Even the Prophet, Peace Be Upon Him, once had to pray in a puddle of mud.

She lifted her foot onto the bench. She whispered the words: *Bismillaah ar-Rahman ar-Raheem Allahu la illaha ila hu.* She gripped the handles of the snips with two hands. *No slumber can seize Him nor sleep. His are all things inside heaven and earth.*

She angled the blades between the plastic band and her shin. *Who could intercede in His presence without His permission? He knows what appears before and after His creatures. His throne extends over the heavens and the earth.*

She squeezed the handles hard and felt the plastic snap. A tiny bird bone. The device chirped. A red light blinked. She pulled the monitor off her ankle and threw the beeping thing behind a bush.

—

Back in the car, the gray-haired woman looked relieved. She pulled the Honda away from the curb and they drove without speaking. Sahro shivered in her down coat. The woman pulled a fleece blanket to the front and set it on Sahro's lap.

"Rest now," she said. "Everything will be okay."

She patted Sahro awkwardly on the arm and turned the heat on high. Sahro reached into the front pocket of her knapsack and pulled out her bottle of black seed oil, unscrewed the cap, and squeezed a dropperful onto her tongue. They were passing streetlights, weaving among buses and trucks. And soon they sped along a highway. High-rises on the right, a river to the left, a long bridge strung with pearls of light. A terrible hollowness entered Sahro. Her head pulsed. She couldn't get warm. She was no longer a flashing dot somewhere on a computer screen but a fugitive now, a flame. A green rock. Diaspore: *a dispersal of gas.*

They drove out of the city and Sahro drifted in and out of sleep. She dreamt of her grandmother outside her hut in the Hawd. Her *ayeeyo*'s voice in her ear, reciting the family names. She dreamt of the villa on Via Sanca in Mogadishu, her cousins Dalmar and Ayaan, the neem tree in the courtyard, the turquoise sea.

When she woke again, she was discombobulated and shivering. She didn't know at first where they were and it hurt to swallow. A razor felt lodged in her throat.

"You had a good long sleep," the woman said cheerfully and added they were already hours north of New York City

Had she really slept that long?

The gray-haired woman offered her a bottle of water.

"Are you feeling better?" she asked.

"Yes," Sahro lied, and took the offered water.

"You had me worried," the driver said.

Sahro didn't answer. She drank water from the glass bottle.

She rose in her seat beneath the blanket, and something flashed in the dark. Moths in the headlights. Thousands of white moths, she thought at first. Then she rubbed her face and looked again at the white flakes flying into the headlights.

"Can you believe it?" the driver said. "It's snowing—in May!"

Sahro inched closer to the dashboard and clutched the fleece to her neck. She'd never seen snow before. Not home in Xamar or in the Hawd or the whole time in detention or inside Angela Simms's apartment. She'd seen snow only in photographs and movies, in postcards in Ayaan's room. They didn't even have a word for snow in Somalia.

She looked at the woman driving, then back at the windshield. The white flakes flew into the glass, millions fleeing out of the dark. The wipers clicked. The snow kept coming. And with each mile north the world turned whiter and whiter than Sahro had ever seen.

3

The groundskeeper woke to tapping on the windowpane—fluttery, insistent—as if the weather wanted in. The sashes shook. The glass ticked. A late spring storm orchestrated around Blue Mountain. Teddy Fletcher dozed again in the studio apartment above the monastery garage while wind raced around the walls and circled back and slammed the big bay doors downstairs.

His dog howled at the foot of the bed, and Teddy hushed her and rose heavily on one elbow, heart racing. Sleet pelted the windows . . . or was it snow? Any kind of weather was possible at three thousand feet in Vermont in May.

Cora growled and settled beside Teddy's foot. The digits blurred beside the bed. 3:55. He threw off the covers, breathing hard. He wouldn't sleep anymore that morning with the hammering wind, the hail or snow. Whatever the precipitation, he'd need to plow the roads and fill the Ford once more with salt.

He sat naked at the edge of the bed—a large man with curly red hair and beard—and groped for his prosthesis against the wall. Covering his face against the glare, he switched on a bedside lamp and grabbed the prosthetic liner and unrolled the cold silicone over his fleshy stump. He padded the stump with a ply of cotton, then fit the prosthesis over his thigh. When he stood, the leg's socket locked with the liner's pin: the metallic click the sound of the start of each day.

In the small attached kitchen he spooned sugar into his coffee while listening to the weather band. NOAA was issuing warnings. Wind advisories. Ice accumulations. Downed power lines. A half foot of snow had already fallen in Hart's Run. All the North Country was affected. Vermont's Northeast Kingdom hit the worst.

Teddy sawed a slice off the sourdough loaf the monks had baked; he knifed a gob of butter. Cora watched from across the room.

"You're not going to get up this morning, are you?" he asked.

The dog lifted one ear but otherwise didn't move. She'd already repositioned herself on top of Teddy's pillow. Part pit, part collie, she was twelve, maybe thirteen—he wasn't sure. He'd found her outside the base at Fort Irwin, all ribs and bitten ears from fights. She'd followed him since that day, eventually all the way east back home.

After he'd washed and dressed, Teddy took his coffee and bread and struggled with his boots by the door.

"So," he said to the dog. "Yes or no?"

Cora yawed but didn't rise, yet when Teddy swung open the door to the garage downstairs, he heard her toenails click across the floor, past his leg.

—

Staff Sergeant "Teddy" Fletcher Jr. (Eleven Bravo) had returned to Vermont after a decade away. He'd served half those years overseas in the longest war—twice deployed in Afghanistan—but the even longer one came later: the hospital stays and VA clinics, the rehab rooms and surgical suites. He returned to Vermont when his father was dying in the hospital in Hart's Run. At thirty-two years old, he flew home for the first time since his injury, his homecoming more bitter than sweet. His father was already on a ventilator, his mother in the nursing home, his ex-fiancée (and her newest baby) living with a new boyfriend. Everyone knew about Teddy's injury in Afghanistan, the Purple Heart, his rocky recovery, but everyone pretended nothing had changed, despite his disability and the extra pounds he'd put on since. He slept in his child-hood bedroom, in the house that belonged now to his sister. A galling arrangement, he on the bottom bunk, his surly teenage nephew on top. His sister's husband wouldn't allow Cora in the house, so he had to tie her up outside. He found himself growing testy inside the old house. A day after his father's funeral he borrowed his sister's car and drove up to Blue Mountain to get away.

For thirty years Teddy's father had worked as the groundskeeper at the monastery on Blue Mountain. Teddy himself had spent weeks working alongside his father there, mowing the monastery's fields in summer, working the woodlot in fall, staying overnight above the garage during deer season. The mountain always seemed to Teddy like a second home, safer than the one in town. The monastery sat on old Abenaki land, but Teddy's father liked to call it "ancestral Fletcher land," because their surname dated back to the first White settlers in that part of the world. In the old overgrown graveyards on Blue Mountain, you could still find the "Fletcher" name fading from the old marble slabs. The monks had bought the entire mountain back in the 1960s, yet Teddy always felt, like his father, an atavistic pull to the land. All eight hundred acres. He loved to hunt and fish in the woods up there on the mountain's slopes and in the rushing brooks.

The day he drove back to Blue Mountain, the private road to the monastery was already closed to the public, the boom gate locked across the road at the tollhouse. It was late October, the leaves already off the trees. *BLUE MOUNTAIN MONASTERY*, the sign read.

MONASTIC ENCLOSURE
PRIVATE ROAD
VISITORS STRICTLY
FORBIDDEN

Teddy keyed the code into the electronic pad (he remembered the numbers) and the metal boom lifted off its mount. He drove up the winding road to the cloister, parked in the field in front. He hadn't been back in ten years, but the place looked exactly as he recalled: beautiful and quiet, the unmowed meadow aflame in goldenrod. The cloister at the top of the field, all contemporary concrete, wood, and glass. The apse of the church angled above the meadow like the jutting prow of a landlocked ship.

Teddy let Cora out of the car. She bounded off, flushing birds. Teddy lumbered up the meadow. He was out of shape and still getting used to walking with his prosthesis. He hiked behind the cloister and took the path that led to the orchard. Cora raced ahead to the rows of trees, then stopped and barked at someone up a ladder.

When Teddy reached the tree, he called off Cora. He saw a monk in a cream-colored tunic, unperturbed in the branches, harvesting apples into a canvas sack. Teddy recognized him right away. Christopher Gathreaux waved to Teddy as if they'd just seen one another a week before, but when the monk climbed down the ladder and pulled off his hood, he greeted Teddy with an enormous smile and hug.

"Thanks be to God you've returned," the monk said, beaming ear to ear.

He held Teddy by the shoulders and stared into his face and called him the Prodigal Son. In Teddy's ten-year absence, "Brother" Christopher had become "Father" Christopher, the new abbot of the monastery, though the man looked exactly the same, the same wire-rim glasses and flannel-gray eyes, the large head and jug ears, the self-conscious grin. The only difference perhaps the thickness of his glasses and fewer hairs on his shaven head. The monks of Blue Mountain never quite seemed to age, Teddy thought; their faces only got shinier, more polished—like old doorknobs, much-handled, carved of wood.

The monk squatted and Cora tunneled into his tunic, tail whipping as Christopher rigorously rubbed her face and she licked his chin.

"Easy girl," Teddy said, but the monk waved him away and let the dog cover him in kisses.

Afterward, they talked about Teddy's disability and his father's passing. Christopher asked what Teddy had in mind for his future. He was due to retire from active duty any day now. Did he have a job lined up, the monk inquired. Was he thinking about returning to school?

Teddy wasn't sure. Everything was up in the air.

Father Christopher reached into his canvas sack, handed Teddy an apple, took one himself, and shined it on his tunic.

"Cheers," he said, and lifted the apple and bit.

Teddy followed suit, and they stood for a while eating apples, looking over the autumn orchard, not speaking.

Finally, the monk broke the silence.

"Have you ever thought about coming back here?" he asked. "To work for us?"

He looked at Teddy with raised eyebrows. He said the monks were looking for a new groundskeeper, someone to replace his father, may he rest in peace, and even though Teddy had been gone for a few years, nothing much ever changed in the monastery, and few people knew the mountain—the fields, the roads, the plumbing—as well as he. On top of that, Christopher added with a smile, Teddy knew how to deal with cranky old monks.

Teddy was touched by the abbot's offer, the confidence he had in him—despite his disability—a confidence Teddy didn't yet have in himself. He wasn't at all sure back then if he could handle the job.

Christopher waved a hand.

"I'm sure you have a lot on your mind," he said. "But if you're interested, we could all give it a try."

The man took a last bite from his apple and tossed the core into the grass and said it wasn't a bad year for the Northern Spies.

—

The Ford was loaded now, the tires chained, the spreader filled with salt. Cora lay on her paws in the passenger seat while Teddy reviewed the checklist in his head. *Chain saw. Brake fluid. Wipers.* A habit formed when he was a truck commander overseas. The SOP before heading outside the wire in Afghanistan. *Flashlight. Knife. Two-stroke oil.* Standard Operating Procedure. *Beretta pistol beneath the seat.*

He capped his thermos and set the truck in gear. The headlights made a theatre of the snow, a scrim of swirling white in dark. He drove out of the garage and dropped the plow and a jolt ran up his thigh.

Teddy knew the monastery roads practically in his sleep, all fifteen miles of asphalt and switchback that climbed from the valley three thousand feet to the top. He'd been repairing the private road long before he ever had a driver's license, patching potholes with his father each summer. He knew every ditch and culvert and where the frost heaves formed. Since his return, he'd slipped back into the way of life he recalled from his childhood: the monks in their cream-colored habits, their hoods and bells, the quiet rhythm of their days. The weight of the weather in the North Country proved a kind of ballast; it grounded Teddy in ways he'd forgotten before his return. He liked the ocean outside San Diego but never felt at home in Southern California. He'd missed the New England weather, the mushroomy smell of the woods. He'd accepted Father Christopher's offer on a trial basis at first. Two years earlier, when he left Walter Reed, he wasn't sure he'd ever get behind a wheel again. It wasn't so much the new leg or the pain but the sudden terror that sometimes seized him on the road. A white pickup rushing past. A trash bag fluttering on the shoulder. A man standing on a highway overpass. Anything could send him into a spiral. The doctors had showed him illustrations of the part of the brain. The amygdala. The place where it happened—fight or flight. They showered him with drugs, which made matters worse. But driving inside the enclosure on Blue Mountain usually felt safe.

In time he'd taken over the loft above the monastery's tool shop and garage—his father's old unfinished "office"—and converted the space into a studio apartment; hung Sheetrock, plumbed a small shower and sink, a Pullman kitchen. The monks were happy to have Teddy near, close enough to call in a pinch, and Teddy was content to be far from Hart's Run and the gossip of his hometown. The monks were easy to get along with. He already knew their idiosyncrasies, the way they lived inside their own world up there (*up their asses,* his father used to say). Always hatching half-baked ideas as to how to pay for the property's upkeep (brewing beer or tapping trees for maple syrup. Shiitake mushrooms. Alpaca wool). If, as a teen, Teddy didn't quite understand why a group of grown men would isolate themselves on top of a mountain in New England, he understood their motivation better now. He partly envied their isolation and regimen, the seeming ease of their lives, everything already decided for them, down to when to wake and what to eat and wear. It was not unlike the military.

A blast of wind shook the Ford. The cab shuddered. Snow shot into headlights. Teddy kept a steady hand on the joystick, feathering the plow, feeling the depths of new snow. They were entering Falls now, the flakes fatter, wetter, mixed with rain, the sky a wash of gray. He cracked the window and let in cold air, dawn already arriving. The chains rang on the road—*chunk, chunk, chunk*—a reassuring sound: iron on asphalt.

At the bottom of the mountain freezing rain swept across the valley. Birches bent, encased in snow and ice. Teddy opened his window by the tollhouse and typed numbers on the frozen keypad. Cora rose and sniffed the air while the boom gate lifted across the road. The two-lane highway beyond lay unplowed, the snow glazed in a sheet of freezing rain. Teddy pulled onto the roadway. Ice crunched under the tires. Cora stood on all fours, hackles raised. She let out a low, menacing growl.

She'd caught the scent of something on the air. A fox or cat. Maybe a moose or bear out of hibernation. Ice pinged off the windshield. Then Cora exploded into barks and lunged at the glass. Teddy's face went pale. A person stood on the highway in the sleet. A small figure in a yellow raincoat. Cora howled and pawed the dash. Teddy slowed and braked. Who'd be outside in the middle of nowhere in an ice storm? Had it not been for the dog's barking, Teddy might have believed he was seeing a ghost.

He shouted for Cora to sit. He tried to catch his breath. He set the emergency brake; when he looked up again, the small figure was waving him to the side of the road.

"*Stay!*" he shouted to Cora.

He shouldered open the door and dropped to the road. Fire shot up his leg. Sleet pelted his face. The person stood a few yards away, shouting something through the downpour. A woman's face beneath the hood. Gray hair, oval glasses. Rain on beet-red skin. She looked frightened and cold, feeble, old; she pointed down the bank to where a small red sedan rested one hundred feet off the road.

Cora was barking madly back in the cab, the woman already picking her way down the slope. Teddy saw the skid marks now in the slush where the vehicle had fishtailed and spun and gone off the road. He started down the icy slope, following the yellow raincoat into the swale, choosing his footing with care. The woman had reached the red Honda and was struggling with the passenger door, trying to get it open. As Teddy approached, he felt a tingling in his leg, then saw a slumped figure behind the fogged glass. His leg went liquid; a ringing rose in his ear. He dropped and tried to regulate his breathing. He hated the word *flashback* as much as the word *trigger*. For nothing ever flashed "back" or "triggered"; it was there all the time, on the surface of the skin, the phantom limb just under the flesh, nerves still alive, as real as living tissue.

The figure's head swiveled in the passenger's window. A Black woman's face appeared in the glass. A red cap. A startled look in her eyes.

The woman in the yellow coat was shouting something about the door, the ice, the snow. She looked at Teddy with exasperation now.

"Could you *please* help! I can't open the door!"

Teddy rose. The feeling came back in his knees. He stepped toward the passenger door and gripped the handle. He waved the woman inside back from the door. With one hard pull, the door flew open. The woman inside sat hunched and shivering, covered in a blue fleece blanket. The older woman reached inside to help her out, and Teddy watched the two emerge fitfully from the car, the older White woman supporting the younger Black woman's weight. She was tall and wore jeans and a down coat beneath the blanket. Her eyes dark, distrustful. She looked at Teddy briefly, then away. Her lips looked as if they were turning blue.

His questions kicked in first. The SOP. Standard Operating Procedure: Was she injured? Teddy asked. Bleeding? In pain? Did she know her name? The date? Where was she from?

The young woman looked up at Teddy with a blank expression. Could she even understand what he said?

"We need to get warm," the older woman said and started up the slope.

Something finally clicked with Teddy. The woman was right. Hypothermia took less than twenty minutes to set in, especially in wet and windy weather. He needed to get them someplace warm and safe ASAP.

He helped steady the girl on her feet and they started back up the slope. The blanket kept slipping off her coat, and the down was matting in the rain. He grabbed her arm unthinkingly; her skin felt ice to the touch.

At the truck, Teddy ordered Cora out of the cab, then helped the young woman into the Ford. Her eyes were open now, watchful, dark, suspicious. The older woman had disappeared and returned out of breath, lugging some bags. Teddy piled their luggage in the back while the older woman climbed in. He whistled Cora back into the cab, then pulled himself up behind and shut the door.

Freezing rain leapt off the glass. The wipers thunked. The older woman sat beside him; he could feel the seat shake from their shivering. He turned the heat on high. He needed to concentrate, to calm his nerves, his racing heart, to think of where to bring them. No nearby place was open at that hour. He doubted they'd reach Hart's Run with the icy roads, and calling the rescue squad was out of the question. There was no cell service in the valley.

He set the Ford in gear and gunned the engine and carved a U-turn in the highway.

He steered back to the tollhouse and punched numbers in the pad and sped up the slope. The cab smelled of wet wool and something pungent, different, an oil or perfume. Cora panted, tongue out, surveying the young woman in distress, who sat doubled over now, her mouth moving. She was uttering something beneath her breath, words half whispered, a foreign language. Was she talking to herself or praying? Teddy glanced at the older woman, but her eyes were shut as well. Cora leaned forward and set her front paws across the older woman's lap and rested her chin on the young woman's shivering knees. The dog looked back at Teddy as if for assurance, but Teddy was lost in thought. The monks forbade visitors and he was weighing where to bring the women. His tiny apartment? The old Guest House? The cloister? None were ideal.

Above the Falls the sleet turned back to snow. Heavy and wet and falling fast at elevation. The windows fogged with the heat and breath, the panting dog and wet clothes. Pins of sweat pricked Teddy's face beneath his beard. He cleared the windshield with fingers. His leg felt aflame. He itched all over. He wanted to open the window to let in some air. He wanted to open his leg to let in some space. Sometimes it happened with no warning, in a car or cinema or an aisle of a grocery store. The smell of barbecue. Liver in cling film.

He gripped the wheel tighter. Cora stood and leaned back into him. He could feel the dog's heart beating against his ribs or maybe his own heart beating into her back. He had to concentrate, to get everyone behind the wire safely. Back to base. It wasn't far now. A few kilometers. How many times had he woken from this dream, near but never close enough? Another few minutes up the mountain. Another mile. You kept your squad safe and worried last about yourself.

Cora looked back at him—and they drove upward, into squall.

4

Father Christopher walked the empty cloister in the dark. The Office of Vigils didn't begin for another forty minutes, but he hadn't slept all night. With all the howling wind, the electricity cutting in and out—the generator kicking on and off—he'd tossed and turned throughout the storm. When the worst seemed over, he'd gotten out of bed and wandered the cloister, checking doors and windows, the library and scriptorium, the Chapter Hall and kitchen, making sure everything was closed and sealed up tight.

Now, at four a.m., he entered the unlit church, the only light the red glow from the Sanctuary Lamp flickering in its glass flue. He made his way to the choir stall and sat in the abbot's seat. Snow ghosted dimly outside the tall altar window. The shadowy church looked clean and spare in the dark, the waxed wooden floors, the orthogonal timbers of interlocking spruce. Christopher liked arriving early before the others to prayer office and sitting alone in the empty space. It gave him time to close his eyes and collect himself. The Office of Vigils held a special place for him and the monks of Blue Mountain. Their Order had been charged for centuries with the task of waking before dawn and keeping watch through the dark for the new world to come. Seeing through the dark was part of their vocation, though lately Christopher had found it increasingly difficult to get out of bed before dawn.

He sat in the blond wood stall now and set his elbows on armrests, hands outstretched, palms open. The church smelled of frankincense and citrus cleanser. He tried not to dwell on the storm or damage to his apple trees or the paperwork piled on his desk. He followed his breath instead, inhale and exhale, and the slowing beat of his heart, and after a few minutes he settled into his seat, and that old feeling returned, which he hadn't experienced in so long—a feeling that he'd arrived at home.

In the old days, it used to happen faster. Years ago, the moment Christopher sat in the choir stall before prayer office, a pleasant calm always washed over him. He often felt like a passenger on a plane taxiing before takeoff. A feeling of surrender, of leave-taking, of someone else in control, while the engines keyed and roared and he ascended into air. But the feeling of lightness came less and less these days to Father Christopher. Ever since he'd been made abbot of the monastery, he felt more pilot than passenger, that even in church during prayer, he couldn't just sit back but needed to keep track of all the dials and details of flight, the workings of the office and the whole monastery that rested squarely on his shoulders.

Christopher's mentor, the old abbot Father Edward, used to say, "The monastery's a small ship, the abbot its captain. Your job is to keep the craft moving, the sailors meaningfully occupied and fed." Two years earlier, when Father Edward had announced his retirement, the whole community pleaded with the old abbot to stay. No one at the monastery had Father Edward's gravity or charisma; no one could fill his shoes. But Father Edward was firm. He'd served the Brothers faithfully for decades and at eighty-four he wanted to pass his remaining days as a true hermit outside the confines of the cloister. It was time, he said, to leave the cenobium and "live with the antelopes."

The monastery elected a new abbot. Much to Christopher's horror, he was chosen by all—even though Brother Bruno had been angling for the postition. Christopher didn't think he was equipped for the job. He was a hesitant public speaker, nervous and rambling, uncomfortable with being a mouthpiece for the monastery and the Order and, in theory, God. Plus, he'd only gone to art school and not to seminary, and he'd have to first become a priest. But Father Edward assured him it was no obstacle. He couldn't refuse the will of the community. Obedience was part of monastic life. Clearly his brothers, Edward said, saw the abbot inside him even if he didn't. And Father Edward wasn't going far, only a few hundred yards away to the stone building they called the Guest House. Near enough yet removed from the daily regimen inside the cloister. Christopher could always visit him anytime—which he did, often, to deliver Edward his mail or supper or bring in firewood or for confession or simply to sit with his old friend. He'd gone to him every day for the last two years, until the old man sickened and died the previous fall. Christopher hadn't been quite the same since.

The sound of footfalls broke Christopher's meditation. Sneakers squeaked out in the Cloister Walk. Brother Minh, the novice, was arriving to ring the bells for Vigils. Christopher listened with his eyes closed to the squeaking tread, the whoosh of the curtain in the corner, the click of the wheel and rock of the headstock overhead. The middle bell banged. The Angelus. Once. Twice. The third toll was a mistake— Christopher would have to school Minh on the ropes once more. Ease up on the rope. Drop the shoulders.

He breathed evenly into his belly and tried to collect himself again, but soon other sounds filled the space: the shuffle of arriving sandals. The organ bench scraped. Pages fluttered. And now the monks were all arriving in the dark, feeling their way in the shadows, as they did each morning, and seven times each day, so accustomed to each corner of the cloister, most could make it to their seats in total darkness. Christopher identified each monk by his footwear. The clap of Brother Bruno's clogs. The sandpaper of Ramon's Birkenstocks. The stomp of Anselm's boots. Lastly came the tap of Father Teilhard's walker as it loudly crossed the nave despite the two tennis balls padding its feet.

Christopher opened his eyes to the sight of robed figures settling into seats, switching on, then off their tiny reading lamps in the choir stall. Heads shadowed under hoods. Nine monks that morning—three missing—some wearing heavy sweaters or down vests over cream-colored tunics and slate scapulars. Then all the stall lights went out and the men sat for a moment in total darkness. Their coughing stopped. Their clearing throats. The silence grew deeper, more pointed. Christopher felt cold air against his skin. He waited an extra beat, then made a fist and rapped his ring against the wood of the stall—the abbot's sign to begin. Brother Bruno's voice rose from the dark.

"O Lord, open my lips, and my mouth will proclaim Thy praise."

The others soon joined in, standing in the stall, and the office began in earnest, five men on one side of the choir, four on the other, facing each other with the lectern and the lamp in between. Brother Luke sang the Invitatory, and Anselm at the organ gave the key, and the men chanted the opening psalm. It was Psalm 129 that morning, *De Profundis. Out of the depths I cry to You, O Lord. Lord, hear my voice!* They alternated each verse responsively, from one side of the choir to the other, so the men's voices washed back and forth like waves barely overlapping on a shore. Outside the altar window, the day was just beginning to take shape, the sky the smallest brushstrokes of plum blue. Christopher was reminded just then how gorgeous Vigils could be, with the men's voices reverberating in the choir and the snow sifting heavily outside the glass. Christopher's sister Ana, the biologist, once asked him skeptically what exactly they did all day in the monastery. He gave her the easy answer. Being a monk was a life of song, he said. "We sing."

They were a contemplative Order, the monks of Blue Mountain, their days spent in work and prayer. It said as much over the monastery's front door entrance: *Ora et Labora*, Prayer and Work, the old Benedictine motto carved into the wood. Their routine set to the season and the hour, the Divine Office laid out in ancient texts. *Lectio, Meditatio, Contemplatio, Oratio.* Reading, Meditation, Contemplation, Prayer. Each monk had his own job or craft and chore, and there were always community meetings to attend—Chapter meetings, lectures, chant practice, paperwork, housekeeping. Having lived on Blue Mountain for nearly twenty years, it still astonished Christopher how busy a contemplative monk's life could be.

The men finished the first nocturne and hymn and the reading from Romans 9 and started the second set of psalms. They chanted The Prayer for Renewal, Psalm 101. *For my days are vanishing like smoke, my bones burn away like a fire.* Christopher knew the words by heart, as did most of the men. Singing the psalms was their primary task, and each week they cycled through all 150, so the words became second nature . . . *I have become like a pelican in the wilderness, like an owl in desolate places.* Christopher mouthed the words now and thought of Father Edward. Not a day passed that he didn't miss his friend and confessor's stable presence in the monastery. Ever since Edward's death, Christopher felt as if he were on the brink of falling and no one was there to catch him. It wasn't so much Edward's dying as the manner in which he passed. His last terrible days Christopher alone had witnessed and kept secret. He wanted to protect the others in the cloister from the old abbot's last ravings, but the experience had shaken him. Worse, Christopher hadn't chosen a new confessor yet despite the community's insistence he do so. What was he waiting for?

He'd promised Brother Bruno, the prior, he'd choose a new confessor as soon as spring arrived.

Father John stepped to the lectern and read the second reading from the Book of Ruth. Then the next psalm started, 148, and as the chant flowed back and forth from one side of the choir to the other, Christopher relaxed again into the music, the praise of *sea monsters and deeps, fire and hail, snow and frost, winds that obey His words.* For he could always lose himself in the chant, in the breathing back and forth. *Mountains and hills, fruit trees and cedars . . . reptiles and birds on the wing.*

In the altar window, the morning had turned a potter's glaze, smalt blue. They were nearing the end. Another psalm. A versicle and response. The doxology. And before Christopher knew it, he gave the final blessing and dismissal from his seat; the office was over. The day begun.

The men shuffled slowly out of the stall, their cream-colored robes swaying side to side. No one spoke. Father Teilhard's walker clicked. Father John, Simon and Anselm, hoods down, recessed on either side roughly in the order of seniority, Brother Bruno and Ramon, Luke and Brother Minh, each figure vanishing toward the rear of the church.

Father Christopher alone remained behind. The Great Silence wouldn't end for another few hours, not until after Mass. He waited until the last footfall echoed in the church, then made his way to the altar and stood by the cold glass and faced the morning's dark. The snow still fell out there, without its former fury, as if in slow motion now. The dawn already held a hint of gray. Winters in Vermont at three thousand feet were hard to endure most years—they seemed to last forever—but this last had been the longest Christopher could recall. For five months they'd lived in a cloud. It was hard to keep up the spirits, especially with all the new weather: the Polar Vortex, the bomb cyclones. The warming summers. The world needed praying for more than ever before. Yet if the monastery was a lighthouse, as the Danish philosopher had said, who, Christopher wondered, could see their light, obscured as it was in the clouds?

5

Back in his apartment above the monastery garage, Teddy Fletcher played over that morning's events in his head: the shivering women in the Ford, the young Black one, the older White one. The drive up the mountain through the snow. It was not yet eight in the morning, but Teddy had already taken off his wet clothes and removed his prosthesis and swallowed two Ativan for his nerves. He'd fed Cora and switched on the police scanner and the weather band and poured himself a third coffee. He tried to rest now in his underwear, airing his stump, listening to the drone of the radios, a different frequency in each ear. He'd learned to monitor multiple channels while on patrol in Afghanistan— the company and battalion and local net—picking up vital words and phrases between the static. Hearing the right frequency in the Hindu Kush could mean the difference between life and death.

He sat with the white noise now looking out the small window at the already-melting snow, a tightness in his chest, his mind racing, rehashing the last few hours, the surprise of them. He'd driven the women to the monastery's empty Guest House and helped them inside. He'd turned the electric heat on high and built a fire in the old wood-stove and brought blankets from the closet for the young woman while the older woman made sure she was getting warm. When he suggested he call the rescue squad, the gray-haired woman looked flustered. All they needed was to get warm, she said, and then they'd be on their way. There was desperation in her voice, an entreaty in her eyes. Teddy could tell they were in some kind of other trouble—and he wondered now if he'd done the right thing. He'd acted decisively, but maybe he should have woken the abbot first? Asked his permission? Perhaps he should've just driven them to town or phoned the police—or should phone them now. The women obviously weren't tourists (it was too late for skiing, too early for camping). They'd been heading north, probably to Canada. The international border lay only fifty miles away.

In the old days, the illegals came from the north. But in the last few months, ever since the presidential election, a steady stream of foreigners had started trickling the opposite way. Teddy read about it in the local papers. Undocumented men and women and sometimes whole famlies coming north, slipping through the fields and forests into Quebec. South to north, like a river running in reverse.

Late last fall, he'd been clearing culverts at the bottom of the mountain, when a black SUV pulled up and parked in front of the monastery's tollhouse. Two uniformed men stepped out of the car and walked past the boom gate. It was early December, black-powder season, and Teddy thought at first they were game wardens, until they came closer to where he was working. One man wore the olive-green uniform and campaign hat of the Customs and Border Patrol. The other was dressed entirely in black.

Teddy stood in a ditch and rested his shovel, mud on his arms. The Customs agent squatted and took off his campaign hat and introduced himself. He was a slight man with a salt-and-pepper mustache. He said they were doing a tour of the area. The other man wore mirrored sunglasses and stood hands on hips, chewing gum and surveying the meadow. He wore a full service belt: radio, wrist restraints. Revolver. He seemed barely into his twenties. He looked as if he worked out at the gym.

"You guys are a long way from the border," Teddy observed.

The young man in black stepped forward and put a hand on his holster.

"New rules of engagement, sir," he said with a grin. "Jurisdiction's expanded to one hundred miles from the border. There's a lot going on up here. Have you seen any unusual activity lately?"

Teddy couldn't see the young man's eyes behind his mirrored glasses. His accent sounded Texan. He was probably a recent transfer. Teddy heard they were sending new agents north.

"What kind of unusual?" Teddy asked.

"Strangers," the man said. "Foreigners? Folks you don't recognize?"

He didn't have to say: *Black ones, Brown ones, Asians.* Teddy knew exactly what he'd meant.

Teddy said no, he'd seen no strangers, but the man seemed not to be listening anyhow. He'd reached into one of his pockets and held a business card between two fingers.

"Agent Fusco," the man said. "Number's on the card. Call if you see anything. Appreciate your vigilance."

The man leaned over the culvert and held out the card. Teddy looked at the older Customs agent, who smiled at him almost apologetically.

"Just doing our job, sir," the older man said and set his hat back on.

Teddy set down his shovel and reluctantly took the young man's card.

The older agent thanked him; the young one raised a finger in a half salute, then the two men turned and headed back to their vehicle. The initials on the back of the younger man's shirt read: ICE.

———

By eight thirty, showered and rested, Teddy was back in the Ford with Cora. The monks' "Great Silence" had ended by now and he could finally see Father Christopher about the women and ask what to do. He drove the narrow road to the cloister, plowing as he went, the snow deeper but lighter and easier to plow at the higher elevation. Puffs of white fell from phone lines. The clouds were beginning to disperse high above. Through his open windows, he could hear birdsong; he'd almost forgotten the season but knew that snow, however deep, never lasted long in May.

He let Cora out of the cab at the back of the cloister. She shook herself and wagged her tail and sniffed the snow. He felt a bit calmer now, the Ativan kicking in. Cora ran to the back door of the cloister—the entrance to the abbot's quarters—and waited, tail whipping, beside the door. She knew exactly who they were going to see. Up on the second floor, down the long carpeted hallway, before Teddy could even knock, he heard the abbot from the other side of the door say, "Come in."

—

Father Christopher sat behind a desk piled high with papers and books, an old PC and monitor. He wore a black watch cap and cable-knit sweater over his tunic and scapular. Cora raced around his desk and lifted her front paws into the monk's lap. Teddy didn't bother to correct her; he was used to Father Christopher indulging her; it made him secretly happy that the monk didn't mind the dog's presence—even encouraged her—despite wet paws.

The abbot nodded Teddy toward the chair opposite his desk. He was still rubbing Cora's muzzle roughly with two hands.

"Good morning," he said, looking up. "I see you've survived the storm?"

"Yes, sir," Teddy muttered and set his cap on his knee.

The abbot looked tired that morning. He finished with the dog, and Cora came over and stood beside Teddy.

"Why so early?" Christopher asked with a serious expression.

Teddy was suddenly unsure how to begin. He pointed Cora to the floor, and she circled and lay down and looked back at Teddy. He was thinking for some reason of the abandoned pets people always dropped off at the monastery's entrance in the mistaken belief that the monks would adopt them. In the last few years, whenever he'd found a litter of kittens left in a box or lost dog down at the tollhouse, he dealt with the animals himself and called the animal control officer. He never bothered Father Christopher with the news.

He began telling the monk now about the women in the storm, the older White woman and the young Black one, their car off the road. How both women had risked hypothermia—especially the younger one—and he'd had to make a quick decision, though he wasn't sure it was the right one.

"I brought them to the Guest House," he finally said. "It was the only place I could think of. They're recovering there now. I wanted to tell you as soon as possible."

Teddy swallowed and let his words register. The abbot sat listening with no expression; then he slowly nodded and made a long, barely perceptible sigh.

Teddy was used to Christopher's silence, his slow way of considering things. All the men on Blue Mountain seemed to operate on a slower RPM, everything moving at half speed—the exact opposite of the military, where decisions were made in a snap and reactions came swiftly, where, if you contemplated anything too long, you ended up dead.

He watched the abbot now swivel forward in his chair and stand, walk to the window, and peer out. He clasped both hands behind the back of his tunic and turned to Teddy.

"Are they okay?" he asked. "Both women?"

"Yes, sir, they're resting," he replied.

"Do they need medical attention?"

Teddy hesitated. He ran a hand through the red curls of his beard.

"I don't think so," he finally said. "The younger one, the foreigner, looked like she caught a bad chill. She was shaking all over. I suggested calling 911 but the older woman, the driver, didn't seem to like that idea."

The abbot looked up with sudden interest.

"Foreigner?" he asked.

"Yup." Teddy shook his head. "I'm pretty sure of it. African. Maybe

Middle Eastern. Dark-skinned. She was speaking something foreign, maybe Arabic?"

He looked at Christopher, who gazed back and said nothing. Then the abbot removed his glasses, one temple at a time, and held them delicately in his left palm.

"Why didn't the driver want you to call 911?" he asked.

Teddy shook his head. "She didn't say. I'm guessing she didn't want the trouble. The rescue squad would've taken too long anyhow to arrive. So . . ."

He looked up and didn't finish his thought. Christopher raised an eyebrow and gave Teddy a meaningful look, then turned to the window again.

Teddy sat back heavily in the chair and relaxed his shoulders. The hard part was over. He'd gotten out what he needed to, the debriefing done. Now it was up to the abbot to make the decision. He could call the police or the Border Patrol or let the two women stay—it was all the same to Teddy. Teddy would do whatever Christopher wanted. He'd follow the chain of command. *Do your job and don't ask questions.* That was the rule that had kept him alive overseas. *Keep your squad safe. Leave no one behind.* Everything else was an abstraction, even the mission itself: the Global War on Terror. He wasn't even sure now what that meant.

The abbot sank into his swivel chair. He let out a long exhalation and began cleaning his glasses with the cuff of his tunic. He asked Teddy more questions: Did he know where the women were driving from or where they were headed? Where was their car now and in what condition? Was he sure the foreign woman didn't need a doctor?

Teddy answered as best he could. Their car was still down the swale off the shoulder on the river road. He had no idea where either woman was from. They had packed bags and New York State plates, and on the back bumper of the Honda was a blue sticker with different religious symbols that read *Coexist*. He suspected the women were on their way to Canada, that the foreign girl was illegal.

The abbot said nothing. He set his glasses back on his nose and sat without speaking for a long time. Teddy allowed the silence to deepen. He'd grown used to the monks' long silences, the caverns in their conversations he'd learned not to leap into but to let pass. Cora looked back at him from the floor and thumped her tail, then set her chin back on her paws.

"Does anyone else know they're here?" Christopher finally asked.

"No, sir," Teddy said.

"Good . . ." the monk said, distracted. "Maybe we should keep it that way . . . for now."

Teddy nodded and the two men sat in silence again. The abbot shook his head and smiled mysteriously, for reasons Teddy couldn't fathom. It was just his way, the monk. The private thought. The peace that surpassed understanding. The clouds broke outside the window, and sudden sunshine filled the room before fading just as quickly.

"I suppose I'll be making a trip to the Guest House this morning," the abbot said almost cheerfully.

He smiled over the desk at Teddy; then his face turned suddenly solemn.

"And you?" he asked. "Are you okay?"

"Yup," Teddy said. "I'm good."

Christopher stared at him a moment longer.

"You'd tell me otherwise," the abbot asked, "right?"

Teddy nodded and flipped his cap back over his red curls. Cora stood and shook herself and started wagging her tail.

"She can read us better than we can," Christopher observed, a finger on his chin.

He looked at the dog, and Cora trotted over, tail whipping, and the abbot leaned down and scratched her muzzle again.

Teddy pushed himself out of the chair.

"I'll call you later," Christopher said. "I might need your help."

"Yes, sir," Teddy said and made his way to the door and called the dog. Before he left the room, Christopher stopped him.

"It sounds like you did the right thing this morning," the abbot said. "An act of mercy. Bless you."

Teddy shrugged and didn't answer. He wasn't sure at all about mercy, let alone if he'd done the right thing.

6

Christopher looked at the clock on his desk and let the words sink in: *The Guest House. Two women. A foreigner.* It was just after nine in the morning, halfway into the monks' work period. He'd napped through Lauds and Mass, finally catching up on some sleep, and woken a little before the groundskeeper arrived. He'd hoped to get out into the orchard during the work period to check on his apple trees, the saplings he'd covered before the storm—but now this. *A foreigner. African. Maybe Middle Eastern.* He partly wished to know nothing, to have been told nothing, that Teddy Fletcher had taken matters into his own hands. Wasn't that the role of the groundskeeper after all? To keep people off the grounds, out of the enclosure? Teddy's father wouldn't have been as accommodating as his son. Ted Sr. took perverse pleasure in escorting trespassers out of the enclosure and calling the state cops on them. Father Edward had called Ted Sr. the monks' "redheaded bulldog." Teddy Jr. had a bigger heart and sense of service, for which Christopher was grateful—most of the time.

He surveyed the papers on his desk and let out a long sigh. Bills and letters, next year's budget, the half-finished homily on Peter of Tarentaise—all of it would have to wait. Maybe it was for the best, the unwanted distraction. He was tired of penning homilies besides.

He stood and snaked a long gray scarf around his neck and climbed into a quilt-lined vest. He wondered why Teddy had brought the women to the Guest House, to Father Edward's "hermitage," of all places, the very spot Christopher had avoided all winter, unable yet to deal with the dead man's closets and drawers. Why couldn't Teddy have taken the women to his own apartment above the monastery garage? Why to the very site of Christopher's pain?

He made his way now along the hall and down the back steps, hoping to run into no one, to not have to explain anything. The May morning felt raw outside, but the bluebirds were back despite the snow, and in the kitchen garden, the rows of radishes and peas were already poking through the melt.

The Guest House came into view, the small stone cottage trimmed in red. Lamplight glowed in the casement window, and Christopher stopped in his tracks, overcome by a sudden pang of remorse. How many times had he seen that same warm glow in the window on gray mornings, a welcoming beacon, a sign of Edward's presence? In winter they'd sit by the woodstove and talk about everything from Edith Stein to the color theories of Kandinsky. Their conversations sometimes lasting days. No subject too strange or taboo—Tibetan sand mandalas, Cassian's *Conferences*, the surgical piano technique of Thelonious Monk. And just as often, the two men sat together in complete silence, watching the flames fall to ash, not needing words at all.

Christopher thought of Edward now as he approached the Guest House with growing trepidation. Footprints lay in the melting snow, evidence of that morning's activity. He clomped up the wooden ramp they'd built for Edward's old age. A tang of woodsmoke hung in the air. He composed himself, then knocked lightly on the door and went in unannounced—his only impulsive move.

"Hello," he shouted, and closed the heavy door behind him.

The smell stopped him short. An unfamiliar odor. Wet clothes, a perfume. Pungent, oregano-like. A fire blazed in the woodstove in the front room. A drenched down coat hung on a chair back, a pair of small white sneakers, tongues turned out, in front of the flames. *Do they want to set the whole damn place on fire?* He bristled. He hurried across the room and swung the stove door shut and slammed the damper rod down. The flames shrank instantly behind the glass.

When he turned, a small gray-haired woman in round glasses stood in the hall. She wore a brown pantsuit and stepped forward and held out a shaky hand.

"You must be the abbot," she said, attempting a smile behind her glasses.

Christopher studied the woman. The close-cropped hair, the nervous look, the rosacea—or was it frostbite? She retracted her hand and looked suddenly distressed. Christopher thought she might burst into tears.

"I hear you've had a terrible fright," Christopher finally said, softening. "Thanks be to God you're okay, that Teddy found you."

"Yes," the woman said anxiously. "I don't know what we would have done if he hadn't been there . . ."

She swallowed hard, then looked at Christopher.

". . . He probably saved our lives."

"Are you sure you're okay now?" Christopher asked.

"Yes." She nodded unconvincingly.

"And how is your friend?" he asked.

A pained expression crossed the woman's face. She looked down at her hands, then at the woodstove.

"She's running a fever, I'm afraid," the woman said.

"I'm sorry," Christopher replied. "Does she need a doctor?"

She avoided his gaze again and looked down the hall, then fluttered a hand in the air.

"I really don't think it's necessary," she said. "She just caught a chill. She needs time to rest."

She looked Christopher in the eyes for the first time, her face flushed now. He could see her uncertainty and doubt. She was biting her bottom lip. Hazel eyes behind glasses.

Christopher tried to frame the question as gently as he could.

"Do you *not* want to call a doctor," he asked, "because you're worried about her safety?"

The woman looked directly at Christopher but gave no answer.

"It's okay," Christopher assured her. "I think I understand your situation. You were headed north. Yes? That's not a problem."

The woman said nothing. A log spat in the fire. She put a hand to her neck and let out a long breath and then began pacing the room.

It all came out in a flood of words. Yes, they were heading to Canada, and her passenger was from "some other place," but the woman herself was just a volunteer, only a driver—an escort—and knew little about her passenger. She was only helping out. Being a good citizen. They were supposed to be at the border hours ago, then *this* happened and her cell phone had no service and she couldn't reach her contact and she worried about her passenger, her *client*, and wasn't sure exactly what to do.

She looked at Christopher pleadingly, then apologized and asked him to forget everything. She looked again on the verge of tears.

"You're safe here," Christopher said at last. "You have nothing to fear. This is a monastery. A sanctuary. How can I help you?"

He was a little surprised by the certainty in his words—and the sudden effect they had. The woman burst into tears.

"One second," he said and held up a hand.

He hurried to the kitchen and ran the tap. He filled a glass with water and returned to the front room, where the woman was still standing, wiping her cheeks now.

"Drink," he said.

She took the glass with shaky hands. He watched the muscles in her neck as she swallowed. She put the glass down and mouthed the words "thank you"—though they came out without any sound.

"Now," he said. "How can we help you and your friend?"

"I've got to get my car back on the road," the woman explained. "I need to send a text. My phone doesn't work . . . and . . ." She gestured toward Edward's old bedroom. ". . . she's in no shape to travel."

Christopher assured her the phone wouldn't be a problem; all she needed was the passcode. The car, he said, if it runs, the groundskeeper,

Teddy—the man who'd saved them that morning—might be able to get it back on the road. As for her passenger . . . her *client*—Christopher glanced down the hall.

"I'm sure she'll be fine," the woman interjected, nodding a little too assuredly. "I gave her Tylenol and had her drink a lot of water. I'm sure it's just a touch of fever. By tonight or maybe even this afternoon we'll get out of your hair."

Christopher listened and said nothing. He wondered about the woman in Edward's room. Was she really okay? Was she warm enough there? Edward's old bedroom tended to get drafty. Christopher used to plug in an electric heater at night during winter to keep the old man warm; he'd have to fetch it from the front closet.

The gray-haired woman held her cell phone in hand now and was waiting for Christopher.

"The passcode for the phone," he said, "is Northern Spy. One word."

The woman nodded and quickly typed in the word—wrong at first—she thought he'd said "Northern *Sky*."

"*Spy*," he corrected, "like 007."

"Oh," she said and tried again while he walked to the stove and opened the damper a turn. He was already thinking of practicalities. Food. Tea. Coffee. Towels. Breakfast. How could he bring anything from the refectory kitchen without alerting the others in the cloister? He'd have to call Teddy Fletcher about the woman's car.

When he looked up again, the woman was staring at the fire.

"It was a moose," she said softly, turning her gaze to Christopher.

"A moose?" he inquired.

"In the road. In the snow. I swerved to miss her."

"Did you?" Christopher asked.

The woman nodded but said nothing and neither did Christopher. They stood a moment, listening to the tick of the iron stove, the flame growing again behind the glass. Christopher surveyed the drying clothes on Edward's old armchair. The black down coat. A red baseball cap. A green silk scarf. He wondered where the other woman—the foreigner—was from. *African, maybe Middle Eastern*—but stopped himself before asking.

"You must be hungry," he said, turning to the woman. "I'll bring some tea . . . or do you prefer coffee?"

"Either is great," the woman said.

He realized he didn't know the woman's name, and neither did she know his. Perhaps it was best that way. Cleaner. The less one knew of the other.

"Make all the calls you need," he said. "There's tea in the kitchen in the upper cabinet and a kettle below, and I'll bring some milk and breakfast in a little while, and please," he added, "stay inside." The monastery grounds were technically off-limits to visitors, he explained, and he didn't want to give any of the monks a surprise.

"Of course," she said. Her face looked drained now.

He gave her a smile and turned to the woodstove. It was full enough for now. He'd come back later and load it again.

"Are you warm enough?" he asked.

"Yes, thank you," the woman said.

"Just leave the stove as it is. The damper is a bit tricky."

She looked as if she had something to say.

"What is it?" Christopher asked.

The woman waved her hand with the phone.

"Nothing," she said, then looked around the room and stepped close.

"Her name is Sahro," the woman said, confidentially, nodding toward Edward's bedroom. "She's been through quite a bit."

She swallowed and looked Christopher in the eye, then whispered: "She's from Somalia."

7

Sahro was four years old when they came to kill her parents—though she never learned the exact details, the who or why or exactly when. Sometimes over the years an image rose in her head, clear as a photograph: sunlight falling through breeze blocks in a room. Her mother facedown on the concrete floor. A yellow jerry can. The turquoise sea. Was the memory real, or one made up later on? The silence, the flies. Her father shouting, "Hide!" Blood on canvas boots. Water dripping somewhere in the room.

Later she learned her aunt had found them, her father outside in the courtyard, her mother in the kitchen, Sahro miraculously alive, hidden under a tarp behind some jerry cans inches from her lifeless mother. In the chaos of the days that followed, when everyone was fleeing the district, her aunt sent Sahro north with neighbors. It was safer north than in the city and Waardo gambled on the mercy of Sahro's father's family, however complicated the clan and web were made.

She remembered little of the journey, the long drive north. The sea of legs and swaying lorry. Bundles of bedding and rice. How she slept or ate or the number of nights, she didn't know. She knew only that at some point she was taken off the truck and left with others beneath an acacia beside the road. And sometime after, having slept, she was shaken awake by an old woman she'd never seen before squatting on heels in front of her face, a woman wearing a red wrap and rubber flip-flops who smelled of woodsmoke and leather. A string of black beads hung from a bony wrist. She held Sahro's chin in her grip, pulled her face one way, then the other, muttered something to herself, and let go.

"*Kaalay,*" she said and stood and took Sahro's hand and gestured for her to follow.

Sahro trailed the old woman in the red wrap and flip-flops into the scrub. They passed low bushes and thorn, a landscape of sand the shade of cinnamon, lizards skittering between rocks. The old woman held her beads and muttered as she walked, her words incomprehensible yet somehow soothing to Sahro, a kind of rhythm or coo, something familiar from the world back in the city with her mother and father, the breeze blocks and oil tins and view of the turquoise sea.

In the afternoon, a man and camel appeared in the bush accompanied by a procession of skipping goats. Black-and-white, hairy and horned, they nibbled at everything in sight. The old man lifted Sahro on top of the camel and secured her with a rope to a wooden saddle. Then all of them continued into the twilight—the man and woman, goats and camel—Sahro perched on top.

Their camp consisted of a dozen huts, thorn-wood fences, corrals for goats and sheep, hobbles for camels. Sahro was put to work right away tending baby goats. She learned from the old woman how to separate them from their mothers in the mornings and when to reunite them later. How to feed the weak ones and orphans from old soda bottles filled with milk. She helped carry water from the well and fill the troughs and watched how to hobble the mothers and milk them; after, the old woman always gave her a tin of milk, frothy and sweet and warm from the teats of the mother goat.

—

One afternoon the old woman motioned Sahro into the *aqal* and sat her on the straw mat inside the hut. She rummaged among the bedding and pots and pans and produced a yellow-and-tan Nescafé tin and opened its lid. She sat and took Sahro by the elbows and placed her between her legs in her lap, then took an old photo from the tin and brought it in front of both their faces.

"Look," the old woman said, tapping the photo with one finger.

A man and woman, both dressed in white, stood smiling on a beach. Clove-brown faces radiant in the sun, the blue behind. They looked young in the photo, but their features registered anyway. Her mother, her father. Sahro stared at their two faces side by side, and her chest began to burn. The old woman ran a finger on the photograph around Sahro's father.

"*Ismail*," she said. "*Wiilkaygiiyow.*"

Her voice cracked a little and she pulled Sahro tighter to her chest and they stared at the photo together for a long time.

"Ismail," she said. "My son."

—

From that day on her grandmother taught her the names, the long line of ancestors, her father's lineage. Each afternoon they sat outside the hut and her grandmother recited the names and Sahro repeated them back one at a time, each in order, like beads on a string, until they made a long chain leading back, her *ayeeyo* said, to the Prophet Himself, Peace Be Upon Him. That lineage, that chain, her ayeeyo said, was the most vital thing she owned: the rope that anchored her to the past and the future. A network of clan and sub-clan, the nomadic vine. If she knew the names, if she could recall them all, she'd never be lost in the world. If she knew where she'd come from, she'd know where she was going. She'd always have the names to hang on to.

At night, she slept in her ayeeyo's hut and learned how to handle the fire and bank the embers and blow them alive in the morning. How to mix the flour and soured milk for canjeero and let it ferment overnight. To circle the mix on the steel. How to peel cardamom pods and prepare tea and sugar for *shaah cadeys*. And when her grandfather slaughtered a camel, she was put in charge with the other children of keeping flies and birds away from the drying jerky.

At *dugsi* she wrote with charcoal sticks on narrow wooden boards and learned Arabic letters. *Alif* and *Ba*. The dotted *Ta* and *Thaa*. The school a shed of thorn-wood topped by a sheet of shiny tin, a floor of pure white sand. She learned the prayers by rote and when to pray them, the surahs and whole sections of the Qur'an. She loved everything about dugsi, the poles of light that leaked through the tin. The Arabic words and swooping script. She memorized whole surahs without knowing their exact meaning, but the sound seemed enough for Sahro, the Qur'an a kind of music, the sentences a camel she could ride. The teacher wore a white robe and small wire-rim glasses. He was bearded and young with hazelnut eyes, a gentle face, and a voice like velvet. Imam Torino, they called him, because—someone said—he had an Italian ancestor, though Sahro wasn't sure what that meant or if it was even true.

One day at dugsi, a group of men arrived in jeeps and vans. The school had been cleaned, the sand neatly raked, and a new milk-blue Somali flag hung from a makeshift pole. Arab men in kufiyahs and thobes clustered into the shed. A man in sunglasses gave a speech, then Imam Torino called some of the students and asked them to stand and recite Qur'anic verse. Sahro heard her name and Imam Torino was waving her to the front of the class. The men in kufiyahs watched; the other children did too. She picked her way to the front, and Imam Torino put a hand on her shoulder and asked Sahro to recite *Surah Ad-Duha*, The Morning Brightness.

The men waited. Sahro cleared her throat.

"By the morning brightness," she began, hesitantly. "By night when it grows still, your Lord has not forsaken you, nor does He hate you."

She stopped and looked up. Imam Torino urged her on.

"Did He not find you an orphan and shelter you," she said, closing her eyes now, "find you lost and guide you, find you in need and satisfy your need? So do not be harsh with the orphan and do not chide the one who asks for help; talk about the blessings of your Lord."

She stopped and opened her eyes. Imam Torino was beaming. The men in the kufiyahs were nodding too. She'd only forgotten a few words.

Afterward, Imam Torino gave the group a short speech about orphans and Islam; though Sahro had never thought of herself before as an orphan, it was clear the teacher was talking about her, an *orphan*, someone special, for wasn't the Prophet Himself, Peace Be Upon Him, an orphan too?

Later, the Arab men presented the students with new Qur'ans, gold calligraphy etched on their covers, pages thin as tissue. The first page inscribed: *A Gift from the Royal Family of Saudi Arabia.*

—

Sahro cherished her new Qur'an. She kept it wrapped in a piece of silk her grandmother gave her. She studied the script whenever she finished her chores or when out with the goats in the afternoon. Dried leaves inside the pages marked surahs she'd already memorized. *The Night Journey. The Cow. The Fig.* The Arab script seemed a kind of magic; it created a spell—that's what Imam Torino told her—that if you recited certain *ayat,* they protected you from trouble, that the words inside the Qur'an were unlike any others. They came directly from the Prophet, Peace Be Upon Him, and therefore had supernatural powers. They alone had been touched by Allah.

Sometimes in the afternoon, alone, Sahro put the book aside and found the Nescafé tin inside her grandmother's hut. She'd pry open the tight-fitting lid and take out the photograph of her mother and father; each time the burning came back into her chest. Old memories emerged: the whitewashed floor, her mother's black curls. Her father's big laugh, the smell of his small beard. She couldn't stay with the memories long (*men holding her mother down, blood on the boots, the terrified look in her eyes*). She'd put the photo back into the Nescafé tin (*the sound of flies, her father screaming, "Hide!"*) and smash the lid down and lock the images inside. Like djinn, they were best to keep bottled away.

Still, she asked her grandmother often about her mother and father, but her ayeeyo always told her the same thing: Her father went south to study in Mogadishu. He met her mother at university. They married. End of story.

When Sahro asked for more, her ayeeyo waved a hand dismissively and changed the subject; if Sahro persisted, her grandmother grew sharp and said *enough*. Some things were better off left unsaid.

—

Years passed in the northern scrublands—the Hawd—along with the seasons. The dry and wind and rains. The *xagaa, jiilaal,* and *gu*. They moved camp according to the weather. Everything depended upon the rains—which camels or goats would live, how much milk they'd have for the season, if there'd be enough to eat at all. It had worked that way for thousands of years, her grandfather said. Her people had learned to make milk from rocks, meat from stones. He told her about the twenty-eight Stations of the Moon, how the planets traveled like nomads themselves in the sky, appearing and disappearing in different seasons, and how once upon a time you could tell the weather from the stars—but all that had changed and the weather was no longer predictable. The seasons were broken. The dry seasons lasted longer and sometimes the gu failed to come.

One year when Sahro was around seven, the rains never arrived. The family moved higher into the hills, north toward Ethiopia. Each week they had to move again, forced farther and farther into the highlands, seeking elusive water and pasture that never appeared. The men went off with the camels, and the women set up camp. Sahro learned from the older women how to build the aqals: how to fetch gob wood and thorn and lace long, bendable poles into each other; how to weave the wood into a braid; then cover the frame with cloth or plastic or whatever tarps or rags or hides were on hand. The finished aqal became a solid structure, sturdy in the wind, easily taken down or built again. She learned each part, piece by piece, noun and verb. The language of the nomadic lands. The perfect expression, flexible, lightweight, sturdy. They walked their homes with them into the scrublands.

She remembered that period as a time of taking down and setting up huts, catching lizards and larks, barbets and grubs—anything to eat. Of being hungry most of the time, their goats growing thin and dying, the camels too. Butchering the old ones. A constant ache in her belly. The pots of water her ayeeyo put on the fire with a pinch of salt and dried grass. How Sahro would wait long into the night for the "soup" to cook, often falling asleep while waiting. And that was her grandmother's point; the soup wouldn't stave off hunger, but waiting for it might put Sahro to sleep.

During those nights beside the fire, or inside the confines of the hut, her grandmother told her stories, the old Somali folktales. The *Sheeko Soomaaliyeed*. Tales of rulers and queens. Animals who transformed themselves into people. The Hyena-Man, Qori-ismaris. The cannibal woman named Dhegdheer, or the beautiful Queen Aweelo who ruled over the whole country. She told her too how Somalia got its name. *So mal* meant, in the old nomadic language, "go milk." The nomads were always welcoming to guests. It was part of the nomadic code. So when a stranger showed up out of the scrub, the herder would greet them with the words "so mal." Go milk. Go milk the camel and have some food. Everyone knew how to milk a camel or goat. And that's how the country got its name: Somalia. A way of welcoming a stranger.

The stories distracted Sahro—at least momentarily; they swaddled her in her grandmother's words and kept the dark at bay, the hyenas and hunger. The wind at the flap of the hut.

But soon the drought grew worse. The plants and trees wilted and died. The water holes grew dry. A camel could last thirty-two days between watering points, a goat fifteen. Sheep even less. Then animals began dropping, and everyone left the scrublands, packed their aqals and tents, fled to the cities. North to Bosaso. West to Hargeisa. Some even south to the capital, Mogadishu, also known as Xamar. At least there was food in the cities. Government tents. The Red Crescent, the Red Cross. News traveled along the nomadic vine. A message sent to Mogadishu. To Aunt Waardo, Sahro's mother's sister in Xamar. Word came back: Send Sahro. It was safer now in the city. At least there she'd have a chance to survive.

—

One night around that time, Sahro stood with her grandfather under the stars. By then he'd shown her the planets and where each constellation appeared in the night sky: the Sky Camel, the Trench, the Den. The *Jid-Cirir*—the Milky Way—where the cruel son scattered his mother's bones across the night. The constellations were like separate clans, her grandfather told her. Each had their own section of sky and they often fought, but some stars could travel between sections. These stars belonged to many constellations but wholly to none, and in this way they were unusual and unique, like messengers able to travel safely between hostile worlds. Sahro was like those stars, he said. She had that ability too; she'd already shown it. She too could travel between worlds unharmed. It's what made her special.

Sahro listened. She didn't quite understand. She hardly remembered her Aunt Waardo, or the city by the sea. She didn't want to leave her grandparents, her home. She knew she was different. An orphan. Imam Torino had told her so. Still, she had so many questions. About her mother and father, about the conflicting clans, the constellations, the names her grandmother forced her to learn. But she didn't know what to ask or even how. All she knew was that she'd be tested, over and over again. Imam Torino told her in school that *ichtabar* made people perfect. Testing made them true. Ichtabar often took the form of a journey, and her own test was once more about to begin.

8

The monastery kitchen smelled of baking bread, and a large cauldron of soup simmered on a stove. At ten a.m., Christopher found the kitchen empty—the stainless steel counters, the green tiled walls—his timing fortunate. Brother Benison, the cook, had stepped away for a moment. Christopher hurried into the room and slipped into the larder. He filled a canvas sack with coffee, sugar, tea. A box of cereal. Two cans of tuna. A loaf of bread. In the walk-in cooler he added eggs, butter, cheese, apple juice. A jug of milk.

He managed to exit the kitchen before Brother Benison returned.

Back at the Guest House he found the gray-haired woman asleep in the armchair beside the woodstove. He tiptoed to the kitchen and unpacked the food and took out plates. On his way back through the hall, he couldn't help but see through the open bedroom door the young Somali woman, at least the outline of her body beneath white blankets. She was asleep in Edward's bed. Black hair on a white pillow. Christopher instantly averted his eyes and scurried past.

Now, at eleven a.m., he sat in the refectory with the others and took his midday meal—lentil soup and tuna salad. "Dinner" was the community's largest meal of the day. At that hour, the work period over, the monks sat around four long wooden tables set in a square and ate their common meal while listening to *Lectio Divina*—divine reading—a DVD or a book on tape or a live reader, or lector, one of the monks chosen that day for the task. The readings at mealtime ranged from religious books to biography, travel narratives to newly published novels. Often the novels they choose for luncheon *Lectio Divina*—Father Edward wryly observed—was more trashy than divine.

That week they were listening to a book on tape about the 1966 Florence flood and the famous "mud angels," the volunteers who'd come from all over the world to help clean Florence's artwork and streets. The topic greatly interested Christopher, but his mind was elsewhere that morning. He kept worrying about the women in the Guest House. Maybe he'd been rash in letting them stay. Surely someone would find out sooner rather than later. Secrets were impossible to keep in the cloister. Despite all the cant, monks loved to gab. Back when the monastery used sign language during the Great Silence (years before Christopher ever joined), the community had a universal sign for "idle chatter": two arms crossed at the elbows and ten fingers flapping. Father Edward always used the gesture to admonish his monks. The impish grin and wildly fluttering fingers his gentle way of saying: *Shut up.* Christopher missed Edward now more than ever; he could certainly use the old man's advice, if not his humor.

When dinner was over and the dishes cleared and the Office of Sext had come and gone, Christopher went to find Brother Bruno in the library, his usual spot at that hour. Bruno was sitting behind a computer in a corner in a slant of noonday light, his face—big glasses, black beard—reflected in the computer's screen. He didn't look up when Christopher appeared but grunted to let him know he knew he was there.

In the old days, internet access had seemed anathema to the idea of monastic life. What was the point of closing yourself off from the noise of the world—of *fuga mundi*—if you let the world and all its noise in digitally? The rules of the enclosure were much stricter before Christopher ever joined. Everything the monks read or listened to was first vetted. Books. Magazines. Cassette tapes. All approved by the Order with a stamp of *Nihil Obstat*. There was no TV, no cable. The news came filtered through the abbot, who alone received and read the papers that came by post. In this way the monks were insulated from the weekly ebb and flow of the news. They could step out of the present and enter a different octave of time, a deeper narrative. They could live inside what they called "Kairos time," the Dreamtime of monastic life.

But in the past few decades the monks had had to adjust to the internet. By the early 2000s a whole new generation had grown up with social media and the web. If the Order wanted to attract new vocations and survive, they'd have to adapt. Some of the older, solemn professed wanted nothing to do with the internet and its distractions. A debate simmered in the cloister for years between the purists and the adapters. Christopher sympathized with each side. Distraction in the monastery was an inevitable and perhaps necessary part of a monk's life. If a young monk couldn't deal with a little second-guessing or social media ennui, maybe he wasn't cut out for the life of a monk? Maybe the internet could act homeopathically; a little dose of online annoyance might actually effect a cure by driving the monk back into his cell and making him want to pray—or read a book?

Back then Brother Bruno was one of the most ardent purists. He argued that monks and books were practically synonymous; that monks had *made* books, copied books, safeguarded the printed word for thousands of years. Why give that up now for fleeting images on a screen? "We have our own internet," Bruno intoned back then. "We've had it for two thousand years. *It's called prayer!*"

Two decades later, ironically, Christopher always found Brother Bruno behind the computer screen in the afternoons, surfing the web. Christopher ribbed him now and then but tried not to rub it in. Though Christopher did wonder: when *was* the last time Bruno had actually read a book?

—

"Have you got a minute?" Christopher asked.

Bruno looked up with a curious expression and closed the browser with a mouse. He turned to Christopher and set both hands on his knees.

"Sit or walk?" he asked gruffly.

Christopher gave him a wan smile. *Sit or walk?* had always been Father Edward's question whenever he met anyone for spiritual direction. Both men knew the right answer: Walk. *Solvitur ambulando.* It is solved by walking.

Bruno pushed off his knees, and Christopher followed him out of the library and into the hall. They made their way across the stone floor to the Cloister Walk, where Christopher soon began telling Bruno about the morning's events. Bruno listened intently, inclining one ear toward Christopher. As prior of Blue Mountain, Brother Bruno was the monastery's second-in-command after Christopher. Both men had entered the cloister in their late twenties at roughly the same time. Both had been schooled by Father Edward, their novice master, but the two men couldn't have been more different in temperament. There was a time when everything about Bruno irritated Christopher, his piety and self-righteous opinions, the way he corrected people in choir practice, his rigid adherence to "tradition" (even the way he sucked his teeth after a meal). Bruno had gone to seminary and lived with the Carthusians for a year, which lent him an air of superiority, especially toward Christopher, who'd only attended art school and had little theological training. But Father Edward treated both men equally and relished their differences. Edward, who'd been a Jesuit, believed in the concept of *agere contra*, "to act against," as a way of growing spiritually. If someone rubbed you the wrong way, you could use them as sandpaper to smooth your own edges, to balance your own prejudices, to find the sweetness hidden inside their bitterness. Once during confession Edward explained that Bruno was the vinegar—the acid—to Christopher's oil. You needed both to make a meal or eat a salad. What Father Edward never said but seemed to imply was that the oil always calmed the water; it usually ended up on top.

Over the years Christopher had gotten used to Bruno and Bruno had softened toward Christopher, who now felt a grudging comfort in Bruno's presence, a kind of counterweight. They'd both made it through the novitiate together and through the decades after, even though their politics were often at odds. They'd both picked up some of Father Edward's mannerisms (the tilt of the head, the look at the floor, the hand-clasp behind the back), so much that being around Brother Bruno now was the closest Christopher came to being around Father Edward. At least they shared a similar body language, if not always the same worldview.

Christopher finished telling Bruno about the women in the Guest House. He didn't go into any detail. He didn't tell Bruno that one of the women was from Somalia and likely undocumented, or that the two women were on their way to Canada. What was the point in opening that can of worms? Instead, he played down the situation and said it was only an act of mercy, letting two stranded strangers spend the night.

They'd reached the north end of the Cloister Walk and were looking out the large window into the garth, where the midday sun was warm against the white colonnades.

"So," Bruno said, touching his chin with two fingers. "Let me get this straight. Their car skidded off the road and they nearly froze and one of them is sick but nobody saw fit to call an ambulance or 911?"

"No," Christopher conceded.

"Don't you think that might be a good idea?" Bruno asked.

Christopher didn't answer right away. He began walking again and Bruno followed.

"I didn't want to disturb the community," Christopher said. "I don't think we need the drama of an ambulance or rescue squad. Besides, they're already on the mend. The accident happened hours ago."

Bruno shook his head but said nothing. Christopher continued walking; he could sense Brother Bruno's disapproval, his turning over the matter in his head. They walked side by side like skaters, hands clasped behind their backs. The plaster walls of the Cloister Walk were carefully inlaid with objects from around the world, tiles and tesserae from Rome, a mosaic from Constantinople, a chunk of travertine, even a mani stone from Tibet. The design Edward's idea, the inlaid mosaics and niches and ceramics for each Station of the Cross. Christopher said the women would probably just spend the night and be gone the next day. He was only telling Bruno out of due diligence. He didn't want to hide anything from the prior.

"I'm not sure it's a good idea," Bruno offered, unable to contain himself.

"Which part?" Christopher asked.

"Both," he said. "Letting the women stay and not telling the others. Everyone will find out sooner or later."

Christopher nodded noncommittally.

"You'll have to call a community meeting," Bruno said decisively.

"I supposed there's no getting around it," Christopher mused.

"And then everyone can have their say."

Christopher shook his head but made no reply.

They came to the other end of the walk overlooking the little quadrangle outside the glass. The weeping birches and pollarded willows, protected from the wind, had already let out their golden catkins in the melting snow. A "weeping garden" in the garth was also Father Edward's idea. A tiny Gethsemane in the heart of the cloister, the center of their lives.

Christopher turned to Bruno.

"Can you wait before telling anyone?" Christopher asked.

Bruno clasped his hands in front of his stomach and looked out the window at the willows.

"How long do you want me to wait?" he asked exactingly.

"Twenty-four hours," Christopher said. "One day."

That's all he was asking. A day might do. He wanted to keep the monks innocent as long as he could.

9

Throughout the day Teddy Fletcher wondered about the women in the Guest House and what the abbot had decided to do. In the morning he'd half expected to hear the siren of an approaching emergency vehicle, the rescue squad or state police, climbing the access road. But in the afternoon Father Christopher phoned and asked Teddy if he could recover the woman's car from the side of the highway. Drive or tow or winch it up the bank. He wanted to help the women get on their way. Teddy was surprised by the abbot's involvement. He said he'd give it a try, though it would be easier the next morning when the ground was frozen again.

"Maybe you can try it earlier than that?" the abbot suggested.

"Sure," Teddy replied, he'd do it that evening, then asked if the "foreign woman" was feeling any better.

"To be honest," the abbot said after a beat, "I'm not at all sure."

—

At six p.m. Teddy was back in the Ford for the fourth time that day. Cora joined him in the cab. Fourteen hours had passed since he'd found the women that morning in the blizzard, but it almost felt like days. He drove now with the late sun slipping through the trees. The snow had all melted from the mountain, and the sound of robins came through the cab window. He used to love this time of year, before the mountains greened. Spring turkeys and wild leeks. The season of long twilights and whistling woodcocks overhead.

Down by the highway the valley was already sunk in shadow. He pulled on the truck's low beams and flashers. The woman's car lay where they'd left it hours ago, half-hidden now in twilight. He backed the Ford as close to the bank as possible, cut the engine, and told Cora to stay in the cab.

He picked his way down the spongy bank. Spring peepers belled loudly from the swale. A damp cold rose from the earth. He heard a car approach on the highway and stood motionless, undetected in the half dark, as the vehicle flew past. He didn't like being down in the valley at this hour. Twilight always brought danger in the Hindu Kush. The enemy liked to attack at dawn and dusk.

New boot prints lay hardening in the mud. Large, fresh, alarming— they led straight to the Honda. A new fluorescent green sign hung on the car's passenger-side window. Teddy read the "Abandoned Vehicle Warning." The vehicle's operator had seventy-two hours to remove the car from the state highway before it was towed at the owner's expense. Teddy read the time and date entered by hand. The trooper's name: *B. Desautel.* Was it Brendan or Brian? Teddy forgot all their names. His sister would know which one became a cop. So would his ex, who'd married into the Desautel clan.

The keys lay on the Honda's dashboard. Teddy tried the ignition, but the battery was dead. He got out and inspected the vehicle for damage, then headed back to the truck for the block and cable.

Not two months into his first deployment, Teddy found out about his fiancée's affair. Teddy's sister told him. She'd seen Karen and Dale Desautel at the Bog, the local pub. They didn't even try to hide it. Everyone knew Karen was already pregnant and Teddy overseas, but the Desautels were snakes (his sister reminded him), every one of them. Years later now, Teddy felt mostly relieved to have little to do with Karen Petit and her family's drama. The Desautels and LaCrosses. The Beaudrys and Petits. The Prues. He'd joined the military in part to get away from the valley's five families, their infighting and feuds. Fort

Bragg offered a fresh start, a way to get out. But now that he was back, the name "Desautel" still rattled—he had to admit.

He dragged the snatch block and cable from the truck bed. The river road was growing dark. The Ford's flashers painted the swale behind in an eerie orange glow. Back at the Honda he rigged the snatch block and the pulley and hooked the cable to the undercarriage, then trudged back to the truck.

Some days in the Hindu Kush his squad had spent hours rescuing their own disabled vehicles. MRAPs and Humvees and gun trucks. The terrain in Barmal Province tore up tires, and their top-heavy vehicles always ran into ruts or bogged down in sand or mud. One afternoon during his second deployment they were convoying to a new outpost on a road little more than a moonscape. A steep slope dropped sharply to the right. A pothole to the left. Lopez, the driver, jerked the wheel and suddenly they were airborne, rolling to the right, plummeting through empty air. The sky upended. Teddy's stomach flew into his throat. When they stopped moving, he hung upside down in his harness, Lopez too. They called a head count. Lopez, Doniger, Cody, Dee; they all hung in their harnesses like bats. Teddy climbed out the way he'd trained; and when they all emerged uninjured, Byron Dee started laughing and the others joined in, slowly at first, then uncontrollably, like a bunch of schoolboys. Even Teddy couldn't resist the laughter, or the razzing they gave Lopez for driving them off a cliff.

The rest of the platoon by then had scrambled down the scree and set up a wide perimeter. The medic checked for injuries. The on-site commander made a quick assessment; the lieutenant called for assistance.

After the excitement, the ridicule and ribbing from the others, Teddy turned somber. Why did it have to be *his* vehicle? *His* guys? He'd already been a target because of his red curls and size, because he was from Vermont. The hillbilly. The Yankee. The Red. He knew he'd get shit now for the rest of the mission. Especially after they tried recovering the vehicle without success. In the end, they had to abandon and destroy his gun truck. A new RG-31. Better to blow it up than leave it behind for the enemy.

He thought of that day nine years earlier now. The late-afternoon light in the Hindu Kush. The laughter and embarrassment that followed. The decision to pack the MRAP with explosives. The night coming on. Some locals appeared out of nowhere and lined up to watch on a nearby ridge. Yes, the Americans were going to blow up their own fucking truck. Put on a show for Haji. Millions of dollars' worth. A squad was sent to keep the locals at bay. Everyone took cover. When the upturned truck exploded, the Americans whooped and hollered; what else were they to do? Fireworks! The Fourth of July! They loved blowing shit up. But Teddy secretly felt ashamed. He caught Lopez's eye over the others, and they smiled wanly at one another—then both looked away.

—

Teddy pulled on gloves and started the winch. He watched the cable lift off the ground in the dusk. The line reached all the way to the Honda, where it caught the undercarriage and jerked the car an inch. For a moment the Honda seemed to dig deeper into the mud, and Teddy thought he'd rigged the tackle wrong and cursed—but before he cut the winch, the Honda's front tires freed themselves and the car rose from the mud. He watched it being dragged in the twilight, all the way up the slope, until it reached the road.

Later, after he'd jumped the Honda and driven it behind the toll-house, after he drove the truck there too, he let Cora out of the cab. She shook herself and stretched, then trotted to each wheel of the Honda, sniffed the muddy tires, squatted and peed. It was fully dark now. Teddy could hear the river across the road. A woodcock high overhead. He'd promised Father Christopher he'd give the woman's car a quick inspection. He let the battery charge while he looked under the hood and beneath the carriage with a flashlight. The vehicle seemed largely unscathed. The women had been lucky. The car could've easily rolled—wet snow was the worst; and once a car rolled over, it was never the same again. The metal suffered extrusions. Compressions. Unseen stress fractures to the frame. Nothing ever aligned again. Teddy knew all about it from vehicles he'd driven in Afghanistan. Even if you couldn't see the damage on the surface, the steel was never the same. Metal had a memory of its own.

10

Sahro Abdi Muse woke later that night to moonlight streaming in a window. She thought at first she was inside a dream, the light so strong and blue, it looked like liquid pooled in the room. Moonlight lacquered the floor and spilled onto the walls and lapped at the sides of her bed. A blue insistence. A tide. A bell was banging somewhere in the night. She felt hot and chilled and realized all at once her body was burning with fever.

She rose with a pounding heart, shivering violently in sweat-damp sheets. She didn't recognize the room—the low ceiling, the moon-washed walls—and for a few frightening seconds she had no concept at all of where she lay, what continent or country, what time zone or town—if the blue was actually liquid or light, harmful or healthy—whose bed. She tore the wet sheet from her skin and wrapped the top blanket around her fevered body. She shut her eyes and let the tremors pass. Images from the other night assailed her: Snow on the windshield. The gray-haired lady driver. The animal in the headlights. They'd driven off the road in the ice. Was that last night or the night before? And where was this room sunk in blue silence and light?

She listened for a long time to the quiet. Her throat was parched; she needed to pee but was afraid to leave the raft of her bed. Could she possibly be in Canada or somewhere else, and why was the moonlight so blue?

A clock ticked somewhere in the room. A wooden chair stood in a corner, an upright dresser in the moonlight, a crucifix on the wall above.

The animal came back in a flash, a camel with a hump on its head. She remembered the coldness in the car, the windshield encased in ice. The heat not working in the Honda. A large man with a red beard and a limp. His truck. A dog. She reached for her ankle and felt the monitor missing, and a fresh panic bloomed in her chest. How much time had passed since she'd taken off the device on a park bench in Manhattan? How long had she been lying in the blue?

She stood unsteadily and wrapped a blanket around her shoulders and found her shirt and jeans, her undergarments, folded on a chair by the bed. A cell phone on top beside a note. Who had folded her clothes and left them there? Who had left the note?

She dressed quickly, shivering the whole time, and covered herself again with the blanket. She flipped open the phone and before checking the texts read the handwritten note by the light of the screen.

> *Sahro, you had a fever. It was safer for me to leave*
> *with the car. You're in good hands. The abbot knows*
> *everything and will take care of you. You are inside*
> *a guest house of a monastery. Your contact will come*
> *and get you in a day or two. I'm sorry about every-*
> *thing. Don't be afraid. You are safe here. —Jane*

Sahro read the note again but couldn't quite comprehend. What, or who, was "the abbot"? What was a "guest house of a monastery"? Who was "Jane"? She tapped the app on her phone and looked at texts. She'd missed a dozen messages. Half from Aunt Waardo. The cousins sending prayer hands. Fartumo and Ahmed asking for an update. An urgent text from the sanctuary people and the contact in Canada, a man named Hassan. More messages from Waardo with growing alarm. Then several from Jane, the driver—the small gray-haired woman (it was coming back now). Sahro scrolled through the messages, her heart beating in her throat. The driver saying she was leaving that morning. Instructions for

Sahro. The contact, Hassan, joining in, writing that he'd come as soon as he could to pick up Sahro. Finally, another private text from him: *pls call as soon as you can.* Sahro closed her eyes and tried to calculate the time since the accident the other night—for she remembered now going off the road. How long had she been lying there asleep? Was it almost twenty-four hours now?

She set the flip phone down. Her head throbbed. It was too much to think about. *You're in good hands. The abbot knows everything.* She was shivering again, her body racked with chills. She stood and staggered across the moonlit floor into a small bathroom. She lowered the seat of the commode and sat. The same blue moonlight spilled over the bathroom tiles, the sink, the tub, a small shower. Through a square window she could see the shape of mountains in the night, the silhouettes of spiky trees. Her teeth chattered in her head, yet there was something calming about the moonlight, the tall trees through the window, the quiet of the place, everything sunk in silver and indigo and the stars shining visibly above.

She twisted the tap at the sink, let the water run, and lowered her mouth to the spout. She was so parched, she drank gulp after gulp, hungrily, as if she'd never tasted water so fresh before. When she closed the tap, her teeth hurt. Her lips felt numb. She looked at the mirror above the sink and saw the ghost of her face staring back, gaunt, hollow-eyed in the glass.

She stumbled through the bedroom and wandered into a hall, half expecting to find someone. In another room orange embers glowed behind the glass of an iron stove. The room was warm. More windows. More blue light. An armchair sat beside the stove. A small table, a bookcase against one wall. Some stacked wood. She recognized her own down coat hanging on the back of the chair. Her red ball cap. She snatched them both and hurried back into the bedroom and shut the door.

She buried herself beneath blankets and piled her coat on top but couldn't get warm. She shivered in the damp sheet and clutched the phone in one hand. *You're safe*, the gray-haired woman wrote. *The abbot knows everything.* But where exactly was she, and what was a "guest house"? The name sounded somehow ominous. It reminded Sahro just then of the place that floated above the Kana Kaaba in Mecca. The Bait-ul-Ma'mur or the "Much-Frequented House" where millions of angels visited each day, replaced by millions more the next. She repeated the English words to herself: *guest house*. Was she inside the Bait-ul-Ma'mur among angels? Who were the hosts? Was she falling into light or into fire?

She lay back and listened to the night, the stillness of the room. She tried to reason it out. She was not yet in Canada, she knew, but someplace north. In the country, the woods, the mountains. A place of spiky trees and blue moonlight. A place filled with something else she didn't recognize right away. A sound or maybe not a sound at all but the lack of it, something she hadn't heard in so long—silence—spreading all around her like silk.

11

Sahro didn't recognize the city of her birth when she returned there at eleven years old. Xamar, the capital, frightened her. The rubble and ruined buildings. The armed men in Toyotas and jeeps. The loud market with its colorful crowds and piles of electronics and melons and cut-up fish. She was used to the northern scrublands—the Hawd—the quiet country, the camel's pace. Plants whose names she knew, familiar trees and birds. In the noisy capital she had no reference point or guide. The afternoon she arrived, filthy and exhausted from days of difficult travel, she stood outside a pink-walled compound on Via Sanca with all her belongings in one vinyl bag. She banged on a dented gate and waited. No one answered right away. A peephole slid open—an eye appeared—and just as quickly slid shut. After a few minutes the sheet metal banged, bolts unclicked. A door within the gate creaked open and a large woman in a gold floral wrap pulled Sahro inside by the elbow and locked the gate behind her.

She found herself inside a leafy courtyard with red bougainvillea in bloom. The woman in the floral dirac stuck a hand on her hip and frowned. Sahro didn't recognize her Aunt Waardo, but the woman then pulled her to her chest, one minute wiping away tears and thanking Allah, the next frowning and pushing Sahro an arm's length away. It happened so swiftly; before she knew it she was being dragged across the courtyard, behind a wall and curtain, her aunt tossing her hands in the air, grumbling about the girl's filth, her tangled hair, how her father's people *obviously didn't know how to keep anything clean.* She made Sahro strip naked behind the curtain and scrubbed her head and neck hard with caustic soap. Another woman shortly appeared with a razor and together they cut and shaved Sahro's raven hair to the scalp, Waardo shouting the whole time about *injirta*. No one brought lice into *her* house.

Sahro endured it all. She didn't protest or cry. Even when her black locks fell around her feet and two small girls peeked behind the curtain and pointed and laughed at the naked bald-headed girl. Sahro simply glared back—and stuck out her tongue.

—

Those first weeks she rarely left the villa. The pink-walled compound sat in a once well-heeled neighborhood north of the city near the airport. Its sandy courtyard and leafy neem tree in its center seemed almost opulent to Sahro, especially the second-floor balcony and its view of the Indian Ocean a kilometer away. The neighborhood's wealthy residents had long since fled the city for overseas. Aunt Waardo had taken over the place after the collapse, fending off others with cleverness and bribes while enduring the worst of the war. She was a large, formidable woman with dramatically arched and scowling eyebrows; she wore her irritability like a perfume, something meant not to attract but repel. Waardo was the eldest of six siblings, including Sahro's mother, none of whom were still alive. With no children of her own, Waardo had raised several of her siblings and then their kids. Most had fled Somalia, south for Kenya or north to Yemen across the Gulf. Waardo never talked about those terrible years, nor the unspeakable things she'd seen. Sahro knew better than to ask, especially about her mother and never her father. She knew intuitively what couldn't be spoken—her father's name, his clan. Both sides of the family shared that silence, the code of things best left unsaid.

A dozen cousins occupied the villa on Via Sanca, each related somehow to Sahro by oath or by blood. Waardo and her half brother Uncle Cabdi Rashid, his stepkids, Sahro's older cousins, Dalmar and Ayaan.

Adam and Hussein, the twins, and the young cousins, Little Ibrahim and Leylo and Cumar.

Most of them had teased Sahro the first days after she arrived. The nomad, they called her. The hick. The bald-headed girl from the north. The *Laaxo* with lice. She smelled like a goat, they said. Like camel testicles. Her skin as rough as a lizard's.

One afternoon that first week she watched the twins, Adam and Hussein, trying to catch a rooster her aunt had brought for their family's supper. The two boys lurched and stumbled and lost their grip on the panicked bird. After a few minutes, exasperated, Sahro leapt down from a limb in the neem tree and snatched the rooster by a wing and wrung its neck in a flash. She held the still-flapping bird straight out with a stiff arm. Back in the north, she'd had to dispatch goat kids quicker than that.

"Fools," she muttered and glared at the boys. She dropped the fluttering bird and walked away.

From then on they dubbed her the *wiilo*. The tomboy. She preferred it to "hick" and soon proved she could climb the neem tree fastest and outfight all of her cousins, even the boys.

—

Her aunt put her to work right away, cooking and cleaning for the younger cousins, scrubbing the sinks and latrine. She slowly came to understand this other family, her mother's side, and how she was just one piece of a larger puzzle. It was almost as if she'd discovered overnight a whole new section of sky, a constellation her grandfather never told her about, one she never knew existed. Half aunts and uncles, cousins and nephews, third and fourth removed—a whole galaxy spread across the globe. Not only those living inside the villa, but others who lived overseas in cities whose names she hadn't yet learned: London and Oslo, Abu Dhabi, Columbus, Johannesburg. The extended family, the nomadic network, who wired money back and forth, north to south, from the wealthier places to the poorer, a little here, some there, sent through *xawaalad*—money transfer. Aunt Waardo oversaw it all as best she could from the villa on Via Sanca, pleading and arguing and threatening the others, arranging payments and marriages, fighting on the phone through messages and texts. Waardo was always going off in her big burka to wait in line at the money transfer agency in the city's center. Sometimes she returned with bags of fried sambusas or camel meat from the butchers or sweet red xalwa candy from the confectioners—a VHS cassette hidden beneath her burka. On those afternoons news spread quickly in the compound, and by nightfall, after evening prayers and supper, after the pots had been scrubbed and stacked against the walls, the cousins would gather in the courtyard around an old VHS player and Zenith console and watch whatever pirated tape Aunt Waardo had managed to find. Bollywood musicals usually. *Janwar* or *Disco Dancer*. No one spoke a word of Hindi, but they made up their own storylines and plot, and the songs were easy to learn. Sometimes Aunt Waardo returned with American films. *Pale Rider*, *Top Gun*, *Rocky*, *Rambo*. Sahro always tried to sit near her older cousin Ayaan on nights with American films. Ayaan knew English, at least enough to translate Sylvester Stallone.

Ayaan Farah was two years older than Sahro, but her older cousin seemed so much more sophisticated, Sahro couldn't believe they were actually related. Ayaan was tall and beautiful with long, wavy hair. She wore reading glasses and Western clothes—jeans and T-shirts—under a silk wrap. She didn't play games with the others out in the courtyard but mostly kept to herself. She was always sitting on the balcony of the second floor outside her flat, head buried in a book. Sahro had been secretly watching her for weeks, a little afraid of the older girl with the long hair and cinnamon skin, the way she floated around the others—confident, aloof—her mind obviously elsewhere. She and her brother Dalmar lived across the courtyard on the second floor with their stepfather, Uncle Cabdi Rashid. Like Sahro, Ayaan and Dalmar were orphans as well.

One afternoon Sahro was sweeping the courtyard, when Ayaan leaned over the balcony and motioned her with a finger.

"Tomboy," she said. "Wiilo."

Sahro looked around and pointed to herself.

"Who else?" the girl said. "Leave the broom. Come up and join me." She gestured to the staircase with her chin.

Sahro set down the hand broom and walked to the stairs. Ayaan waited on the balcony, watching. It was the most the girl had ever said to her before.

Upstairs, Ayaan took Sahro's hand in hers and led her along the pitted balcony. Her head wasn't covered and her hair went down to her waist and she wore green glass bangles around one wrist. The flats upstairs were larger, airier, and Sahro could see parts of the city beyond the villa's walls. They walked through a red-curtained doorway into a dark, rectangular room with a small window in the rear. It took a moment for Sahro's eyes to adjust to the dark, and then she saw all the postcards taped to the concrete wall, the row of books, a mattress with a maroon silk throw on the floor.

"This is all yours?" Sahro asked, incredulous.

"Of course," her cousin said.

Sahro stepped to the wall and examined the postcards. Pictures of cities and skyscrapers, towers and mountains. the Kana Kaaba lit at night.

"Wait here," Ayaan said. "I'll be right back. "

She left the room, and Sahro gazed at the other pictures. A snowy mountain. A Norwegian fjord. A beach somewhere filled with nearly naked White people. She eyed the row of books lined up against the wall. Paperbacks and hardbacks, new and old. She'd never seen so many books in one place.

Ayaan returned carrying two bottles of Fanta and handed one to Sahro.

"Don't tell anyone," she whispered and put a finger to her lips.

Sahro took the bottle. The cap was off, the glass cold. She didn't ask where it came from. She knew Uncle Cabdi Rashid liked to drink Vimto and Fanta when he chewed qat in the afternoons.

Ayaan folded her legs and sat on the floor and gestured for Sahro to join her. Her cousin clinked her bottle and they sat for a while not speaking, the Fanta a burst of sweet in Sahro's mouth. The red curtain lifted and let in a breath of hot air, the smell of blooming jasmine from the courtyard.

"Tell me," Ayaan said nonchalantly, looking at Sahro for the first time. "What is it like up north, the place you came from?"

Sahro shrugged and sipped the Fanta; she wanted the orange liquid to last forever.

"What do you want to know?" she asked.

"How did you travel here?"

"Bus," Sahro said, "and truck."

"Was it safe?"

Sahro put down the bottle.

"Nothing is safe," she said, quoting her grandmother. "But I am here, *alhamdulillah*."

Ayaan looked at her queerly, with a little smile.

"How old are you?" Ayaan asked.

"Thirteen," Sahro lied.

Ayaan laughed; she seemed to know Sahro was lying. There was a large gap between her two front teeth Sahro had never seen before. Ayaan *never* smiled.

Her cousin asked her more questions and Sahro answered, hesitant at first, unsure why Ayaan was interested. Who cared about the scrublands, the *miyi*, the bush. Her camels and goats. No one had asked her before at the villa; they'd only made fun. The *laaxo*, the nomad, the hick. But Ayaan seemed genuinely interested, and the more questions she asked, the more Sahro spoke—about her grandparents and camels and milking goats in the morning and going to dugsi—until she grew self-conscious and took another sip of soda and changed the subject.

"Whose books are those?" she asked, nodding toward the row against the back wall.

"Mine," Ayaan replied and explained that most had belonged to her parents. They'd both been schoolteachers before they were killed in the war.

Sahro nodded and said nothing. Ayaan sipped her soda. The only books Sahro ever knew were the Holy Qur'an and the flimsy Somali language primers they used in school, yet here in her cousin's room were dozens of books composed not by the Prophet—Peace Be Upon Him—but by mere people. It seemed a little scandalous to Sahro that her cousin lived with so many inside her bedroom.

"Do you want to look?" Ayaan asked, eyebrow raised.

She set her Fanta on the floor and took Sahro by the hand and brought her to the books against the wall. Sahro ran a tentative finger across the spines, feeling the different textures—paper, cloth, cardboard. There was something immensely pleasing about their shapes, their bright colors (blue, yellow, orange, green) stacked side by side, like bolts of perfectly folded fabric in a seamstress's shop. The titles on their spines were written with the Roman alphabet, just like Af Soomaali, the Somali language, but Sahro couldn't recognize the words.

"What kind of books are they?" Sahro inquired.

"All sorts," Ayaan said.

"Religious books?" Sahro asked.

Ayaan shook her head and said no.

"They're mostly stories. English stories. American stories."

"*Sheeko?*"

Ayaan nodded.

"Western sheeko," she said. "Some are called 'novels.'"

Sahro seemed surprised, a little confused. She asked if the people in the stories were good people.

"Not always." Ayaan shrugged. "Some good, some bad."

What good were books about bad people? Sahro wondered but

didn't ask; she didn't want to seem stupid. A breeze lifted the curtain on the door and let in a saturation of afternoon light.

"Can you read Somali?" Ayaan asked.

"Yes," Sahro said. Of course she could read Af Soomaali.

Ayaan strode to her bed and picked up her reading glasses and returned. She selected a book from the row. A paperback with a bright orange cover—the same color as the Fanta—and a black silhouette of a bird. Some foreign words as the title.

Ayaan stood next to Sahro and held the cover in front of her face.

"Here," she said. "Give it a try."

Ayaan stood close, towering over Sahro, holding the book in her hand. The smell of soda on her breath. Sahro sounded out the Roman letters to herself on the book's cover but the words made no sense.

"Is it English?" Sahro asked.

"American English," Ayaan said. "Go ahead," she urged. "You already know the letters."

Sahro blushed and studied the book cover again, suddenly shy in front of her older cousin, the skin under her lip growing damp. Then she began sounding the words out loud.

"*I ka-noo . . . waahay . . .*"

She looked up at Ayaan, who gave her an encouraging nod, and she started again.

"*I ka-noo waahay tahay caayjee baard syeng.*"

Ayaan clapped her hands.

"Good!" she said and spoke the title slowly: "*I Know Why the Caged Bird Sings.*"

She looked at Sahro and winked.

"Not bad," she said, "for a tomboy."

—

That afternoon they made a pact. Ayaan promised to teach Sahro English words if Sahro told her some of her grandmother's folktales. They could each learn something from the other. They were both orphans after all, Ayaan said. They had to stick together,

Sahro was surprised by her cousin's proposal, surprised she had anything to offer someone as sophisticated as Ayaan. She was thrilled to learn a little English but happier to spend time around Ayaan. And so each night, for the next few weeks, they met at the neem tree in the center of the courtyard. After Sahro performed her prayers and scrubbed the supper pots and put the cousins to bed, she'd meet Ayaan at the foot of the tree and they'd climb together to the top. There, among the branches, with a small flashlight, Ayaan would teach Sahro ten or twenty English words. Nouns. Prepositions. Verbs. Sahro would write them down with a sharpened pencil in a school notebook, their definition in Somali beside. In this way, over the weeks—then months—her English grew. Each word became a blade, a key that opened a world. Sometimes they'd read from the book with the orange cover and the silhouette of the bird, just so Sahro could get the English in her mouth. Other times Ayaan gave her words that came out of her own head. After thirty minutes or so of teaching Sahro new words, her cousin would grab Sahro's notebook and shut the cover and switch the flashlight off and say now it was time for a story. She'd sit back on the limbs and look at the dark over the city and wait for Sahro to begin.

Ayaan knew English words and the names of foreign cities and the characters in Turkish soap operas. She knew how to braid hair and paint henna on hands in beautiful patterns; but Sahro knew the stars overhead and how to milk a goat or cush a camel or read the direction of the qibla in the constellations—things Sahro had never considered of value before, but second nature, a little like the knowledge of her own knees. Yet at night now up in the neem tree, when she showed Ayaan the Stations of the Moon, or told her tales of Queen Aweelo or Faay Geedi, or any of the other Somali folktales—the *Sheeko Soomaaliyeed Xirirooyen*—her older cousin fell quiet and listened to Sahro speaking. Ayaan had never heard the folktales before. Not the tales of Dhegdheer, the famous cannibal woman. Dhegdheer, who grew up beautiful and obedient but had to marry an older wealthy man. Dhegdheer, who became tall and fat and strong as a horse and gave birth only to girls, which angered her old husband, who beat her. When she couldn't take his beatings anymore, Dhegdheer cut the old man's throat and ate him. And that began her reign of terror, of eating men for food.

When Sahro recited the stories and saw the look of interest on Ayaan's face, something flowered inside Sahro, something she hadn't known was there. All Sahro had to do was close her eyes and imagine the hut in the scrublands, the wind at the flap of the aqal, the fire, and her ayeeyo's gravelly voice, and the tales came tumbling out, fully formed. She always began the traditional Somali way, the way her grandmother taught her.

Sheeko, sheeko.

Sahro would say when she was ready.

Gather here. Listen, I have a story.

Then Ayaan would respond from the dark.

"Sheeko xarir."

Make your story smooth *as silk.*

12

The spring night passed on Blue Mountain. The temperature moderated each hour. The moon went down at two. The monks all slept in their cells, in narrow beds built into the walls, in rooms of birch and pine. Brother Bruno and Anselm. Father Teilhard and Ramon, Simon, Jonah, and John; Brother Benison and David, Luke and Minh. Each monk had arrived at Blue Mountain over the decades, from near and far; from California, Da Nang, Rio. Kansas and Queens. From Boston, Zurich, Cincinnati, and San Juan. Each man drawn to the monastery, for his own mysterious reasons, like metal filings to a larger magnet. They slept now in their cells, each under blankets, soundly asleep, as the May night passed overhead. All except for Father Christopher, who alone lay awake long after midnight, unable to sleep. So much had happened in the past eighteen hours, he hadn't had time to process it all during the day; he lay in bed turning over Teddy's call earlier that evening about the woman's Honda, the warning notice from the state police. When he'd gone to the Guest House after, the gray-haired woman insisted she leave right away. It was no longer safe, she said, for her to stay. Someone from Canada would come in a day or so to pick up the Somali woman when she was more fit to travel. In the meantime the young woman could recover there in the Guest House—the driver suggested—under Christopher's vigilance and care. The woman apologized profusely for imposing on the abbot, for putting him in such a hard place, but she didn't know what else she could do.

Christopher didn't know what to say. He kept thinking of the three strangers who appeared by the oaks in Mamre in the heat of a summer day. Abraham running to meet them and falling at their feet. The curds and milk, the calf and bread. How could he turn the visitor away?

Yet now at night, in the dark of his study, he felt the full weight of his decision. The safety and care of the young stranger lay in his hands. What if she didn't get better? What if something more serious was wrong, or he was breaking the law by harboring her? He'd have to deal with Brother Bruno and come clean with the rest of the community. Bruno had given him twenty-four hours; half that time had passed. He'd have to call a community meeting in the morning. There was no hiding the young woman anymore. He'd have to tell them all who she was and where she was from.

—

He knew he wouldn't sleep that night. He rose and put on a robe and powered the PC on his desk. Ever since he'd seen the young woman asleep in Edward's bed, the image stayed with him—her body beneath the blankets. The stranger. A Black woman. African. Muslim. The fact of her body in the old abbot's room both troubled and intrigued him—the mystery of it all. How else did she end up on Blue Mountain, in Edward's old bed, if not by Providence?

Christopher sat in the gray glow of the computer and typed words into the search engine. He knew nearly nothing about Somalia—the country and culture, its people or food. He didn't even know what language Somalis spoke. He sat now and began to educate himself online, scanning everything he could find related to Somalia. He read about a country of nomads and traders; an ancient Cushitic people who herded camels and goats, who sailed dhows across the Arabian Sea, clockwise from their coast to Aden, then Bombay, and back home with the winds all in one season. He read about Europe dividing the country, Italy seizing the south, England the north. The colonizers exploiting clan divisions and making everything worse—ethnic Somalis in the north, Somali Bantu in the south; Darod and Hawiye, Dir and Isaaq. He learned about the actions (or inactions) of his own Roman Catholic church in

Mogadishu, the forced labor they ignored or encouraged. He read long into the dark about Somalia's independence, its heyday, the gradual, then swift, collapse of the country. The foreign armies. The American invasion and pullout. The U.S. support of warlords. The CIA's involvement. The promise of oil. He took it all in: Extraordinary rendition. The "black sites." The Global War on Terror. And the deeper he read, the more he discovered, not only about Somalia, but his own unhidden history—for it was there for all to see—his complicity and the overlapping of their lives: he inside a cloister on a mountain in New England, she from halfway around the world. Weren't they part of the same system, no matter how separate each seemed on the surface? Didn't he—Christopher Gathreaux—benefit from the same bloody history from which he drew his livelihood? Rome and its violent past, the U.S. and its more recent plunder? It was easy to pretend otherwise in the cloister. To live inside their own bubble, inside a dream of their own autonomy, invested in tunics and robes. The problem with living inside a bubble was how easily it could be popped. Every outsider was, potentially, a pin.

The year before he made his simple vows Christopher's sister had asked him: wouldn't it be better for him to use his faith to actually help others or provide a service for the poor? He told her back then that monks *did* help others, that the monastery was a lighthouse to all. He quoted Thomas Merton and compared the cloister to a power plant and explained that contemplative monks and nuns were like unseen engineers sending out invisible currents of prayer, keeping the planet in sync. In the economy of the spirit, he *was* serving others all the time.

His sister just rolled her eyes, yet her question stayed with him still (as it did with most monks he knew). The contradictions of monastic life could never be fully squared. The mystery and faith. The doubt and belief; they were two sides of the same coin. You could never have one without the other.

He typed new words into Google—"Somali recipes"—and scrolled through pages of popular dishes. Sambusas and canjeero. *Basto* (pasta),

Somali rice and goat. What could he bring the young woman in the morning to give her comfort, to make her feel less alone? Somali bread was called canjeero or anjero or sometimes laxoox. It was basically the same, he read, as Ethiopian ingera, the spongy flatbread—or pancakes—Christopher had sometimes eaten in SoHo when he lived in New York City.

Perhaps he could make her Somali bread? Canjeero drizzled with honey or maybe maple syrup? A simple gesture: bread?

He read multiple recipes. The monastery kitchen had no teff flour or sorghum or millet. But he found a recipe that called for other flours instead and sent the page to his printer.

—

Downstairs in the kitchen, he gathered ingredients from the larder. White flour. Wheat flour. Cornmeal. A bottle of yeast from the walk-in. Warm water and sugar to start the yeast. It was almost four in the morning now, dark in the kitchen windows; the bells for Vigils would toll in fifty minutes. He followed the recipe by the light over the stove, sifting flours into a ceramic bowl, adding the wet ingredients to the dry. Now he had to wait, according to the recipe, and let the mixture ferment for at least twenty-four hours (forty-eight even better). The dough needed to sour and bubble before it could be baked on a hot skillet.

He covered the bowl with a dish towel. He looked around the kitchen. Where could he keep the bowl warm enough but out of sight? He didn't want Brother Benison finding it and asking questions.

He put away the flours and stored the yeast, washed the counters and scrubbed his hands. He cradled the covered bowl in his arms and shut off the lights. He'd bring the bowl upstairs to his study and set it in a sunny window. There it would keep warm throughout the day and overnight. By then he'd have called the community meeting and all the monks would be aware of the young woman in the Guest House. By then all would be revealed. The mixture soured. The fermentation started. Then the real baking could begin.

13

By the time Sahro entered high school, she and Ayaan had grown inseparable. They traveled everywhere together, to school and market, to mosque on Fridays, to the Lido Beach on weekends. Ayaan's brother Dalmar had joined them by then. Dalmar had sprouted overnight and towered over his tall sister now. They looked so much alike, brother and sister, that people mistook them for twins. Dalmar had the same smooth cinnamon skin and slanted eyebrows. The same lustrous wavy hair and gap between his two front teeth when he smiled. He'd been a promising soccer player when younger, but his asthma had grown worse, and he had to drop the sport. Like his sister, he was a bit reserved and serious, and Sahro didn't like to share Ayaan with him at first. But soon, to her surprise, she didn't mind Dalmar's company, his joking and thoughtfulness. His occasional moody silences. The three became a unit, seen together so often the neighborhood kids called them the *Bajaj* after the ubiquitous three-wheeled scooter cabs that patrolled the city's streets. The nickname irked Dalmar but Sahro secretly liked it. A Bajaj was swift and could travel places other vehicles couldn't. Three wheels, she reasoned, were more stable than two.

Soon, however, they couldn't go very far. Fighting broke out in the city. The streets became unsafe. Car bombs and kidnappings, terrorist attacks became part of daily life. Sahro, Ayaan, and Dalmar huddled inside the villa, tried to make the best of it, but even there life was growing untenable. Ever since Ayaan turned sixteen, her stepfather had been trying to marry her off to one of his wealthy clients. Uncle

Cabdi Rashid made no secret of his efforts. He'd bring men by in the afternoon for a qat-chewing session and show off Ayaan. An arranged marriage with an older, well-off man would greatly benefit the family, but Ayaan had other plans. She wanted to emigrate overseas, to travel to one of the places pictured on the postcards in her room. London in particular, where her half sister lived in a flat in Streatham. Soon, Ayaan said, she'd leave Mogadishu and do *tahriib*, illegal immigration overland. The last thing she wanted, she told Sahro, was to stay in Xamar and marry some old fart who already had another wife. But her stepfather was a practical man with many business ties. Ayaan could help them all, especially with a well-appointed marriage. Tahriib was dangerous besides, a gamble at best. Half the young people who tried to migrate to Europe never made it the whole way. Many ended up in the Mediterranean, drowned.

It was around the time of the new instability that Uncle Cabdi Rashid redoubled his efforts. London was a pipe dream but marriage a sure thing. He needed to secure Ayaan's promise, or at least good faith. What was she waiting for? They quarreled back and forth in the flat upstairs. Sahro would often hear them late at night. Uncle Cabdi Rashid's curses and threats. Ayaan's shouting back. Sometimes their arguments lasted hours, fueled by a long afternoon session of Uncle Cabdi Rashid chewing qat and sipping cola. Sometimes Dalmar joined in too, defending his sister, which only enraged their stepfather more. The arguments always ended with Cabdi Rashid shouting the same refrain: *The only respectable place for a woman is in her husband's house or in her grave!*

Afterward, Sahro and Ayaan would meet in the courtyard and commiserate. They'd climb to the top of the neem tree and look out over the city. Sahro would try to soothe her older cousin with a story or folktale, but Ayaan wasn't interested in fables anymore. They'd talk instead about tahriib, Ayaan getting out of Xamar, away from the villa, from her stepfather and the cursed country. It was just a matter of time,

Ayaan said. She'd figured it all out. Her half sister in Streatham had been sending her money on the sly.

—

Summer began. The days grew irritable and hot, yet the Lido Beach remained off-limits. The religious militias patrolled the area, boys in pickups bristling with semiautomatic weapons, making sure everyone was properly clad, the sexes appropriately apart. Some days Sahro went with Ayaan nonetheless just to stare at the enticing waters, she and Ayaan entombed in full niqab, the ocean cool and opalescent and tumbling in the breeze, but they didn't dare go in. It was much too risky. They'd skulk off instead to the Nasiid Travel Agency and Internet Café, the empty room in a concrete building hidden off the Corso. There they'd meet Dalmar and spend hours surfing the internet on an old desktop computer, watching YouTube and chatting with friends on Facebook. Dalmar's friend Maxmuud Xirsi owned the "café" and let him use the computers in exchange for labor. Everyone called Maxmuud Xirsi "Mad Max" for his English trainers and tie-dyed shirts, his defiance of the militants, his goatee. Maxmuud knew all the YouTube channels and was gaining a reputation himself as a rapper, mixing the traditional Somali *jaycal* and *heebo* with hip-hop and rap. At his place, they'd watch music videos of Farxiya Fiska and K'naan, and Sahro learned about the London poet Warsan Shire and watched her readings in English, and often they watched Ayaan's favorite talk show, *Sheeko Sheeko*, filmed in Toronto, featuring a rotating panel of Canadian Somalis sitting around a table speaking about life in Canada and in the *qurba joog*. The panelists were young and smartly dressed, the women in lipstick and leather jackets or traditional hijab. They seemed incredibly glamorous to Sahro— confident and good-looking, occasionally breaking into a sentence or two of Somali. Sahro grasped only some of the English, but their words mattered less than the way they moved on the screen with such assuredness and ease and open flirtation, their faces so familiar, their gestures too, but something magical had happened to them overseas. Some mysterious transformation in the diaspora. Oftentimes, staring into the computer screen, Sahro would see her and Ayaan's gloomy faces reflected back in the glass. What if they too were on the other side? Would they be made happier, smarter, more beautiful, better dressed? Certainly they'd have more money.

After hours of watching the show or scrolling through Facebook feeds, looking at posts from around the world, Sahro always felt a little sick. She could see the defeat in Ayaan's and Dalmar's faces as well, the mix of pride and jealousy, envy and despair. Three losers who'd never left Somalia. They'd step out of the Nasiid into the hot wind off the Corso, assaulted by the heat, the smell of burning and sewage, Ayaan in front, Dalmar sullen and cautious behind, wary of every passing vehicle, a loose anguish lacing them together until they hiked back up to the villa and opened the dented metal gate and locked it safely behind.

—

One morning when school was back in session, a group of militants clad all in black burst into Sahro's classroom flashing rifles, faces concealed behind black scarves. They took the teacher at gunpoint, separated the boys and girls, and lined them against opposite walls. Sahro could hear shouting out in the hall. Bursts of gunfire. Canvas boots. Something inside her went cold. A memory of childhood. A flash of blood. She stood terrified, unable to speak or move, and watched as if from the wrong end of a telescope as the soldiers started with the boys, shouting and pushing and lining them up by the door. Dalmar had left the class-room minutes earlier. Did they get him out in the hall? And Ayaan in the other classroom? Sahro thought of running out of the room to try to find them but stood frozen in place. The boys were being marched out of the room at gunpoint. Two soldiers stayed behind. A tall man swathed in black with a long beard and a bandolier of bullets across his chest slapped one of Sahro's classmates because she was wearing only a bati and hijab and part of her foot was exposed. He lectured the girls on modesty and wearing the full-body niqab and said they'd be back for them soon, that they should be preparing themselves to be wives rather than wasting their time in school.

Then just as quickly they left. Some of the girls started sobbing. Another volley of gunfire echoed outside the room. Then came the roar of an engine in the courtyard, a truck speeding away. Sahro rushed into the empty hall. Had they taken Dalmar? Where was Ayaan? The compound outside was empty, the school gate left open, the truck with all the boys and schoolteachers gone. The girls fled through the open gate. Sahro turned and saw Ayaan wearing only her bati and headscarf, walking beside another tall figure covered in her green jilbab.

"Sahro," she hissed before Sahro could ask any questions.

She snatched Sahro's elbow and steered her quickly out of the compound and down the street. The jilbab was too short for Dalmar, and Sahro could see his large sandaled feet beneath. She caught his face for just a second, shaken and sweating inside the jilbab. He'd hidden inside the latrine to escape the soldiers, she later learned. It's where Ayaan had found him. They walked the whole five kilometers back to the villa. Dalmar hidden inside the fabric, embarrassed and enraged. He didn't say a word the whole time.

From then on the three rarely left the villa. They stopped going to school. Each day a bomb exploded somewhere in the city. Sahro would feel the shudder of the blast, then hear the boom seconds later. She'd climb the neem tree to see which neighborhood had been hit, how close, and watch the black plume after rising into the blue.

One afternoon she was hanging laundry on the roof when a loud explosion shook the villa's walls and birds flew out of the trees. The blast was nearer than usual. A fireball rose over the Corso. She finished pinning her cousins' clothes. She heard car horns, then sirens, the sounds of mortar fire. Sometime later—twenty or thirty minutes—

Dalmar appeared in the courtyard, out of breath, his face varnished in sweat.

"You must come," he said and took her arm, a tightness in his voice she'd never heard before. On the way through the courtyard, slipping on flip-flops, she heard only the word *Nasiid*.

Outside, a Toyota was waiting, the driver a friend of Dalmar's. They piled in, Sahro by the window, and zipped down toward the business district, dodging pedestrians and potholes and people on bikes. The traffic grew heavy and stopped. Dalmar and Sahro leapt out of the car and ran the rest of the way. The air smelled acrid; black smoke billowed above. People were shouting, some covered in dust and blood. At the corner near the Nasiid, the blackened skeleton of a bus smoldered in flames. A donkey cart had upended and lemons lay everywhere in the street.

Most of the injured had gone to the hospital, they learned, and they started off on foot. It wasn't far, a mile at most. The smoke thinned and they jogged in the heat. The stores were closing, people peering out of shuttered grates. It was almost noon, time for Zuhr, afternoon prayers.

They found Ayaan an hour later, unconscious in the hospital's hall, lying on the concrete second floor. Her head was wrapped in gauze purple with dried blood, her niqab too darkened and heavy, the fabric partly burnt. Her arms were wrapped as well, a white powder on her skin. The hall bustled with injured men and women. People were shouting for IV drips, for drugs. There weren't enough antibiotics or beds, not enough drugs or blood, and the generators in the hospital kept cutting in and out. Sahro sat on the floor and nestled Ayaan's head in her lap. Dalmar went off to try to find a doctor or nurse or anyone who could help.

"Where is the pain?" Sahro whispered into Ayaan's ear.

She cradled her cousin's head in her lap, the bloody gauze matted in her hair. Her skin whitened with some kind of powder. Her beautiful cousin. If she could find the right place, she would hold a hand over the hurt and say the dua for healing, or blow her breath over it to take it away—as her grandmother had done to her many times in the Hawd. But where was her cousin's hurt if not everywhere? On her head and her hands, her arms and under her skin?

Sahro rocked Ayaan back and forth and said the dua anyhow—*Oh Allah, Sustainer of Mankind. Remove the illness, cure the hurt. You are the One who cures*—but she hadn't the breath or the hands or the time to cover all the hurt inside her cousin's body.

III

14

Teddy Fletcher woke the next morning to a riot of birdsong. The spring night had brought a flood of migrants from the south, and he lay in his bed listening to their song. Warblers mostly. He knew their calls, having studied them one summer and he tried now to remember their names: *Black-throated blue, Bay-breasted, Golden-winged.* He heard a Redstart and a Common Yellowthroat, then the gobble of a turkey calling from out in the fog.

Years ago, on a morning like this, Teddy would already be hunkered down before dawn in a blind, shotgun in one hand, turkey call in the other. Part of the thrill of hunting spring turkey was catching the ear of an amorous tom with a lure, establishing a rapport, drawing him in. On a good morning in May, he'd sometimes bring home a fifteen-pound tom for the family in Hart's Run.

Teddy lay in bed now and listened to the gobble again. Cora sat up, alert at the end of the bed. It was late in the morning for Teddy—almost eight a.m.—but the night before he'd been up later than usual. Having delivered the woman's Honda to the Guest House, he got a ride with Father Christopher back down to the tollhouse to pick up the Ford. Before Christopher dropped him by the truck, he thanked Teddy for all his help that day.

"Do yourself a favor," the abbot said. "Take tomorrow morning off—or better yet, the whole day. You've done more than enough for one day."

Teddy shrugged and said he was fine, but lying in bed now, feeling the moist May air slipping through the open window, he thought: maybe he would take the day off. He hadn't hunted in so long, not since his return from Afghanistan. Maybe he'd pattern his shotgun or build a blind in the woods as preparation for the next day. Maybe it was time for him to start hunting again.

He took a long, hot shower that morning and washed his hair and beard while Cora stayed in bed. Afterward, toweled, he put on his prosthesis and fished the Browning pump action from under the bed. He took out his .22 as well, the Marlin .35. The gun bags too, cleaning kit, and ammo. When he stood, he saw the light flashing on the answering machine. Someone had apparently left a message while he was in the shower. He leaned over and pressed the button, expecting to hear the abbot's voice. He was wrong.

"*Good morning, Mr. Fletcher,*" the voice said. "*This is Agent Fusco with Immigration and Customs Enforcement. I got your number from Trooper Desautel at the state barracks in Hart's Run. I'm calling about a suspicious vehicle abandoned on the river road, Route 46. Please give me a call as soon as you can. 802-345-8899. Thank you.*"

The message stopped; the machine beeped. Teddy stood in his towel, steam rising from the red hairs on his chest. Cora cocked her head and gave him a quizzical look. He leaned over and played the message again—while outside the sun broke through the morning fog.

15

A half mile up the mountain, Sahro Abdi Muse woke at the same time to a warm glow in the bedroom, a similar sound of birds outside the window. Her body still ached but her fever had broken and she felt clearheaded and rested for the first time in days, maybe weeks. She rose and checked the texts on the burner phone, recalling what she half remembered from early that morning—or was it the night before?—the messages from the driver about someone named "Abbot" who was to take care of her, and more messages from the contact Hassan. There were four new texts from Aunt Waardo, two from Fartumo and Ahmed. Everyone worried and waiting to hear from her. She replied to each with a quick message. A thumbs-up emoji. She was okay, *mashallah*, she'd write back soon.

In the bathroom she scrubbed her face and neck and arms, then studied herself in the mirror. Her cracked lips, puffed cheeks, rings beneath her eyes. Her hair was matted and tangled. She needed coconut oil, a shampoo. But first she had to find out where she was and how long she'd been lying in that room.

She threw an olive silk scarf over her head and wrapped it around her neck and opened the bedroom door. She called out loud to anyone who might be there. Sunlight fell from the end of a hallway; a clock tapped somewhere in the quiet. She waited and called again, but no one replied. She followed the sunlight on the floor and found a kitchen, the room bright and airy. Faded wallpaper printed with violets and ferns. A moist breeze came from an open screen door, a rushing sound of water or wind—she wasn't sure which. Someone had placed yellow flowers on a table in a blue glass vase.

She stepped through the screen door onto a stone porch. The sun felt luxurious on her face. She leaned against the porch rail and let the warmth soak into her skin. She needed to do her prayers. How many had she missed? That morning's salat and the one the night before. Those from the day before that. She closed her eyes and felt sleepy, then heard a faint knocking and looked around, alert, suddenly self-conscious, aware someone might be watching. She hurried back into the house, pulling her scarf tighter to her neck, then saw a man in the hallway wiping his shoes by the door. He was White and tall and wore eyeglasses and a long cream-colored kaftan with a hood. His back was turned and he was bent down now untying his boots. When he stood and saw her, he placed a hand over his heart and nearly leapt.

"My God," he said. "You scared me."

He froze and swallowed and kept one hand on his chest. Sahro froze too. The man's face turned tomato red. He didn't say anything for a moment. His head was square and jug-eared and he held a straw basket in his hand. His clothing seemed so unusual for an American. Sahro reached inside her pocket for her knife.

"Are you feeling better?" the man asked.

Sahro nodded warily, wondering who he was. If this was his home.

He raised his basket and apologized and made a little bow and said his name was Christopher. He was the abbot of the monastery. He'd met her the other night but she was probably too sick to recall. He was glad to see she was up and awake and hoped the worst of her fever was over.

"I've been praying for you and your safety," the man said and lifted the basket again. "I was just dropping off something for you to eat. . . . May I?"

He nodded behind her toward the kitchen, but didn't wait for her reply.

He swept past her down the hall. She watched him cautiously and followed and observed while he unpacked his basket in the kitchen, announcing each item as he placed it on the table: Bread. Cheese. Hard-boiled eggs.

He held up a large thermos.

"Lentil soup," he said and looked at her. "Good for the blood."

He was talking fast now, as if to himself, about keeping up her fluids and drinking lots of water and something about God's will and her being safe there, at the monastery, and she felt suddenly light-headed and woozy. She leaned against the wall. The kitchen spun a little. When she caught herself, the man was close and looked at her from behind his little glasses with alarm.

"Do you feel okay?" he asked. "Should we get you back to bed?"

He rushed to the table and grabbed a chair and pulled it over to the wall for her to sit.

Sahro waved the chair away.

"I'm okay," she said and shook her head. "I'm fine."

She took a deep breath and asked where they were. "This place— what is the name?" she asked.

"Here?" he asked.

"Yes." She gestured around her, a finger in the air. "Here."

"Blue Mountain Monastery," the man said.

She repeated the Somali words for "blue mountain" to herself— *Burr Bulug*—but didn't understand the last one, which she repeated out loud: "*monstery*."

She looked at him with a questioning expression.

"What is a *monstery*?"

The man's face broke into a smile.

"Mon-*ah*-stery," he corrected her.

She repeated the word again and asked what it meant.

He folded his arms and searched the ceiling, then looked back at her.

"Do you know what the word 'sanctuary' means?" he asked.

"Yes." Sahro nodded. Of course, she knew.

"A monastery is a kind of sanctuary," the man said. "A place people go when they are running away."

"What kind of people?" Sahro asked.

"Religious people usually," he said. "Men," he added. "Women have their own type of monastery. But anyone who needs protection is welcome here. Men. Women. Christian. Muslim. You are safe here," he said.

She put a hand to her chest.

"*Jazakallah*," she said. "Thank you. May God bless you."

"And you," the man replied, smiling again.

He clasped his hands together and looked out the screen door. She could hear the birds again and the sound of rushing water.

"Are we near Canada?" she asked.

"Close," the man said. "About an hour by car."

"Then we are . . ." she asked, "where exactly?"

"In Vermont," he said. "The state of Vermont."

She repeated the word: *Vermont*, a place she'd never heard of. The man said she was free to stay in the Guest House at the monastery as long as she wanted, that he understood her situation and knew someone was coming the next day or so to pick her up and drive her the rest of the way to Canada.

"In the meantime," he said, "you should sleep and eat and get better. That's the important thing. I'll bring you food from the monastery kitchen and you needn't worry about anyone coming here. The grounds are off-limits to the public and the monks keep to themselves. All you have to worry about is getting better."

He smiled and the skin on his his face creased. His eyes behind his glasses were powder blue.

"Thank you," Sahro said, then asked the man what monks were.

"Monks?" the man repeated.

"Yes," she said, "the word. What does it mean?"

"Monks are men," he said, "like myself. Religious men. That's what we're called. Monks are like . . ." The man paused and looked out the window, then back at her. "Like Sufi men or Imam? I'm not sure what you'd call it in Somalia or in Islam."

She repeated the word to herself. Monks. She wasn't exactly sure what he meant, or if there was an equivalent in Islam. She was still a bit wary of him. She'd seen something in a film once about White American men in hoods and robes carrying crosses and wanting to kill Black people.

The man started moving around the small kitchen, opening cabinets, setting a plate and bowl on the table. A fork and a spoon. Sahro watched as he filled a glass with water from the tap and brought out a jug of juice from the fridge.

"I'll just set all this up before I leave," he explained. "The soup will do you good. So will the apple juice."

He opened the thermos cap. She watched him with a mix of curiosity and caution. A White man. A Christian. A *monk*. In Mexico the priests wore outfits with collars and often a crucifix around their neck and they were the ones, along with the nuns, who offered shelter and food to the migrants. The religious ones were generally good, but some tried to turn you into a Christian or secretly fed you pork and said it was chicken.

The man was pouring soup into a bowl. He seemed to read her mind and glanced up.

"Halal," he said, nodding at the soup. "We don't eat meat at the monastery."

She blushed and he gestured for her to sit and emptied the whole thermos and screwed the cap back on, then stood a moment hovering beside the table.

"I should wash," she said. "I need to say prayers."

"Of course," the man said, and flushed a little himself. He put the thermos back in the basket and wiped his hands on a dish rag. Sahro felt suddenly, tremendously, tired from the effort of talking. All she wanted to do was crawl back into bed. She watched steam rise from the soup into the sunlight. The birds were calling again outside. She needed to send Waardo a text.

The man picked up his basket and made a slight bow. He said he'd come back in a few hours to check on her and bring her supper. Was there anything else she needed?

"No." She shook her head.

"Blessings," he said.

Before she could thank him, he rushed from the room, down the hall, and she heard the door close behind.

16

In the weeks after Ayaan's death, Sahro hung around the villa with Dalmar, heartbroken and aimless, unable to process their loss. Ayaan had become Sahro's big sister, her best friend and confidante, the one she admired and shared stories with at night. Sahro relied so much on her cousin's confidence, her knowledge of English and the outside world, her plans for migrating overseas. She was the front wheel of the Bajaj, which steered the other two; without her Sahro and Dalmar felt directionless.

At night now Sahro climbed the neem tree alone. She thumbed through Ayaan's old books and wept. Was there any point to learning English anymore? Ayaan was going to be the pioneer who led them out of Somalia to Europe, the *sahan* who scouted for hopeful signs and hazards, good grazing and water. She and Dalmar would follow—that had always been the plan. They'd all studied the route north through the Sahara in the last few months. Hargeisa to Khartoum, Tripoli to Lampedusa. What if Sahro made the journey herself? Now that her cousin wouldn't be leading them to some unknown future—nor helping the family with a job or husband overseas—didn't it fall to Sahro to take her place? She already knew some English, enough to get by, and she wasn't afraid to travel. Hadn't her grandfather told her that she was a star who could journey between warring constellations without harm? That she *belonged to many constellations but wholly to none*?

One evening after the brazier had burned down and Sahro stowed the pots against the walls, she went to Aunt Waardo's room and called through the curtain. Since Ayaan's death, Waardo had retreated ever more into the sanctuary of her small bedroom. She sat there now on a leather stool by the window, fanning herself and watching the street through the window bars. The strong smell of incense, frankincense— *foox*—burning in a clay dish. Sahro stood by the door, against the wall. She wasn't sure how to start; they'd rarely discussed tahriib before, but Sahro said she'd been thinking about it for a long time, and ever since Ayaan died, she felt it was up to her to take her place and make the journey to Europe as Ayaan had planned. Not necessarily for herself, she said, but for the family, to find a job, send remittances, marry, find a foothold, a safe place for her cousins to live. She knew the Sahara route was dangerous—she'd studied the maps with Ayaan—but she'd already traveled as a child through hostile terrain. She was old enough now and knew how to look after herself. Hadn't she proved that already as a child? And wasn't the Prophet Himself, Peace Be Upon Him, an orphan like her, forced to flee his murderous homeland, his birthplace, Mecca, for peaceful Medina, for himself and his family? His flight into exile, his hegira, was a model for Sahro now. What better way to honor her cousin Ayaan?

She said all this now to her aunt in a flood of words. Waardo listened with a skeptical look and afterward said nothing for a long time. Sahro half expected her aunt to laugh or shout her out of the room. But she sat quietly on her stool instead, picking at her fingernails and occasionally fanning herself or looking out the barred window at the evening outside.

At last Waardo let out a long breath. She wasn't surprised by Sahro's thinking. She'd always thought one day Sahro would ask about tahriib. She was so much like her mother, Waardo said. Headstrong. Always dreaming. Nothing could hold her back, not even good sense.

She turned to Sahro and regarded her for a long time.

"And you think you're strong enough, clever enough to do tahriib?" she asked, eyebrows raised.

Sahro nodded.

Her aunt snorted and shook her head.

"What makes you so sure?"

Sahro said she'd already traveled north as a child and south as a teen. Hadn't she done all that alone?

Waardo waved a hand.

"This is different," she said.

In Somalia, Waardo explained, Sahro had been among her own people, who spoke the same language, ate the same food, had the same religion, the same *diin*. There, she shook her head, she'd be among the hyenas and sharks and she was, *wallahi*, a woman—not even a woman, only a girl.

Waardo put down her fan and folded her hands in her lap, and what she said next stunned Sahro.

Had she been a boy, Waardo said, she'd have sent her overseas on tahriib long ago. There'd be no question. But Sahro was a girl and therefore had to prove herself ten times over, had to be smarter and more strategic than a boy would ever be. And yes, the fact that she was able to survive in both the north and the south, in the Hawd and in Xamar, with both sides of the family, was a good sign. But doing tahriib would be even harder. Her life would constantly be in danger. She had to be more than fierce, more than tough. There was only so much Allah could do. One wrong step, she'd fall into a pit.

Waardo fell silent. A distant crackle of gunfire echoed somewhere in the night. The room was growing dark, the incense thick. Sahro didn't know what to say. Waardo flipped open her fan and resumed moving the air in front of her face.

Then she began talking about the city. The Mogadishu she knew as a child, the one she loved growing up—and still loved despite what had become of it. She spoke in a way Sahro had never heard before, about the city's cinemas and colonnades, its beautiful lighthouse and beaches. Xamar, the White Pearl of the Indian Ocean. The envy of Africa. The spaghetti factory and sports stadium and the concerts and parades and dances held outdoors. A lost world she recalled as a small child, with her mother and father, alongside her younger siblings, Sahro's mother included. She spoke of the endless wars since, the armies and militias and the foreign occupiers, the "hyenas in boots," and now "the Youth," al-Shabaab. How all of them would one day leave and the fighting cease and the city would rise again from its ashes. She was confident about it. Their people were strong. She had to believe it would happen. That was the only reason why she'd stayed and endured it all. To keep the place safe and occupied, to keep a foothold for all the exiled family to return to. Here on the Indian Ocean in the old port town. Someone had to stay. It was easy to run, but harder to stay put. No one ever thought of that, *her* difficulties, *her* raising all these children and seeing them off to the *qurba joog*, keeping track of them all. But the moment peace came, they'd all come flooding back, asking for favors. The children of exiles who knew nothing of the country, who couldn't speak a word of Somali, they'd all come back and Sahro, inshallah—her own children among them.

She fell silent and turned aside and Sahro thought for a second her aunt had succumbed to tears, but when she faced Sahro again she was crisp and all business.

"I've been waiting for you to have the courage to ask," Waardo said, curtly. "I will talk to Uncle Cabdi Rashid. The others are too young. You're the right age. With Allah's mercy you might succeed."

Waardo folded her fan in her lap, then raised a hand as if in dismissal. Sahro didn't know what to say. She couldn't see her aunt's face anymore in the dark, only her outline against the window, her silhouette among smoke. Sahro had the sudden urge to walk over and embrace her.

Before she could take a step, Waardo snapped, "Well, don't stand there like a fool; go and get me a glass of water!"

"Yes, Auntie," Sahro blurted, relieved to have the task, and hurried out of the room.

—

In 2014 it cost—at the very least—five thousand dollars to make the journey from Somalia through the Sahara and across the sea to Europe.

Five thousand or more to pay for smugglers along the way and a boat that *might* make it across the Mediterranean. All that money and no guarantee against local pirates—the *magafe*—or police or soldiers or gangs, and no guarantee that the boat wouldn't sink or lack life vests (or a motor) or that Sahro wouldn't be sent back once she reached the other side, wherever that might be.

In the Nasiid Travel Agency and Internet Café, Sahro had spent hours with Ayaan watching the slow-loading pages of Google Earth appear on the screen. They'd tracked the journey from the brown parts of the earth to the green. North Africa across the sea to Europe. Often they toggled down to Street View to see what a city looked like on the ground, a place they might pass through. A street corner in Addis Ababa or Lampedusa. Outside the train station in London or the Metro in Rome. The people. The clothing. The signs.

That was the journey Sahro had imagined for years. The Sahara Route overland. The one she thought of when she met the following week with Aunt Waardo in Uncle Cabdi Rashid's upstairs flat. It was midafternoon, a Friday after mosque, the shades drawn to keep out the summer heat. Dalmar appeared in the doorway and Waardo waved him in. Her uncle sat in his chair, Waardo on a stool, and Sahro sat on the rug beside Dalmar.

Uncle Cabdi Rashid started first. He spoke about Ayaan and the plans she'd had for London. Contrary to what everyone believed, he said, he'd wanted her to emigrate to London but was only afraid for her life and the difficult journey it required. Marriage would have been much easier, but so be it; Allah had decided otherwise. Dalmar had kept the money she'd been saving for London, and that would go to Dalmar. Waardo had savings too; in fact, she'd been saving up for this very thing for a long time. Over the last few days Cabdi Rashid had talked with Waardo and the rest of the family and they'd all decided the best thing to do, the safest thing, would be for Sahro to go together with Dalmar.

Sahro started to protest. She didn't need a chaperone or extra baggage. She was quite capable of going on her own. And what about Dalmar's asthma?

Cabdi Rashid waved a hand and shook his head.

"You need a man as an escort. It is the only way."

Sahro looked at her aunt, who sat with her arms crossed, expressionless.

"Do you agree?" she asked Waardo.

Waardo nodded.

"Yes," she said.

Sahro glanced at Dalmar. He was trying not to smile.

"Did you know about this?" she asked.

Dalmar shrugged and picked at something on the rug. Then Waardo started speaking. She'd consulted with the whole family overseas. Fartumo and Ahmed in Ohio, the cousins and nephews in Norway, those in London and Dubai. They in turn had talked to others—contacts, smugglers—and everyone agreed the Sahara was no longer safe, the journey too risky. People were drowning in boats, jailed in Libya, killed in the Sudan. But there was a new route, another way to go. Not to Europe but to North America. It took a lot longer and cost more money but the chances of success were slightly better. You flew from Nairobi or Kampala to Dubai, where you could get a student visa. Then you flew to a city in South America. From there you traveled by land all the way north to the United States. When you reached the U.S. border in the place called Texas, all you had to do was tell the border guard there you were from Somalia and you were asking for "asylum."

"And then?" Sahro asked.

"They let you in," Dalmar said, unable to contain himself.

"Show us." Cabdi Rashid nodded at Dalmar, who stood and unfolded a paper he'd held in his hand. He came close and squatted beside Sahro and flattened the printed map with the palm of his hand. His forehead gleamed in the heat. Sahro leaned close too and studied the colored map of the Americas, North America attached to South by a strip of land that looked to Sahro like an umbilical cord between two continents (but who was giving birth to whom wasn't clear). Each country had its own color, pastel pink or yellow, orange or red or blue. Each with an unpronounceable name: *Panama, Costa Rica, Nicaragua, Guatemala.*

Dalmar placed his index finger somewhere in the middle of the big continent to the south.

"You start here," he said. "Then go north."

He ran his finger up the map, following an imaginary line through the isthmus all the way to the southern border of Mexico.

"You get on the train here." He tapped the map. "It takes you all the way to the United States."

He looked up at Sahro and smiled. She hadn't seen the gap between his front teeth in months—the same smile as Ayaan's, the same lips and mouth—and it made her suddenly sad, for it should have been Ayaan sitting there, having this conversation, making these plans. Somehow it didn't feel right.

The United States was a good country, Aunt Waardo said, famous for its fairness, its legal system. Its laws. Uncle Cabdi Rashid agreed. There were good jobs in America, he said. Jobs that paid well that Americans no longer wanted to do themselves, in meatpacking plants and hospitals, food stores and factories. And now, he said, they even had an African American man as president whose father came from Kenya. Which showed—did it not?—how anyone could make it in America. Then Dalmar talked next about American sports teams and rap stars, movies and TV, and how all the houses, people said, came with two cars, and three sinks inside their kitchens. One for water. Another for milk. The third for orange juice.

"Come on!" Sahro made a face and pushed him.

"Wallahi," Dalmar protested, "it's true!"

Sahro just shook her head and said he'd believe anything—but couldn't help smile too.

—

For the next few weeks Sahro let the new idea settle. She studied Dalmar's paper map and wrote down the incomprehensible names in her notebook. *Colombia. Panama. Nicaragua.* And though the whole idea seemed abstract, a journey that might never start or come to fruition, an afternoon arrived when she and Dalmar and Cabdi Rashid met with a smuggler downtown and handed him money, and another day when Sahro and Dalmar bought new clothes and rucksacks and received forged papers. Sahro had gotten used to the idea of traveling with Dalmar and felt partly relieved she wasn't going alone. Still, she worried about the arrangement. She could take care of herself fine, but another person? She'd already lost Ayaan; she couldn't bear thinking of losing Ayaan's brother.

—

Four months later they left the city inside a smuggler's lorry. The rainy season had just begun. A long, silvery light fell over the Indian Ocean. They hid in a hollowed-out section in the back of the truck with two other migrants, evading security posts. When they finally crossed the border into Kenya, they emerged, drenched in sweat, money sewn into the seams of their clothes. Sahro wore the dark blue head wrap signifying she was married. Dalmar a light green macawis and white button-down cotton shirt.

Two weeks later in Uganda at the Entebbe airport, they boarded an Emirates Air flight to Dubai. It was their first time inside a plane. Sahro gripped the armrest as the earth titlted away. Central Africa below. The rich greens and blues of the mountains giving way to reds and browns the farther north and east they flew. They waited twenty-four hours in the airport in Dubai, then flew to Amman, then Istanbul, and eventually—a day later—crossed the entire Atlantic in an Avianca aircraft. Hours later, sleepless, disoriented, they dropped out of the clouds into a cradle of green. Rain was falling over the Andes; water streaked the plexiglass. When the plane set down on the tarmac, the passengers broke into applause. Sahro had never even heard the name of the place on the high plateau outside the plane's window. A city nine thousand feet in the air called Quito. A country named Ecuador. The hard part was about to begin.

17

Christopher called the all-community meeting for one in the afternoon, yet ten minutes before the hour, the monks of Blue Mountain had already gathered inside the Chapter Hall. No one, save Brother Bruno, knew what the meeting concerned, but rumors had already started. Someone had spotted Father Christopher sneaking a basket of food out of the cloister. Another had seen smoke rising from the Guest House chimney. So routine were the monks' lives inside the cloister that the most minute change was noted. Especially the abbot's repeated absences from prayer offices. The old abbot, Father Edward, used to say that gossip was the only thing that traveled faster inside the cloister than the flu. Earlier that morning, after Christopher had hung a notice in the Common Room for an "All Community Chapter," the news rippled through the dormitory, cell to cell, relayed from monk to monk, fast as a phone tree; and everyone made his way downstairs to read the sign himself, handwritten, tacked to the bulletin board, beside the weekly schedule, beneath the clock:

URGENT
ALL COMMUNITY CHAPTER
1 PM, TODAY
ATTENDANCE MANDATORY
—FR C

What could it be about? Why the urgency?

No one in the cloister quite knew.

At 12:58 Christopher stepped into the Chapter Hall. The afternoon had turned cloudy and the room felt stuffy and close. The monks were already seated in high-backed chairs arranged in a formal U. Christopher strode to the front of the hall and sat in the center seat—the abbot's "throne"—and arranged his papers. As prior, Brother Bruno sat to the right at one end of the U, and next to him sat Father Teilhard (with his walker), then Anselm, John, and Simon; then Brother Benison, David, Ramon, and Luke; and lastly, to the left the novices Jonah and Minh. Each week on Sunday afternoons the community met for Chapter meetings in the hall, where one of the men delivered a talk on a spiritual topic related to the liturgy or season or a book they'd all been reading. Both the meeting and the hall were given the name "Chapter" because, historically, in their Order, the room was reserved for reading and discussing chapters from *The Rule of Saint Benedict*. The Chapter Hall on Blue Mountain served many purposes—meetings for scheduling, job duties, daily chores, anything pertaining to the running of the monastery. On Tuesday nights they gathered for a film: *Netflix night*.

—

Christopher rose and took his papers to a lectern. He made a motion and everyone stood and shut their eyes.

"May the Holy Family exiled in Egypt be a living model for all those forced to flee their country," Christopher began. "And may Jesus, Mary, and Joseph serve as an example for us here in the monastery while we continue to live our own exile from the world. May the divine assistance always remain with us."

All the men muttered "Amen" and sat, except for Christopher.

He opened his eyes and slowly looked around the hall. He was not a natural speaker; there was a time when he couldn't even face an audience, let alone deliver unwritten remarks. Yet over the years he'd grown more comfortable with the abbacy and all its trappings: the crozier and miter, the chasuble and stole, the whole getup handed down from one abbot to the next since (one could argue) the twelfth century. In time Christopher learned to channel Father Edward's confidence and voice and shape himself to the role. Yet when speaking in front of the community, he often felt like a dry pump that needed priming first in order to issue its water.

He began talking that afternoon about the blizzard the other night, the downed trees and power outages in the area, the extreme weather they'd been witnessing the last few years and how the new weather affected everyone both inside and outside the cloister. He spoke of their supposed separateness as monks, but how that separateness was largely an illusion.

"We have this idea about ourselves," he said, "and others have it about us, that we've 'renounced' the world in order to cut ourselves off from it, to disengage and be apart, but we all know how untrue that is, how we're never separate from the neighbor or the Other, even when living alone on a mountain three thousand feet in the air."

"Some of us here in the cloister" he continued, "misuse the idea of *fuga mundi*—'flight from the world'— as an excuse to simply evade responsibility and pretend we don't live in the real world, or to hide in the hold of our ship, like Jonah, and avoid what's being asked of us. And sometimes the cloister itself becomes the belly of the whale, a warm, comfortable womb sunk beneath the sea, safe from the storms, where we can live in our watery twilight between the living and the dead holed up inside our own leviathan."

Christopher paused and looked around the room. Some of the men had closed their eyes; others leaned forward with curious or unconvinced expressions, as if waiting to hear more.

"It's funny," Christopher said and took off his glasses and held them in one hand. "When Father Edward was alive, he used to sit on the porch of the Guest House, and when a jet passed overhead he'd point his cane at the clouds and complain about 'those damn neighbors upstairs.'

" *'There they go again,'* he'd say, *'making all that racket!'"*

The monks chuckled.

"The thing is," Christopher continued, "he really meant it. He even counted the number of souls passing overhead. Four hundred and something each hour. He even knew the flight numbers of the planes, where they were coming from and going, over the Atlantic or to Newark or Dulles. Somehow, he'd studied the timetables and destinations and made sure he was praying for each passing plane, each body overhead. It was amazing to witness. He felt this necessity in his bones, the reflex toward others; even though he lived alone, sealed away in his 'hermitage,' he never felt separate. It always reminded me of Thomas Merton and his revelation in downtown Louisville. We've all read about Brother Louis's moment on the corner of Fourth and Walnut, when he found himself among the lunchtime crowds after living inside the monastery so long. His beautiful realization, his great relief from the illusion of monastic solitude, that he was just one in the mass of humanity, no different from the rest. But we tend to forget what Merton wrote right after those words. That it was precisely the function of his solitude, his living as a monk, that lent him the clarity that would otherwise be impossible for anyone immersed in other cares; that his monastic solitude belonged not to him, but to *others.* 'My solitude is not my own,' he wrote"—and here Christopher closed his eyes and quoted from memory—"*For I see now how much of it belongs to them—and that I have a responsibility for it in their regard, not just in my own. It is because I am one with them that I owe it to them to be alone, and when I am alone they are not 'they' but my own self. There are no strangers.*"

Christopher opened his eyes. He pulled a handkerchief from his tunic and stepped away from the lectern and wiped perspiration from his forehead. Some of the monks had their eyes still shut, their heads bowed.

"All that sounds good, right?" Christopher asked, looking around the room. "We agree with Merton, don't we? The 'One with them.' His belonging to the others. The 'responsibility'? He owes *them* to be alone?"

The monks nodded. Some of them muttered yes.

"All those big, beautiful sentiments and words—they're easy to say, right?" he asked. "But maybe they're harder to actually live, especially here in the cloister, where we can have all sorts of opinions about who we are and what we believe in. We can talk until blue in the face about Brotherly Love and the Beatitudes and what we owe the Other, the Neighbor, but never be confronted with an actual situation where we have to be in the same room with them, never have to step up or show up. That's the paradox of the monastery—how easy it is to fool ourselves, each and every day"

Christopher set his glasses back on and stepped to the lectern and picked up a pile of papers. Then he told the men about the woman in the Guest House and how she'd come there the other night in the storm, frozen and feverish. He didn't go into details but said she was an undocumented immigrant on her way to Canada, seeking asylum there. As much as he wanted to protect them from knowing that fact, he needed to be up-front and hide nothing. He'd brought them all here today, he said, because he knew how quickly misinformation spread in the cloister, and he wanted to inform them himself and not have to keep things clandestine or hidden from anyone.

He looked around the room. The monks sat upright now in their seats; their foreheads gleamed, everyone suddenly alert. Brother Bruno was shaking his head in the corner in evident disappointment. Christopher stepped to the bank of windows, thumbed the lever on one, and pushed open the sash. Fresh air tumbled into the room, cool and moist, smelling of coming rain. How fast the weather changed on the mountain. He could hear robins outside on the lawn now. A cold front was pushing out that morning's warmth. He opened the next window and the next one and one more until the room felt freshened with new air.

Back at the lectern he said the woman in the Guest House would be staying at least another day if not more, but it shouldn't affect any of them. And while he'd unilaterally made the decision to let her stay inside the enclosure, he wanted the community's input and blessings.

He picked the pile of papers off the lectern and started distributing sheets around the room.

"I put together a packet of readings," he announced, "in the hopes of clarifying any questions regarding our guest."

He finished handing out the pages and pushed his glasses up the bridge of his nose.

"Would anyone like to begin?"

No one volunteered right away. The men were shuffling through the stapled pages. Brother Luke lifted a hand and began reading the first lines from *Exsul Familia Nazarethana*, the 1952 papal decree that established Rome's stance on immigrants and refugees.

"The émigré Holy Family of Nazareth," Luke read, "fleeing into Egypt, is the archetype of every refugee family. Jesus, Mary, and Joseph, living in exile in Egypt to escape the fury of an evil king, are, for all times and all places, the models and protectors of every migrant, alien, and refugee of whatever kind who, whether compelled by fear of persecution or by want, is forced to leave his native land, his beloved parents and relatives, his close friends, and to seek a foreign soil. For the almighty and most merciful God decreed that His only Son, 'being made like unto men and appearing in the form of a man,' should, together with His Immaculate Virgin Mother and His holy guardian Joseph, be in this type too of hardship and grief, the firstborn among many brethren, and precede them in it."

Luke continued reading about the church's *motherly solicitude for migrants*, how the church must look after them with *special care and unremitting aid*, that priests in particular were called to carry out this work. He read a long passage about refugees from different parts of the world—Armenia, Mexico, Russia, Poland, Palestine—and how, in each case, *regardless of nationality or religion*, the church offered safe sanctuary and should continue to show sympathy and *every Fatherly regard for pilgrims, aliens, exiles, and migrants of every kind.*

Luke stopped and looked up and asked if he should go on—there were another few pages. Christopher waved a hand and said, "You get the idea." They could read the rest later on their own. For now they should move to the next reading.

Everyone turned the page. On the next was a passage from *The Rule of Saint Benedict.*

"I'm sure," Christopher started, "you're all familiar with chapter fifty-three, 'On the Reception of Guests at the Monastery.' Would someone like to read it, please?"

Brother Simon raised the page and began to read aloud.

"All guests who present themselves are to be welcomed as Christ, for he himself will say: 'I was a stranger and you welcomed me . . . ' Great care and concern are to be shown in receiving poor people and pilgrims, because in them more particularly Christ is received."

Simon read the rest and stopped. Christopher asked if there were any questions before they continued. Most of the men shook their heads, but Brother Bruno raised his stapled pages in the air, and Christopher called on him.

Bruno, who'd been frowning the whole time behind his beard and thick glasses, put the pages down and sat up straight in his chair.

He said he knew the *Exsul Familia* well, and that it never addressed the key role of monasteries and monastics; that while the papal bull issued by Pope Pius XII was written for the church as a whole, and priests in particular, the apostolic constitution left out, he believed on purpose, any mention of the cloistered religious. He argued that they on Blue Mountain, like all monks and nuns of contemplative Orders, were charged by the Church to do one thing and one thing alone: *Pray without ceasing.* And while he accepted and supported the Church's concern for migrants, there were other churchly bodies—clerics and parishes and non-cloistered communities—better fit for the role and more able to provide refuge for immigrants and aliens. Back in the 1980s, he continued, when he was briefly with the Carthusians, they had to address the same issue of housing illegal immigrants from El Salvador during the Sanctuary Movement. At the time, the Benedictines at the nearby Weston Priory had publicly declared their monastery a sanctuary, and the debate had spilled over into their own charterhouse not far away. After much deliberation and prayer, the Carthusians concluded that the disruption and illegality, not to mention the very public (and frankly unseemly) theatrics of creating a sanctuary at the cloister, outweighed the good it would serve.

"We made the right decision back then," Bruno said, "and it's the right one now. Even though we're not Carthusians, we're contemplative monks nonetheless. Not activists. Our activism is prayer. We can't get involved in the fleeting business of social movements and contemporary politics. It is not what the monastery is built for."

He paused and put his papers down, then quickly ran a hand through his beard. Christopher looked around the room. The others sat in silence, some with downcast eyes. He'd expected opposition from Bruno. He felt a little remorse now about not telling him everything about the woman the day before. How much of his resistance was resentment about not being told?

Christopher thanked him nonetheless for his historical perspective. He said Brother Bruno was right in his description of their duties as contemplative monks, but that each of them had sworn vows of obedience as well to the Order's foundational documents. He asked them all to turn to the next page, where the appropriate section was found.

"Would someone like to read it aloud?" he asked.

Father John from Cincinnati—the only African American in the monastery—raised a hand and started reading from the section *De hospitibus suscipiendis* in the Order's "Constitutions and Statutes."

"Every monastery," John read, "is to continue the tradition of welcoming guests and the needy as Christ. Let those whom the providence of God has led to the monastery be received by the brothers with reverence and kindness, but without allowing this service to impair monastic quiet. Monasteries are holy places not only for those who are of the household of the faith but for all persons of good will."

He set the papers down and looked up, and the monks fell into a general discussion about other faiths and the meaning of "good will" and the nature of the guest's stay and her seeking asylum. Brother Benison asked where the woman was from.

Christopher moved back to the lectern.

"Somalia," he said.

The hall fell silent. They all seemed to chew on the name: *Somalia.*

"Is she a Muslim?" Brother Bruno asked.

"Yes," Christopher said. "She's Muslim."

The room remained silent. Bruno raised a finger and Christopher called on him again.

"With all respect, Father," he started. "I have grave reservations about allowing the woman to stay. When we talked yesterday, you told me she had been in an accident in the storm and you were sheltering her in the Guest House. Never did you mention once where she was from or her legal—or rather illegal—status."

"That's correct," Christopher said. "So the question I ask—in all humility—not just to Bruno, but each of us: Does it matter where she's from? Is our welcoming of guests conditional? Is our love of the neighbor?"

He looked around the room now from monk to monk. Bruno said nothing for a moment; neither did the others.

Father Teilhard, hunched over his walker, lifted a shaky hand. Christopher called on him and Teilhard adjusted his hearing aid.

"Is there a legal issue," he asked, "to hosting the young woman? Are we actually breaking a law?"

Christopher removed his glasses and began cleaning them with the sleeve of his tunic.

"Good question," he began. "I did a little research yesterday into the law. I looked into the Immigration and Nationality Act and the new guidelines put out by Immigration and Customs Enforcement. There was a whole section that addressed 'knowing' versus 'unknowing' transport of noncitizens across state lines—something we are not doing—and another section on the difference between transporting and 'harboring.' I even read some case law, but it was so mandarin and complex, we needn't get into the weeds. Suffice it to say," Christopher concluded, "the law is a lot like Scripture: it's open to many interpretations."

He slipped his glasses back on and smiled. Brother Ramon raised his hand.

"How long," he asked, "will the woman stay?"

Christopher said he wasn't sure. Probably only another day or two.

At the side of the room Jonah the novice lifted his hand.

"What should we do," he asked, "if we run into her by accident outdoors?"

Christopher raised an eyebrow.

"Smile and say hello?"

Everyone chuckled except Brother Bruno, who was whispering something to his neighbor, Anselm.

"Please don't worry," Christopher said. "You won't be running into her. You won't even notice she's here."

Christopher straightened his papers on the lectern.

"There's one other thing," he said, waiting a beat for Bruno and Anselm to stop talking. "Tomorrow, as you may know, is the annual feast day of Peter of Tarentaise. I was going to talk about Peter of Tarentaise in tomorrow's homily, but his story seems too fitting to not talk about now while we're on the subject of guests and contemplative versus active practices."

He set the papers down and moved to the side of the lectern and laced his fingers together.

Most of them, he assumed, knew something about the twelfth-century Cistercian abbot and monk. Perhaps, like he, they'd heard that Peter of Tarentaise had fed the needy and started a tradition in France of distributing bread to the local farmers in spring when their winter stores had run dry, a tradition known as *pain de mai*. Or maybe they knew how Peter assisted travelers who came over the Alps from Italy and set up hostels for them—waystations for migrants. Or perhaps they knew about Peter's reputation as a healer and humble monk, a man who—against his will—was made an archbishop, even though all he wanted was to be a monk. Certainly, they must have heard the celebrated story of how he once fled his own abbey for an even more remote one in the Alps in order to escape the responsibilities of his position. His escape didn't last long. He was found out after a few months and ordered back into service.

All this, Christopher continued, he'd previously known about Peter of Tarentaise, but there was a story he read for the first time the night of the snowstorm. It told of a winter evening in the Alps when Peter of Tarentaise was traveling with a few fellow monks in the mountains. A terrible blizzard overcame them. Halfway home to the monastery, struggling through the snow, they found an old woman dressed only in rags freezing at the side of the trail. The monks didn't know what to do. They gave her the few coins they possessed but knew money would do little in a place where she couldn't purchase shelter or food. Most of the brothers continued on their way, lamenting the old woman's fate, but Peter himself disappeared. When he rejoined the group, he was walking alongside the old woman, accompanying her, and she was now dressed in his warm robe and tunic. Peter himself wore only his hair shirt and scapular and cowl. When they arrived at the monastery, they sheltered the old woman, and Peter was put to bed, sick now from the cold. It took him a few weeks to recover.

Christopher paused and looked around the hall. Peter, he continued, slower now, was the perfect model for them and his example couldn't

come at a more apt time. For he married the two aspects of their vocation so well—contemplation and action—and his example dispelled the
whole notional difference between the two, between Martha and Mary
and who had the better portion. For even as contemplative monks, they
were not forbidden from acting on Christ's example, or by imitating
Peter of Tarentaise—one of the saints of their Order. And what better
example to model than Peter covering a stranger in his own cloth, risking
his own life for an other.

He looked around the hall again and asked if anyone had a question
and turned to Brother Bruno before he could raise a hand.

"Brother Bruno?" he asked.

"I assume we're going to revisit this matter in more depth," Bruno
said, one eyebrow raised.

"Of course." Christopher nodded and said everyone should bring
the papers back to their cells and read through the other writings and
passages and spend some time in meditation and examining their
conscience; that they'd meet on the subject again in a day or two. It
was work every one of them had to do, even if the woman had never
arrived inside the enclosure, for the Neighbor, the Stranger, the Other,
was a piece of who *they* were, and no less a part of the Body of Christ.

Christopher turned to Bruno again, as did the others. He still had
one finger in the air.

"Father Abbot," he asked, "would you consider a community vote
to see where we all stand?"

"No." Christopher shook his head. "Not now. Let's wait until we
all have time to process and pray and search our hearts privately
in cell."

He smiled at Bruno and looked around the hall. Bruno sat back in
his chair. Before Christopher could close the meeting, the novice Minh
at the side of the room shyly raised a hand.

Christopher nodded and Minh stood, hesitating, timid, twisting his
hands together. Minh Pham—his family lived in Da Nang.

"I just like to say," he started . . . then stopped. He pursed his lips. His English was still uneven; he seemed suddenly overcome with emotion.

"It is our duty to help in what we can in Christ our Lord," he said in a rush and sat quickly and looked at the floor.

"Thank you, Brother Minh," Christopher said, then asked if there were any other questions.

When no one answered, he bowed his head and the men rose once more.

"Our help is in the name of the Lord," he intoned.

"Who made Heaven and Earth," the monks replied.

Christopher made his dismissal and the men began moving toward the exit. He didn't lead them out of the hall as he normally would but sat back in the abbot's throne. His legs felt heavy, his eyelids too. He'd slept only a few hours the night before with all his googling and research about Somalia and Somali food and trying to make canjeero in the refectory kitchen. Afterward, back in his study, he'd put together his little packets for the Chapter meeting in the morning, xeroxing various passages and scripture: Matthew 25. Leviticus 19, Luke 16, the Catholic Social Teaching on Immigration and the Movement of Peoples—there was no shortage of appropriate matter. He'd even looked in the library during Lauds and spent far too long reading about the history of the Sanctuary Movement of the 1980s. The Quakers and Jim Corbett. Father Quinones. In the end, he'd left most of the material out.

He watched the men filing out of the hall now with their habits and shaved heads, one after another, Father Teilhard with his walker in the rear. When the last had left and the room was empty, Christopher sat back in his chair and felt the cool breeze blowing in through the open windows. After the sunny morning, it looked all of a sudden like rain. Christopher took off his glasses and rubbed his eyes. He needed to bring supper to the woman in the Guest House. He thought of their earlier encounter. Her elegant reserve, her distrust. Her sea-green headscarf and walnut skin. There was something fierce in her eyes. When she'd asked him what a monastery was, he'd told her it was a kind of sanctuary. A safe place. A place where people went when they were running away. How could he explain to her, he wondered, what they were running from—or to?

18

Everyone arrives at the monastery because of a shipwreck, Father Edward used to say. They crawl out of the sea like Saint Paul and try to find a Malta at the monastery: a rock to take them in. Sometimes a person stays a week or month. Other times they stay the rest of their life.

Christopher Gathreaux arrived at Blue Mountain in his late twenties, confused and disoriented, after his own years at sea. His brief "career" as an artist had already bloomed and faded. He'd lived in New York City, a young painter trying to make it in the art world. His one big solo show at a gallery in SoHo was a bust; not one canvas sold and his work was panned in the press. It was the late eighties and he worked by day as a museum guard at the Frick Collection and lived in a group loft in Williamsburg, but suddenly—after his show—he didn't want to be in the city anymore. Friends were sickening with AIDS and Christopher suddenly seemed to fit in nowhere. Not in the club scene nor the art world, nor in several groups he almost (but never quite) joined—the Gay Men's Health Choir, God's Love We Deliver, the War Resisters League. He attended Mass at St. Joseph's in the Village but even there he kept to himself, partly out of introversion and shyness, partly to avoid the complications of finding himself entangled in a relationship he didn't want. He'd dated both men and women but was never that keen on sex—not half as much as whomever he was with. His indifference, his lack of ardor, always ended up hurting the other. Even back then he thought of sex as a poignant attempt to tunnel back to some original Eros or joy. His conflating one love with the other—the physical with the spiritual—disappointed everyone, but mostly himself. It was easier to go straight to the source—agape, divine love—though he didn't know if it existed or where he might find it in the world that he knew.

By luck, he escaped New York City on a fellowship to Rome. A year at a villa on the highest hill overlooking the city. He couldn't believe his fortune, to leave behind New York and its confusions. For there, along the Tiber, in a new context, he felt oddly liberated and at home. His studio overlooked the ancient city and the back garden with its olive trees and oranges, its fragrant hedges of bay. He couldn't have hoped for a better place to work—but painting was suddenly the last thing he wanted to do.

Each morning, instead, he stepped out of the villa and dove into the city and entered each and every church he passed. He fell into murals and frames, statues and stones; like a fish dropped into a current, he drifted from painting to painting, church to church, square to square—upstream to the Ara Coeli and down to the Gesù, over to Piazza del Popolo and out to Santa Cecilia. Along the Lungotevere, the plane trees glowed like hammered gold in autumn light, and in all the chapels and rooms the same story was going on. Matthew inside a bar. Paul fallen from his paint. The same wrenching narrative, how it struck them in the middle of an afternoon, in a clerk's office or on a hill, that finger pointing in the air, in the Caravaggio in the church of San Luigi dei Francesi: the same light that struck Matthew impaled him. In every piazza and every room in Rome a diorama reiterated the story; even the staircases up to the Janiculum marked by the Stations of the Cross. Every tessera and paving stone and column. There was no escaping the story, the sound of bells banging everywhere, announcing a new page.

Over the course of those weeks and months, something shifted deep inside Christopher. He stopped looking at paintings. He sat in church pews and looked at people instead. Old Sicilian women, young Romanians in leather, Japanese tourists. Ghanaians. Mexican nuns. They all sat in the cold, empty spaces separately but with the same searching look on their faces, an expression he knew so well from working at the Frick. The way people looked when they sat in a room and tried to discern something that wasn't always there. He felt in those weeks a terrible sadness and longing that often left him inexplicably in tears, a feeling he couldn't tell anyone or put into words. One moment he was full of verve, the next plunged into darkness. It was as if those days he saw too much around him and felt a quaking coming off everything and everyone he met, God seething on every surface, bubbling out of stones. He purchased a pair of sunglasses to hide his mania, hoping they'd act as blinkers to keep the world at bay and dim all the visual information rushing into his head. He locked himself in his room at the villa but didn't touch his paints. He found himself grounded instead only inside the massive caverns of churches. He went to Mass each morning, in a different church each day. Sometimes the Masses were in Latin or Italian, other times Swahili or Korean—it mattered little. The weight of the space gave him gravity, the stone columns, the massive pillars. The ancient liturgy and music; they were a muscle memory from when he was an altar boy on Long Island. The ciborium and the pall, the purificator and Communion cups—he liked the opera of it all. He could already feel the tug in his cheek, the hook in his lip. Unsure yet where it was leading, where he was landing.

One evening in late November he watched a cloud of starlings over the Aventine. The birds had been in the city for weeks but he hadn't noticed their habits before. The starlings arrived in fall from the surrounding countryside to roost in the city at night, and that evening on the Aventine he stood in the Orangery and watched with dozens of others the flocks begin their crepuscular flights. One by one the birds lifted into the twilight; then a massive wave rose into the sky. The murmuration moved like liquid, fluid, unconfined, forming in dark creases and folds above the city, a shape that kept shifting, as if erasing any idea of fixity or permanence, their collective body becoming one.

Everyone around Christopher watched, commenting in many languages, staring into the sky over the Tiber as if at a son-et-lumière show. Then the birds gathered above the Orangery in a darkening pool and dropped into the orange trees and pines, encasing branches in cloaks of iridescence and creaking beaks, a million miniature umbrellas flapping open and closed. The noise was so great, Christopher couldn't hear his neighbor speak, a small man in a cream-colored tunic and a thatch of wiry black hair—a monk. Then a white rain began to fall around them. A rain of starling shit. People screamed, pulled jackets overhead. There was no escaping the baptism; the sky seemed to be squirting milk. People ran in one direction or another. Christopher and the monk, for some reason, were laughing, deliriously, wiping crap off their sleeves. Then they were sprinting out of the Orangery and up the road, the small monk shouting the whole time, "*Hurry! Hurry!*" a look of uncontained glee on his face.

Christopher followed him into an alley of pines and up the steps of a church. The man handed him a handkerchief. Christopher took off his glasses and cleaned them, and when he looked up again, the monk had vanished. Christopher stood in the dark, disoriented, adjusting to the dim candlelight, the few parishioners in their seats. He held the monk's handkerchief, and the chanting began. A subtle weave of sound, beautiful, melismatic, strangely familiar. Slowly the monks came into view, silhouettes against stained glass. He saw the small monk slipping into the back of the choir. The chant ended and a new one began, something he vaguely recognized from his childhood, the Salve Regina. When the service was over, he searched for the small monk with the thatch of black hair. He still held the man's handkerchief—it smelled of aftershave—but Christopher couldn't find him in the departing crowd.

He didn't sleep that night in his room in the villa. He stayed awake and thought of the birds, their improvised choreography, their making of themselves something larger, a message or pattern; and he thought of the men in the church and their somehow similar spectacle, their Gregorian chant, their sound.

The next evening he returned to the church on the Aventine for

Vespers. The small monk was waiting outside the church under the pines, the same droll smile on his face. Christopher had washed and folded the handkerchief, and he handed it to the older man, who looked at his wristwatch and said, "You're just on time."

He led Christopher by the elbow into the church. They didn't speak. The monk disappeared as he had the night before, but after the service they met on the church steps and strolled down the hill to a restaurant in Testaccio.

Like Christopher, Father Edward Diamond was an American living in Rome on a retreat, staying at the Tre Fontane Abbey on Via Laurentina. In the States, Christopher would eventually learn, the monk was the somewhat legendary abbot of a monastery in Vermont, a man known for his colorful past: a former physicist, a converted Jew, then Jesuit, then Trappist before joining their Order. None of this Christopher knew that evening when they sat at a sidewalk table and the man ordered in Italian. Christopher was impressed with the monk's calming energy and quick mind, his knowledge of art and religion, music and Rome. Christopher felt immediately drawn to the man, the mischief in his moss-green eyes, the way he talked about monastic life and salvation. They sat long into the night over a bottle of amaro, until the waiters started stacking tables and the lights blinked off in the bar. After, they walked the emptying streets past the Protestant Cemetery and the Pyramid, all the way to the bus station near the old abattoir where the monk was getting on the last bus back to Via Laurentina. Christopher had the sudden urge to ask him for confession—to make confession—something he hadn't done in nearly a decade. Father Edward invited him to visit at the Tre Fontane Abbey on Via Laurentina. There, at the quiet abbey on the outskirts of Rome, Father Edward said, he'd happily oblige.

—

For the rest of his stay in Rome Christopher split his time between his studio at the American villa and the church at Tre Fontane Abbey. The two old institutions—a thirty-minute bus ride from one another—seemed so different on the surface, yet their real estate was equally opulent and equally exclusive. Christopher liked spending hours at the abbey with the quiet monks in their tunics, the even energy that seemed to radiate from the place and the men. Edward lent him books from the library: Merton and Pennington, Suzuki, Saint John of the Cross. Returning to the American villa in the evening, Christopher locked himself in his room and devoured the books, avoided the other residents and scholars, the writers and artists arguing over grappa and wine. White American men and women outdoing each other with words, tossing their opinions at each other like projectiles, lobbing them here and there. He'd always been mistrustful of words, the way they cluttered a room or stubbornly clung to others or got in the way of what he was trying to say, and the more time Christopher spent at the abbey on Via Laurentina, the less comfortable he felt among his fellows at the American villa in Rome. The less he felt he had to say. The more he trusted silence over words.

—

When he returned to the States the following fall, Christopher wrote Father Edward and asked if he could visit his monastery in Vermont. Yes, Father Edward wrote, he could come visit Blue Mountain Monastery, but not until Christopher spent "significant time" exploring other options. Other monasteries, other Orders. Finding out what he really wanted. The abbot said to write again in a year—and not before.

Thus began Christopher's search for a vocation. He borrowed money from his mother on Long Island and spent weeks, then months, on retreats at different houses across the country. He visited the Trappists in Kentucky, the Benedictines in North Carolina. The Camaldolese in Ohio. He traveled west to Wyoming to visit the Carmelites and spent time with the Russian Orthodox in Quebec. He even spent a month at a Zen monastery in the Catskills. Each Order he tried on like a pair of new shoes, seeing which (if any) offered the best support. All were hungry for vocations. None seemed quite the right fit.

When a year passed, he contacted Father Edward, who gave him permission to come to Blue Mountain, and Christopher took a bus to Vermont the next week. Upon Christopher's arrival, an old monk in sandals showed him to his cell, and shortly after Edward himself appeared in the doorway. He marched into the room with an armful of books and dumped them on the bed.

"Get to know the matter," Father Edward said, gesturing toward the books. "Then come to my office tomorrow after Nones. We'll take it from there. Three p.m."

He gazed at Christopher distractedly. The man looked the same—the thatch of black hair, the big nose, the smell of aftershave (Aqua Velva). Then his expression softened and the mischief came back into his eyes.

"Thanks be to God." He smiled. "You've arrived." He scurried out the door before Christopher could say a word.

Christopher lifted books off the bed one at a time. He was expecting theology (the *Summa* or *The City of God*). But the spines read: *The Apple Varieties of New York, Volume I. Rootstock and Pruning Techniques. Apple Genetics; The History of Applejack or Apple Brandy from Colonial Times to Present; La Pomme: Histoire, symbolique, et cuisine.*

What was Father Edward trying to convey? Christopher wondered. What was "the matter" he spoke of? In order to enter some Zen monasteries, he knew, postulants were sometimes given a koan or riddle to puzzle over and respond to before being let in (sometimes they were left outside the monastery's gates for days until they had the "right" answer). Were the apples a reference to paradise or Eden (which the monastery was sometimes called—a "second Eden," a place to regain innocence)? A metaphor for the temptation of the flesh (which he'd now have to give up)? A for apple, the start of the alphabet, a new beginning? Christopher ruminated for hours. Maybe the books weren't a test at all?

At three the next afternoon Edward explained. It was none (and all) of those things, he said with a smile. They were rehabilitating the old orchard on the monastery property and Edward was thinking of ways to improve the stock, or maybe make cider. He wanted Christopher to investigate, find out everything he could about the orchard's existing apples. The trees there had gone feral, the names apparently lost. Now they had to decide which to keep and which to cut down. But first they needed to identify each tree.

Christopher didn't understand. He knew nothing about apples or trees. Why him? The abbot gave him a serene smile as if it were self-evident. Because Christopher was new and came with fresh eyes, he said; because he was a painter and presumably nimble with color and form. Everyone in the monastery, Edward explained, had his own role. Each monk was a kind of crystal in a chandelier; each had his particular genius and fit in where the light shone strongest through them. Comparing the shade and blush of various apple varieties seemed the perfect job for a painter, did it not? Who else was better attuned to the subtleties of the palette?

Christopher started to protest; he knew nothing about cider or growing things.

Edward waved a hand impatiently.

"All the better, then, to learn," he said. "God will provide, and the books will help. Now," he said, putting up his hood, "let's walk."

Outside, the trees were changing on the mountain. It was only mid-September but leaves lay scattered across the lawn. Cinnabar and cadmium orange. The air crisp and cobalt blue. They passed a garden and a grove of yellow birch and entered an orchard. Father Edward talked the whole time about monasteries and apples. How they shared a common history. How the best varieties of apples—like books—were preserved behind monastery walls during the Middle Ages. He talked about the collapse of agriculture in medieval Europe and how the sweet Roman varieties, the Paradise apples, would have nearly vanished had it not been for the Cistercians zealously propagating them inside cloistered gardens.

They passed trees now weighed down with apples. Windfalls on the ground, haloes of yellow hornets. The air spiced with fermentation and rotting fruit.

Edward pulled an apple from a hanging branch, took a bite, and immediately spat it out.

"The problem," he said, wiping his face with his tunic's sleeve, "is separating the good from the bad, the keepers from the spitters."

He pitched the apple into the grass and looked at Christopher.

"There's a lot of spitters in the world," he said and continued walking. Christopher could hardly keep up. The older man's energy astonished him. There was something almost ferret-like about Edward; small and furry, he could easily slip out of reach.

—

Those first fall days, Christopher worked in the orchard alongside an older monk named Father Teilhard. They studied the shapes and colors and tastes of apples. Christopher drew apples, dreamt apples, made lists and tried to identify each tree. Wolf River, Alexander, Duchess, Ida Red. They compared photographs and old catalog copy, descriptions of taste profiles, called in an expert from Cornell. They made maps of the good trees and bad. Which to keep and try to resurrect and which to cull. Christopher learned about hybridizing and grafting and pollinating, the Biblical metaphors never lost on him (nor the irony of monks pollinating apples. Nonbreeders breeding. Apple sex). Christopher knew as well, the apples were Father Edward's way of easing Christopher into the life of the Order. Edward always approached theology through the created world, through *things*, and believed that only the physical could lead one to the metaphysical. The seen to the unseen. The whole point of the Incarnation, that the Word was made flesh. In this case the flesh was apples.

Everything enchanted Christopher those first few weeks on Blue Mountain. The silence. The woods. The autumn colors blazing on the trees. He took music and chant lessons from an old Swiss monk who'd studied at Solesmes. His days were filled to the minute with a structure he'd never known before. Unlike the hours he'd previously spent alone in his studio, he didn't have to think on Blue Mountain. He didn't have to plan. Everything was set for him. A schedule that dated back thousands of years. Work, prayer, singing, reading. *Oratio. Contemplatio. Lectio Divina.* A cell could be a container to hold his erratic thoughts, a place to put himself inside, a vessel filled with tradition. The daily prayers, the Divine Office. The schedule took time to get used to. The waking at three for Vigils, then heading back to sleep for a few more hours and rising again a little later for Lauds. It felt at first like finding his sea legs, acclimating to the unusual drift of monastic time, the greater and the lesser hours, the liturgy a tide that waxed and waned each day, leaving him sometimes sleepy, or newly rinsed, or shivering cold. It seemed those first few weeks as if he'd entered another time zone or country, a different decade or octave of time; that he'd left the twentieth century and entered another, older way of being, with no touchstone to the present but the sky and the clouds and the bells that tolled the time. Each day was an Ember or a Feast or a Saint. Another chapter in the story they kept retelling, their life organized around a narrative that never stopped, that ended in Passion and began in Resurrection. And everything in the monastery served that story. The colors in the sacristy, the kind of incense burned (sandalwood or myrrh). The liturgical seasons (Advent, Easter, Pentecost, and Ordinary Time). The cycle of psalms became familiar, like phases of the moon. A record played over and over. One hundred and fifty songs. Each another groove in vinyl. (Mostly forty-fives, but a few LPs.) He got to know and love them all. Even the Imprecatory Psalms, the psalms of wrath, destruction, and rage; all of them he learned to read not literally, but as metaphors for his own internal struggles, his wild emotions. What the Buddhists called *kleishas*, the Catholics sins. Each psalm had its own personality, each a different human emotion or mood. The idea was to know each one and name them. To call them out. To play them as a chord, each a different key. To reject none. Accept all. And once known, once mastered, the words themselves mattered less than the act of saying the song, of singing something larger than himself. Of making a murmuration and following the thing that wasn't there. The psalms became an extended mantra that lasted a fortnight and repeated itself over and over though the seasons. Each came back with regularity like a friend or a troubled cousin or someone difficult to deal with, all reflecting back a piece of himself, a mirror of humanity. He had to take the good with the bad and learn to love them all, as he had to learn to love—or try to love—each of his fellow monks.

If, those first few months, Christopher occasionally had doubts—as he did, all the time—it helped that he was surrounded by mountains and forests and the beautiful architecture of the cloister. Even their outfits looked good. The cream-colored tunics and pressed scapulars. The Order's founders self-consciously called themselves *pulchritudinis studium habentes*, "those intent on beauty." And beauty intentionally enveloped every aspect of their life, from their simple birchwood cells to the forks and spoons in the refectory, the plates they ate off. "*All the implements of the monastery,*" Benedict wrote in his *Rule*, "*are sacraments.*" The Order took Benedict at his word; everything in the cloister was hand-cast—the beeswax candles, the handblown glasses and thick turned plates—everything crafted or forged by the brothers (or some other craftsperson), nothing cheaply made but meant to last (as per Benedict) "*a thousand years.*"

—

The honeymoon lasted almost a year. Nine months precisely. Longer than most, according to Father Edward. First came Christopher's disillusionment with the other men, the monks' pettiness, their veneer of piety, their egotism and laziness. As a novice, he was forced to spend most of his time with Brother Bruno, the other novice. They shared work details and formation with Father Edward. Within weeks, everything about Brother Bruno irritated Christopher: the way he ate his soup, wore his socks and sandals, quoted scripture, his having to know the right answer to everything. His showing off his seminary school knowledge, his grasp of Augustine and Thomistic thought.

Christopher had expected all the monks in the cloister to be wise and compassionate, introspective and smart. He'd swallowed the whole notion that the monastery was "halfway to heaven," everyone an Arsenius holding the sun in his arms. Edward told him not to confuse the ideal with the real, that monks were no better than anyone, and possibly the worst sinners; that's why they needed the confines of the cell and enclosure: to keep them out of trouble. The real penance of monastic life was not that you lived alone, he said, but with others. You don't get to choose your fellow monks, but they become your family, and that's precisely why they're all there: to learn how to love not God (that was the easy part) but other humans, the Neighbor, the Other, even people you can't stand—*particularly* people you can't stand. Living inside the cenobium meant constantly being irritated and rubbed the wrong way, but that's how people got polished. The grit makes the pearl.

Edward assured Christopher his doubts were not only normal but necessary. He'd have worried about Christopher if he had *no* doubts. Everyone arrived at the monastery, he said, coiled with idealism. Tense and sharp, wired like springs. At some point the tension had to go out of them. It could happen in a hundred ways, but no one stayed in the cloister if they didn't break or snap; it was a little bit like basic training in the army. You had to be broken down before being built up. Novitiate was the place to fall apart. Edward expected it in all his novices (as it had happened to him as a younger man). The picking apart of one's self, the constant uncovering of faults, was like peeling an onion, layer by layer; it was bound to produce tears.

Christopher listened and nodded and went back to his cell but felt as empty as before. He felt fooled by his previous yearning and disappointed in himself. Perhaps it had all been a passing fancy, a chimera. Perhaps he wasn't cut out for religious life. Perhaps he didn't have what Bruno had: a solid enough foundation in scripture and theology, a conviction of his own salvation. As long as he could remember, he'd always felt the presence of God nearby. God or the Divine, Christ or the Holy Ghost—whatever name he called it at the time. Sometimes it was just the sense of something he felt but couldn't see, a knowledge beyond words, warm and peaceful when he prayed, almost erotic in nature, a bliss that had brought him to the cloister in the first place. But now it was gone. The feeling had left him at the monastery—of all places—in the very place where he was supposed to "enjoy" God. He felt like he was suffocating instead. So what if he couldn't make it as a monk? Couldn't he always go back to school or find a job or try to paint again?

He tried to cure his funk with exercise. Long walks. Singing. Daily spiritual direction with Father Edward. Depression, the abbot said, was part of the spiritual life. Christ wasn't kidding when he said, *Blessed are the poor in spirit.* The Noonday Demon was invented at the monastery. You had to plumb the depths to reach the heights. We're the only profession in the world, Edward argued, that not only anticipates a personal crisis, but encourages one. Depression is impossible to avoid; it's where God enters—*through the wound.*

———

By August Christopher had enough. He could barely drag himself to Vespers, his favorite office. He needed a break. The abbot agreed. He should leave the monastery for a period of time. Give himself a month or two. See a shrink. Sort out the source of his depression. Visit friends, family. Travel—whatever he needed to do—and see what happened.

He packed his bag with a mix of regret and relief. Father Edward drove him to the bus station in Hart's Run. Handed him a folded piece of paper. A poem by Robert Frost titled "Directive." A parting gift. He tucked the page in his pocket and hugged Edward and climbed into the bus—and fought back tears. He was a failure. What would he do now? It was the end of summer, the Greyhound to New York City nearly empty, the AC blasting. Through tinted glass he watched the cars on the road, thousands filled with couples or families and kids heading one way or another. All the rushing astounded him, the engines going on all day and night, the slow spill of oil that was the New England Thruway. Did he really want to return to this world? To a possible *career*, to the business and ambition of *being someone*, fitting in? Trying it all again? The rushing and plotting and proving himself with his painting, each canvas only as good as his last, a kind of bandage. Tear one off and start again. Wasn't the whole point of monastic life wearing the canvas himself—*being* the art?

New York City felt exhilarating at first. He wandered from the bus through Chelsea and the West Village, happy to be among so many others on the avenues and streets, the rivers of bodies rushing past, people talking and eating meals out in the open, on the sidewalks, or shouting to one another across subway platforms. He could go anywhere, eat anything, stop for a drink in a bar. He felt a sudden great love for everyone he saw, the enormous herd of humanity, as if he'd never quite truly seen them before. He was part of them and they him and he was just another blood cell in a great body of people no more or less important than the rest.

He stayed with an old friend in Williamsburg. He walked across the bridge each morning for Mass at St. Cyril's. For a week he wandered in and out of galleries with the little money he had. He visited his old haunts, Caffe Dante, the Strand. He saw his mother on Long Island, and his sister drove down from Ithaca. But after a few weeks of drifting he felt unmoored and weightless, as if he were missing part of himself, a part he'd left in the cloister.

One evening he wandered into the Frick Collection on Seventieth Street. He knew the museum better than any in the world, having worked there for two years. He loved the stuffy furniture and potted plants, the porcelain vases and faded rugs. All of it made the art seem more accessible, intimate enough to enjoy in one go, and if you needed a rest from the collection, you could retire to the glass-roofed courtyard, with its marble pool and living plants. To Christopher, the Frick had always seemed more like a church than a museum, the hushed tones of its rooms, each its own chapel, the Fra Angelico in one, Piero in another. The trickle of water in the font. He never tired of its paintings, the Rembrandts and the Turners, the Manet. Each canvas a touchstone and friend, something to contemplate, a kind of mirror he'd find himself in anew with each visit.

One painting he loved more than any other, Giovanni Bellini's *St. Francis in the Desert.* It was one of the first paintings he'd ever noticed as a child. His mother had taken him and his sister on a trip to New York City after their father died. For some reason they'd stopped at the Frick and Christopher stood in front of the Bellini. He was unsure who the mysterious man was on the cliff, or what he was doing there, but something about the saint's expression, his gesture, his opened arms, the chrome green of the canvas, the ultramarine sky—something about the melancholy mood, the light in the laurel tree—electrified him as a boy. What was the man doing and why? Why all the animals, the ominous sky? His sister also noticed all the birds.

Years later, when Christopher worked as a museum guard, the Bellini painting lost none of its mystery or appeal. For hours during his shift, he'd stare at the meticulous landscape details. The rosemary and white mullein. The caper bush and grape vines. The peeping rabbit and hidden heron and stolid donkey. All of it rendered by Bellini with the precision of a naturalist painting, so unusual in a religious painting of its period. A shepherd stood in the background and a medieval town perched on a distant hill. And above it all floated an eerie blue sky with the thin, sinister clouds of Quattrocento paintings; a sky that seemed to portend something momentous or awful about to occur; a sky that created tension and drama (even without its attendant *putti*). Saint Francis stood in the center on the cliffs below. He looked to the left: arms wide, jaw dropped, awestruck, staring at the dawn sun in the branches of a tree, a laurel with its limbs bent toward him as he bent back, the tree and the man a mirroring, engaged in a silent exchange; it looked as if the tree was exposing its leaves to Francis and Francis exposing to the tree his open palms, palms already marked by spots of blood—the stigmata—his wounds as new as the sunlight. Was it a painting about photosensitivity? About chlorophyll and blood, the relation of iron to each? Or both creature's reaction to sunlight—and receptivity to God? Christopher didn't know. But after staring at the painting for weeks while on duty, what struck him was how Bellini, in making his composition, forced the viewer to mimic the exact pose of the painting's central figure. How, whenever he looked at the Bellini at the Frick, he stood with the same stance and gaze as Saint Francis. Another hidden dialogue was going on: the viewer looking in wonder at the painting, and Saint Francis looking in wonder at the tree, and the tree responding to the source of light, which remained unseen. All the action forced one to consider the invisible thing: the origin of the light reflected on the leaves at the upper left corner of the canvas.

Centuries before the modernists, Bellini had captured an idea Christopher had grappled with as a painter. The idea that every painting pointed elsewhere, not to the paint itself but outside the canvas—to a third party. The unseen source of light, to which it owed its authority. That without this other thing, the painting—all painting—was merely an arrangement of pigment on rag.

—

When Christopher returned to the Frick that evening, he hadn't been to the museum in four years. He recognized none of the guards on duty, and no one recognized him. It was late in the day before closing. He visited his old friends, Fra Angelico, Rembrandt, Turner—and saved Bellini for last. Outside the museum windows, a hot August dusk was falling over the city. He stood in the half dark of the room and stared into the canvas. He knew the story of Francis of Assisi well: how he'd rejected a life of luxury and broken with his merchant father to serve the poor, how he became a friend of animals and wrote his canticles to "Brother Sun" and "Sister Moon" and climbed a mountain in the Casentino Forest. One day after spending a month meditating among the rocks, Francis saw an angel floating overhead, tacked to the sky, wings fluttering. He watched the crucified angel in ecstasy, with pain and joy and awe, and once he received that vision, and his own stigmata, Francis's health failed and he died two years later.

What Christopher hadn't known when he worked at the Frick—but knew now—was that all the landscape detail in the painting had an additional layer of theological meaning. The lizard, the rabbit, the laurel tree, the ass—all were invested with symbolic significance. Yes, Bellini loved to paint hills and clouds and sunlight moving across a meadow, lizards and rabbits and ferns and especially trees (trees were often the most alive things in any of his paintings), but he was also a devotional painter. Like Saint Francis himself, he was born, Christopher read somewhere, with "an emotional response to light." A response that "translated into love." Wasn't that the unseen element he was staring at in the painting? The same thing all those people who came to the Frick were moved by and stared at without even knowing it? Weren't they seeing what couldn't be seen: *love*?

It was getting late. The museum was closing. One of the guards kept coming around saying, sir, we're closing in five minutes. He wanted to tell the guard he knows . . . he knows . . . that he used to work there too but wore a different uniform now. He waited to be alone in the room and fell on his knees in front of the *St. Francis*. So what if the guard was watching? Hadn't he seen others break down in front of the canvas before?

Later, out in the hot streets, the sound of sirens filled Fifth Avenue. Dusk had come and gone, the sky a scar of red above the park. He wandered downtown in the heat, past the Plaza, the public library, the traffic thinning and light. He walked all the way to the East Village in the twilight, to Delancey and Orchard Street. By the time he mounted the steps to the Williamsburg Bridge, he knew where he was headed and his direction home.

The Greyhound back to Vermont took eight hours. He paid scant attention to the route, the small cities and mill towns they stopped at each half hour, another stranger getting on or off. He was anxious about returning to the cloister. How would it go? What would he feel? He found the Frost poem Edward had given him before he left and read it again and stuffed it back in his pocket. Why Frost, he wondered, and not a more religious poet? Hopkins or Herbert, Saint Teresa or John of the Cross?

He arrived in Hart's Run in the late afternoon. Father Edward himself had driven to the bus stop to meet him. The strong sunlight in the North Country felt demystifying and clean, a hint of chill in the air. Christopher chattered the entire time, telling Edward about his weeks away, the loft in Brooklyn, the Ukrainian church, his mother and sister on Long Island. He talked until they drew near Blue Mountain. It was the last day of August and already the leaves were changing on the trees, the mountain beginning to blaze. Along with his elation and hunger—he hadn't eaten all day—Christopher felt something else: a sadness, a giving up. A surrender, a kind of death knell. Who was dying? He wasn't sure but suspected it might be himself.

They drove past the small tollhouse and Christopher opened his window and stared at the colors, the orange and red, the narrow road leading up the mountain. Something in the spruce forests, the crisp air, made him feel he'd come home. When the boom gate at the bottom of the mountain closed behind them, he recalled the lines from the Frost poem Edward had given him. Something about a chalice and child's play and pulling up a road behind you and putting up a sign saying, "closed to all but me." Passing into the enclosure that afternoon, the last lines of the poem came to him out of the blue: *Here are your waters and your watering place. Drink and be whole again beyond confusion.*

19

Christopher stomped on the Guest House steps in the rain. It was early evening now and he was bringing supper to Sahro. He folded his umbrella. Before he could knock, the young woman opened the door. She stood in the threshold in a black down coat and clean canary headscarf. Her face looked freshly scrubbed and alert.

"Good evening," she said.

"You're feeling better?" he asked.

"*Mashallah.*" She nodded. "Much better."

Christopher held up the basket.

"May I?"

"Please." She opened the door wider. "*Fadlan.* Come inside."

The orange lamp glowed in the front room but the Guest House felt chilly and smelled of smoke. While Christopher removed his boots, Sahro gestured toward the woodstove and said she'd been trying to start a fire.

"It does not like the rain," she said.

"No." Christopher nodded; the low pressure made it difficult and the old stove was fussy to light. He'd help her in a second, he said but asked if it was okay if he went into the bedroom first to get something there. She gave him a puzzled look and shrugged.

"Of course," she said.

Christopher left the basket by the door and padded down the hall and entered Father Edward's old bedroom. He hadn't been there in months. He tried to ignore the woman's things—clothing folded neatly on a chair, the unmade bed, a blue knapsack—and went straight to the closet. He pulled open the door, and the smell struck him first. Aqua Velva. Edward's odor still on his shirts and trousers, his tunic and scapular, his winter habit (he'd been buried in his summer one). His sweaters hung on hangers in a row, untouched since his death. Christopher gathered the clothes in two arms, lifted them from the rack, and closed the closet door with a foot.

In the front room the young woman knelt by the open stove door, fanning a new smoky fire. Christopher draped the pile of clothes over the back of an armchair.

"I noticed you were cold," he said, wiping his hands. "All these clothes are for the taking." He gestured to the pile on the chair. "If you need anything to keep warm . . . They're all going to be given away."

The woman looked up from the stove and said nothing but kept fanning the flame with a folded piece of newsprint. Christopher arranged the clothes on the chair.

"May I ask," the woman said, "whose house this is?"

Christopher said it was the previous abbot's house, the abbot before him.

He nodded to the armchair.

"These were his," he said.

"His clothing?" Sahro asked.

"Yes." Christopher nodded. "He died."

"*Allah yerhamo,*" she said. "I'm very sorry."

She stood from the stove and walked toward the chair.

"Please." Christopher gestured. "Take anything."

"They are very nice things," Sahro observed.

"Yes," Christopher nodded. "Old but nice."

"How long," she asked, "he die?"

"Last fall," Christopher said. "Six months ago."

The woman made no reply. Christopher walked to the stove. She'd left the door open, the flame guttering. How many times had he tended the same stove while Edward sat in the armchair with a book?

He knelt there now, opened the kindling box nearby, and took out a few sticks, a curl of birch bark, a pine cone, and arranged each delicately on the smoking fire. Then he leaned close, inhaled and blew. The bark ignited, then the pine cone, and the wood caught fire. He left the door open a crack and watched while the interior of the stove began to glow.

When he looked up again, the woman was wearing Edward's coat. Her yellow headscarf against red wool. Christopher did a double take.

She seemed to sense his reaction. Her face clouded.

"Is it *okay*?" she asked, looking at him with concern.

Christopher smiled.

"Yes, it's okay." He gestured to the coat.

"It's just . . . Edward . . . the abbot—that was his name—he'd be happy to see you wearing his coat."

"Oh," the woman said and looked as if she were blushing. She looked up a second later with a perplexed expression.

"May I ask . . ." she started.

"Yes," he encouraged.

"What does the word 'abbot' mean?"

"It's the head of the monastery," Christopher explained. "The one in charge."

"The boss?" Sahro said.

Christopher laughed.

"More like a father than a boss."

"Yes." The woman nodded knowingly. "It's the same word in Somali. *Abbo*. The word for 'father.'"

"Is that so?" Christopher asked.

"*Abbo* or *abbaye*, it means the same thing."

Christopher knelt by the stove, lost in thought. Somali was probably phonetically close to Aramaic. Aramaic was the language of the Desert

Fathers. The word "abbot" had come from her part of the world.

"So you are abbo now?" the woman asked. "The father?"

Christopher nodded and said he had been ever since the old abbot retired and became a hermit.

He looked up and saw Sahro's confusion. She asked him what a hermit was—then lifted a finger in the air.

"Please," she said. "One second. I come right back."

She hurried from the room and left him by the stove and then returned a moment later with a red spiral notebook and pen.

"I must write the words down," she explained, apologetically. "Otherwise I do not learn English."

She sat on the floor beside the fire, cross-legged, pen in hand, notebook in lap, wearing Edward's coat. She asked Christopher for the spelling of the words "abbot" and "hermit." He spelled each out for her and explained what the latter meant and how it differed from a monk. Then he spelled out the words "monastery" and "enclosure" and explained those words too. He wasn't sure she understood it all, but when she was done writing, she looked up and put the pen to the bottom of her chin.

"I have another question," she said. "The words over the door."

Christopher gave her a puzzled look. She pointed with her pen to the front door of the Guest House.

"It's over there," she said. "I show you."

She stood and walked to the front door and waited for him to follow. Then she opened the door and leaned into the rain and pointed above the lintel.

Christopher leaned out too and saw Father Edward's old sign above the door. The words were painted on a piece of wood: *FUGE, LATE, TACE.*

Christopher shook his head, smiling, and ducked back into the room. The woman shut the door behind her.

"What is it?" she asked. "What do the words mean?"

Christopher wandered back to the stove and moved Edward's clothes off the armchair. He lowered himself into the cushion and sighed. Sahro followed and sat again in front of the stove. She tucked one edge of her headscarf behind an ear and waited.

"Fuge, late, tace." Christopher said the words out loud. Then he told her they were an old saying from the earliest Christian monks, the Desert Fathers. The words were Latin and meant more or less "Run away. Hide. Keep silent." Sometimes they were loosely translated in English as "exile, cunning, silence." But either way, he said, they meant the same thing: Find a safe place in the world and hide.

He looked at the woman and saw her confusion. She raised her pen and asked him to please explain each word.

"Fugere," he said, "to flee. To run away. Flight."

"Latere," he said, "from *lateo*, to hide or conceal. To escape notice. And *tace* means simply: 'be quiet.'"

Sahro scribbled in her book, and when she was done she looked up once more with an equally puzzled expression.

"Why are the words on the door?" she asked. "Why are they hiding? What are they running from?"

Christopher let out a heavy exhalation. How could he explain the context of the quote? The complicated history? The Roman Empire. North Africa. Europe. The Desert Fathers. He began telling her about the early Christians, how they were often attacked in their own country. The terrible violence of Rome, the challenge of Christ's message. Some of the early Christians fled to the desert to find a safe place to live and practice their religion, he explained. The Desert Fathers did too as a way of growing nearer to God there. They were the first monks who lived communally and apart from others. They were the ones, he said, "we model ourselves after today."

The woman looked at him for a while.

"Here?"

"Yes," he said, "here."

She nodded and chewed her lip, then asked, "Where was this desert?"

"Africa," he said.

He looked at Sahro with a little smile and explained further: "The Sinai, the Nile Valley. Parts of Ethiopia."

"And the monks traveled there from Europe?" she asked.

"Europe, the Near East, yes," he said. "Some from North Africa."

She listened intently, her pen touching the tip of her chin again, her eyes serious.

"Did they give them welcome?" she asked.

"Who?"

"The people in the desert. Did they welcome the Christians?"

"Yes." Christopher nodded. "I believe so. That's the reason people went there in the first place. To find a safe place."

"Fuge, late . . ." Sahro pointed toward the door, unable to finish.

"Yes," Christopher said. "They were exiles, refugees. 'Fuge, late, tace.'"

Sahro nodded and said nothing, and they sat a moment in silence, listening to the light rain on the roof. Sahro looked at the flame in the woodstove, then turned back to Christopher. She asked if he would write his name and the name of the monastery in her notebook.

"Of course," he said.

She held the spiral notebook and pen out to him, and he took the book and set it on his lap.

"Where?" he asked.

"Anywhere," she said.

He opened the book to the page where the pen lay and saw her handwriting. Neat and small and mystifying. English and Somali words side by side, written with the same Roman characters, the same Latin alphabet, but the orthography suddenly made strange by the Somali. The sentences like a sea of vowels, like no other Roman language he ever knew. He tried reading the script to himself—*ayaa i xanuunaya in yarna waan warwareenayaa*—but the syllables made him swoon.

He looked up and caught the young woman smiling.

"It's not easy," she said, "Somali language."

"It's . . . unusually beautiful," Christopher said, writing his and the monastery's names in the book and handing it back. "I've never seen it before. I thought Somali was written with an Arabic script."

"No." Sahro shook her head and closed her eyes. She explained that it was supposed to be, but at the last minute after independence, Somalia decided to use the Latin instead of Arabic alphabet for the Somali language, Af Soomaali.

"Why?" Christopher asked.

"Typewriters," she said.

"*Typewriters?*" Christopher repeated.

The woman pulled the bottom of her scarf over her mouth to hide her smile. She put the notebook down and explained as best she could that all the government offices back then, previously run by the English or Italian colonizers, had Western-alphabet typewriters. Thousands of typewriters with Latin letters. To replace them all with thousands of new typewriters with Arabic letters would have cost too much—and where would they get them? So they went with the Latin alphabet for official business. But, she said, many people were not happy with this decision.

"Why?" Christopher asked.

Sahro hooked her elbows in front of her knees, leaned forward, and looked at the fire.

"Arabic," she explained, picking her words carefully, "is the language of God. Of Allah. The language of the Holy Qur'an, of Muhammed the Prophet, Peace Be Upon Him. But Latin . . ." She shrugged and looked down at her hands, then up at Christopher. "That is the alphabet of the nonbeliever, the English, the Italian. The colonizer."

Christopher nodded.

"Matter of fact," she continued, "the word *la* in Arabic means 'no' and *diin* means 'religion,' so together, *la-diin* means, in fact, 'no religion.'

Some Somali people had a saying back then: *Laatin waa la'diin*. It meant 'Latin has no religion' or 'Latin has no God.'"

Christopher looked at her, incredulous.

"Wow," he said. "Tell that to the Vatican. *I* need to write *that* down."

Sahro didn't miss a beat but held the notebook toward him, and they both laughed; then Sahro said shyly, "It is what you call a fun?"

"A *pun*?" Christopher asked.

"Yes!" she said and covered her teeth with a hand and apologized for her poor English.

"On the contrary," Christopher said. "Your English is excellent."

Sahro pulled a face.

As it turned out, she explained, she was happy Latin was chosen as the script for Af Soomaali. It made English so much easier to learn. She already knew the shape of the letters and their sounds.

"Where did you learn it?" Christopher asked.

She sat back, suddenly somber. She made a vague gesture with one hand.

"Long story," she muttered.

"The best sometimes are." Christopher raised an eyebrow.

The young woman tried to smile, but the light seemed to have left her face.

They sat listening to the paddle of rain on the roof.

"Someone is coming tomorrow or the next day to pick you up?" Christopher asked.

"Inshallah," she said.

"Do you have everything you need for the night?"

Sahro stood, suddenly formal in Edward's coat, and said yes and thanked him. Christopher stood too. He told her there was supper in the basket. He could heat it up on the stove in the kitchen.

"No problem," she said. She would do it herself.

He hesitated a moment, putting his hands together.

"Okay, then," he said, gesturing to the armchair. "I'll just leave the clothes there. Take whatever you want. You're okay with the stove . . . the fire?"

"Yes." She nodded. "Thank you."

Christopher went to the door and pulled on his boots, suddenly awkward, not knowing how to say goodbye. A bow or a wave of the hand. He stood and grabbed his umbrella and said good evening, and Sahro said good night back and added something in Somali. Then he opened the door and stepped into the rain.

20

Nothing had prepared Sahro for the city in the Andes, the quiet mountains, the cold streets. The safe house on the outskirts of town, where she and Dalmar were driven at night and dropped off along with four other migrants—two men from Cameroon, one from China, another from Afghanistan. They stayed out of sight in a half-constructed house for a week, sleeping on a concrete floor, while their money was wired via Western Union. The smugglers gave Sahro and Dalmar new clothes. Sneakers and jeans, oversized sweatshirts, visor caps.

When they left Quito, they traveled by bus, were instructed when and how to pay bribes, told never to sit together. Those first days passed for Sahro in a cloud of incomprehension and fear. She spoke no Spanish. Not even enough to say hello. On the buses, she became a target of laughter and stares—the tall African girl groped by drunken men. She didn't tell Dalmar about the men, afraid he'd do something rash or draw even more attention to themselves. But at the bus station by the border in Tulcán, she bought three pencils and a pocketknife, all as weapons.

—

After a week of hard travel they reached the town of Turbo on the Colombia coast. She and Dalmar and the Afghani man stayed together at a migrants' hostel in the port. Back home they'd been led to believe the American route was new, that only the lucky few knew about the "back door" through Central America. But now in Turbo, at the crossroads of South and Central America, Sahro saw how deceived they'd been. Dozens of migrants crowded the hostel and town. Men from Africa and Asia, the Caribbean and South America. Haitians and Pakistanis, Brazilians, Senegalese. Women too. All traffic north from South America funneled through the small port town. They were all making the same journey, Sahro learned, to *El Norte,* North America. Everyone heading across the river, into the big jungle called the "Darien Gap."

One night Sahro lay awake in the hostel while rain drummed on the tin roof. Mosquitoes droned around her, her face already swollen with bites. Reggae blasted from a bar across the street. She tried to pray behind a curtain sectioned off from the overcrowded room, but even prayer failed to allay her fear. She missed Ayaan. She missed her ayeeyo. She even missed Aunt Waardo. How easy it had all seemed back in the villa on Via Sanca on the colored map in Uncle Cabdi Rashid's room. All those pink and blue countries that looked so simple to cross. Yet after only a week of travel now, of parasites and stomach illness, her period, the painful hours on cramped buses—of fending off men and having to pay extra bribes at each roadblock and never being sure of what to eat (because there might be pork inside) and choosing to go hungry instead—Sahro had grave misgivings. Dalmar complained and argued; she was afraid he'd get in a fight. She constantly worried about his asthma—he'd been slightly ill since Ecuador too. It helped that they traveled with the Afghani, a young man named Saleem, a fellow Muslim who spoke a little Spanish and Arabic, so between Sahro's English and Dalmar's Arabic, they were able to communicate okay. No one had told them beforehand about the bribes. The harassment and names people called them. Nor did she know about the Darien Gap, the dangerous jungle they had to cross now. If they had enough money, as some of the other migrants did, they could hire a speedboat up the Panama coast and avoid the worst of the jungle. But they didn't have money. They'd have to cross the rain forest by foot—it took three days if you were lucky and swift. Yet they had to pay for that as well, for a smuggler or a native guide. *Plato o plomo.* They'd learned the phrase from Saleem. *Silver or lead.* They had to pay one way or another, with money or blood.

Sahro had learned all this by the time they crossed the Gulf of Uraba in a flat-bottomed boat. It was just after dawn on a cloudy morning and she and Saleem and Dalmar sat in the small wooden vessel with a woman they didn't know who wore dark sunglasses and jeans and a sparkly red shirt. Their guide was a small, bowlegged man in rubber boots who carried a machete and camouflaged pack. The boat driver sat shirtless with a beer beside the outboard engine. Neither of the two said a word the whole time.

By midmorning, they left the boat and started single file through the forest. Sahro carried a small rucksack, two liters of water, a plastic tarp, and everything else she owned. Clothes and knife and notebook, bottle of black seed oil, her Holy Qur'an. In the afternoon the sun broke through the canopy and they hiked through poles of humid light, the air so heavy it steamed around them. They'd been advised to buy rubber boots, but only Saleem had, and Sahro's feet in squeaking sneakers already felt chafed and raw.

They camped in a clearing that night. The coyote pointed his machete at places not to sleep. Under a tree, on the ground.

"*Escorpiones,*" he said. "*Hormigas.*"

Saleem translated. "Scorpions. Ants." Insects were already attacking Sahro's arms. It was best to sleep up in a branch of a particular tropical tree.

They ate by the light of Saleem's flip phone. Packets of salted crackers. Tins of sardines. The coyote sat at a distance and unpacked his own food from a bandanna. Sahro offered the woman in the jeans and sparkly shirt some sardines and crackers. She timidly took a cracker and said *gracias.*

Sahro asked in English where she was from.

"Caracas," the woman said. "Venezuela."

Sahro nodded, though she'd never heard of the place.

"Far away?" she asked.

"*Bastante*," the woman said and made a vague gesture with a hand.

She took off her dark glasses and cleared something from her eye. In the glow of the flip phone Sahro could see the bruises. The woman quickly put her glasses back on, and the two ate in silence for the rest of the meal.

Afterward Saleem told Sahro and Dalmar some of his story in bits of Arabic and broken English. He was a motorcycle mechanic from Kabul whose brother lived in the United States in a city called Baltimore. Both had fought alongside the Americans during the war in their country, but only his brother had managed to get a green card. Saleem left Afghanistan two years earlier, overland through the Khyber Pass. In Karachi he'd stowed away with four others on a cargo ship that flew a Brazilian flag. A week later, believing he'd arrived in Rio, he was arrested and jailed in Hong Kong. Once freed he found another container ship heading across the Pacific, which eventually ended up in Porto Alegre. In Brazil, he'd been jailed and assaulted, robbed and held for ransom. Twice hospitalized. But he knew a trade, and wherever he went he worked on motorcycles. Japanese, American, Indian Enfields—he knew them all. Small engines too. Meanwhile his brother sent him money from Baltimore, where he worked in a pizzeria. Saleem knew about the Darien Gap because he'd read about it. But this was the farthest north he'd made it yet in the Americas.

Sahro comprehended some of his story, enough to get the gist. She'd liked the man from the start. Straightforward and polite, he'd been an anchor for Dalmar. He was twenty-six years old—seven years older than Sahro—but his round, beardless face made him look even younger. Sahro was sure to include him in her prayers—he and the woman with the bruises from Venezuela—later that night.

—

They woke to rain the next morning. Sahro's feet swollen, her arms lacerated by insect bites. She climbed from the tree, tarp over her head. Saleem sat in the clearing in a raincoat, Dalmar under his square of blue plastic. No one had seen the guide that morning. The Venezuelan woman emerged from the forest, wearing an enormous leaf over her head. She hadn't seen the coyote either.

They waited in the downpour for the bowlegged man with the machete. Rain dripped down their faces. Dalmar funneled rainwater into bottles. Sahro went off to wash and do her prayers. Twenty minutes later, rain pounding harder, the coyote still hadn't appeared. Sahro had her suspicions. Saleem was the first to say it out loud. The coyote wasn't coming back. He'd left with their money in the night. Dalmar refused to believe it. He insisted they stay. But after an hour, and no break in the rain, the Venezuelan woman shrugged off her big leaf and said something in Spanish.

Sahro lifted her rucksack and joined her, and they all started walking. They followed the faint trace of litter through the jungle, a trail of candy wrappers, empty soda bottles, batteries—the remains of earlier migrants—toilet paper, bones. The rain came and stopped and started again. The tree canopy grew so thick, Sahro couldn't see any sky.

All morning they climbed a ridge, the footing muddy and slick, but by afternoon the rains stopped and the birds came out. Parrots and macaws. They rested by a rushing stream in the sun. Dalmar and Saleem pulled off their shirts and leapt into the water. The Venezuelan woman walked across to the opposite bank to wash on her own. Sahro climbed the slope to find a private place to pray. She pried off her useless sneakers—better to go barefoot—and sat on the ground and rested her feet.

After her prayers, she sat alone in the dappled light, leaning against her knapsack. She thought of Ayaan and what she'd make of this strange place, this jungle so far away, on the other side of the world. It made her momentarily sad and she sat daydreaming, scratching her bites in the shade above the stream. She watched Dalmar below with Saleem, both bare-chested, sitting in the water. The Venezuelan woman stood a little ways away, stripped to her underwear, washing her long black hair beside the stream. The birds had stopped squawking. The jungle fell silent. Sahro saw something flash in the trees. Then two men in camouflage appeared on the opposite bank. One raised a rifle to the stream. The other grabbed the Venezuelan woman by her arm. They wore boots, bandannas over faces. Dalmar and Saleem turned from where they were sitting in the stream. Sahro couldn't hear what was said but saw Saleem rise, and Dalmar too. Then a bright puff of red erupted from Saleem's shoulder. He crumpled to the water. The report came after. The rifle's crack. Dalmar was scrambling up the bank.

Sahro didn't hesitate. She was already on her feet, knapsack in hand, diving blindly into the jungle. She ran without thinking, upslope, away from the stream, the rattle of gunfire behind. She ran barefoot over roots through thickets and trees. Life in danger knows only running. *Naftu orod bay kugu aamintaa.* She ran without stopping, in disbelief, with the image of Dalmar in her head, the look on his face in the stream, the bullets ripping the water. She ran until sobs clogged her throat and blinded her eyes and she had to stop in order to breathe.

She leaned against a tree, heart on fire, chest heaving. Sweat poured down her face. She kept replaying the scene inside her head: the men stepping out of the forest. The puff of blood. Who were the men with rifles? What did they want? Why hadn't they said anything before shooting? Saleem, back in Turbo, had told them about the lawless Darien Gap, the drug traffickers and gangs—*narcotraficantes, federales, FARC, urabenos*—but the names meant nothing to her then. Maybe she should have paid more attention. Maybe she shouldn't have run. She listened for gunfire or men's voices or any unusual sound. She had to find Dalmar. His asthma, his stomach. He couldn't last long on his own.

Back home at the villa, she and Ayaan and Dalmar had a whistle they used to signal one another across the courtyard. Two contrasting notes—like the call of a dove. A sign to meet at the neem tree. She tried it now. Low at first, then louder, but after a few minutes she grew afraid she'd attract unwanted notice. She headed back down the slope in the direction from where she'd run. She held her pocketknife open in one hand and a big stick in the other. She needed to find her cousin.

The rain began slowly at first; then the jungle darkened and the downpour came. She was suddenly unsure of the direction. The jungle looked all the same around her. Big wet leaves and vines. The canopy pressed close. Silver dripping on green.

She started off through the rain but stopped. She tried to calm herself with prayer, *Surah Al-Baqara*, the dua that always helped. If only she could discern the direction north—the qibla—she could orient herself. There were times growing up in the scrublands on an overcast day, in an unknown place, when they couldn't see the sky and lost the direction of the qibla. Her grandmother told her you could always find the way by asking Allah. You only had to sit a moment and concentrate and give Him your intention and you'd feel the weight slowly grow in your heart. Whatever direction the weight came from—that was north.

Sahro closed her eyes and listened to rain on the leaves. She said Surah Al-Baqara in her head. But she kept thinking of Dalmar. What if they'd caught or killed him or were holding him hostage? What if he got away? Would he head back to the port city or continue north? They'd always planned if separated to call Aunt Waardo back in Xamar. But Sahro was in the jungle. Even if she had a phone, there was no cell service in the Darien Gap. She'd have to wait until she reached the other side. The town called Yaviza; she'd seen it on the map. The frontier on the edge of the rain forest. Perhaps Dalmar would be waiting for her there.

—

She walked all afternoon in the direction she thought she'd fled from but kept getting turned around. When evening came she climbed a tree and waited. She spent the night petrified in the dark, the jungle loud around her, the pulse of frogs and insects, bone-chilling screams, the howls of animals Saleem had named back in Turbo: *Cougars. Jaguars. Pythons, monkeys, wild pigs,* the jungle floor alive beneath her legs.

A mist fell in the morning, a veil of silver. She still couldn't see the sky. She drank water dripping off leaves and ventured in the direction she thought was north. A hollowness filled her body, an emptiness and a low-grade fear. She sobbed on and off that day with the knowledge now that she was definitely alone, separated from Dalmar, that he might be injured or dead. That she might not see him again.

She walked throughout the day, following little freshets and streams. The rain stopped and started. Sometimes the sun bore through the canopy and she tried to orient herself to east and west but decided it safest to simply follow the little streams; at least they'd eventually lead her to the sea.

She tried consoling herself with her grandmother's voice. Her ayeeyo reciting the names, singing her lineage back through the generations, striking her leg with a stick when she left out a name. *How can you know where you're going if you don't know where you've been?* Hadn't she come from a long line of nomads, the original *reer miyi*? Hadn't she moved through hostile terrain her whole life? Her people had survived the harshest place on the planet for thousands of years by knowing when and where to move and how to make milk from stones. If they could survive in such a dry, unyielding land, surely she could pass through a green one filled with water.

By nightfall exhaustion overtook her. She picked small brown leeches off her legs and watched the blood drip from where they'd cut the flesh.

She ate the last tin of sardines in her pack, then fell immediately ill. She passed the night in the cradle of a tree with convulsive stomach cramps. Rain emptied from the sky. Leaves lit up in flashes, lightning overhead. Glossy limbs and dripping silver. She heard nearby howls. She kept imagining faces. What did the monkeys do in the rain? The men in camouflage? The poisonous snakes? Pumas and tapirs—the names Saleem had said. The pit viper called *fer-de-lance*.

By the third day her bowels gave way from bad water. Her temples burned. She stumbled along a stream and saw dancing figures overhead, small people or maybe monkeys who wore grass skirts and hats and made low, hooting sounds. Maybe they'd seen Dalmar? She waved and hollered to get their attention—but they didn't speak Somali; and when she tried English, they were already gone. She drifted in and out of consciousness, her ayeeyo's voice in her head. The hectoring line of her lineage, a camel train leading her out.

Night arrived again, then dawn. She slept and woke and walked and slept again. She watched the flaming birds overhead, orange and red, the fruit bats, the ants. The *hormigas*. Her legs blackened and swollen, hard and hot to the touch. She was going to die—she was sure of it now—just like Ayaan, like her mother and father, like everyone else, and she wasn't sure anymore that it mattered, if she wouldn't be better off one way than the other, her muscles moving or at rest. Wasn't it easier to just stop? To become scattered, a gas, a flame? To leave her bones behind in the jungle if not in the sea? Did it matter where she laid them down? Divested the parts of herself? Nose. Lips. Mouth. The Bight of Benin. The Strait of Hormuz. Each piece Ayaan had named nights in the neem tree—their own private geography.

When she slept she dreamed of Xamar. The gap in Ayaan's teeth. A cave calling the wind, the breeze blocks in the room. Her mother's black locks, the shining turquoise sea. Was it Xamar? The Karaan District? A blood-red moon loomed over the Indian Ocean. Everyone stood in the courtyard, Dalmar and Ayaan. Cabdi Rashid. Waardo. The twins. They were weeping over a body, washing limbs, winding the cloth, the pure white muslin, saying the prayers. She could just make out the hands, freshly hennaed, the legs, alarmed that the face down there was her own.

—

Two days later, along the rain forest's edge in the Guna Yala region of Panama, three women were gathering mangoes on the mainland across from their village island off the Atlantic coast. The eldest in the group was looking for the medicinal bark of the morqauk tree when she stumbled upon the tall, dark stranger. The woman wasn't sure if the *way suppur*—the foreign girl—was alive. Her mouth hung open, her face disfigured with insect bites, feet bloodied and swollen. She called over the other women. They approached the *way suppur* with extreme caution. The eldest woman leaned down and poked the sleeping girl with a stick—and one of her eyes flew open.

They carried her to their dugout and rowed her across the strait to their home on the island. They fed her medicines from the forest. Grated coconut and taro soup, dried fish and palm fruit and ñame. Later, Sahro wouldn't recall any of this—not the three women who found her in the forest, nor their thatched hut on stilts in the Caribbean Sea, nor the week she lay in a hammock surrounded by the women and their half-naked kids, their brightly patterned fabrics and red *molas* the color of blood oranges, the slip of the coastal waters, the smell of ocean, or the clatter of palm fronds overhead.

When she woke it was weeks later in the infirmary of the migrant center in Panama City. She'd been brought there by boat by the Panama Coast Guard, who monitored the waters around the Guna Yala region. The village men had alerted them about the lost stranger.

Who were these people, these women and men, who'd come to Sahro's aid, who'd saved her? Only Allah knew. Allah and his legions of angels whose names were too complicated for humans to comprehend. Had they found Dalmar too? Had they lifted him as well from the rain forest? She asked everyone in Somali and English and broken Spanish. Had anyone seen him? Was her cousin even alive? A tall boy. Nineteen years old. Black. Lanky. Beautiful eyes. A large gap between his two front teeth? The nurses looked at her strangely and said *¿Qué?*

She didn't stop searching for him. Even when she recovered. She asked everyone in the infirmary and all the officials, the police and soldiers, the people at the migrant center where she had been left. But no one could tell her about Dalmar. No one fit his description, or that of Saleem or the Venezuelan. Maybe they were still in Colombia, in the jungle. An African? An Afghani? No papers or ID? How could they even know these people existed? Where was her proof they'd even stepped foot in Panama?

When she recovered, she was given a seven-day transit visa to leave Panama right away. They didn't care where she went. North or south, as long as she left the country within the week. With the last of her money, she called home from the migrant center. She had to tell Waardo the news, hoping Dalmar had called Xamar. But they hadn't heard from him either. Crestfallen all over again, she relayed what she could (and left out almost everything) and Waardo was silent on the other end of the line. Sahro blamed herself; it should've been her. First Ayaan, now Dalmar. But maybe he was still alive, just ahead of her, or behind, on the road. She wouldn't give up hope. She'd never stop searching for her cousin.

——

Those days in Panama were the worst Sahro ever recalled. The uncertainty. The unknowing. The blame. She'd learned to mourn the dead but not the missing. She wanted to go back south, back to the jungle to find him, but Waardo and Cabdi Rashid and the rest of the family—Fartumo and Ahmed in Ohio—said no. Keep going. Dalmar would find his way, inshallah. She needed to save herself. Go north.

Alone, she felt more exposed than ever. No umbrella or tarp or protection, a woman alone. No father or brother or cousin, only herself in the world. She and her God. But Allah had created her and had a plan for her—that much she knew. No matter what was to come, she was in His hands and there was nothing she could do but pray. For He protected the orphan and traveler. The exile and stranger. Hadn't the Prophet Himself, Peace Be Upon Him, been an orphan, an exile, a fugitive from his own land? She was following in His footsteps, as all her people had in the *qurba joog*. And even there, in Panama, in her complete undoing, in the depths of despair, her situation—she knew—was no worse than that of others. Everyone back in Xamar had an equally awful story. Her neighbors back home. Aunt Waardo's friend, even the sister of the woman across the street. She'd lost all eight children at sea crossing the Mediterranean. The life vests they'd been sold with the last of their money were *filled with grass*. At least the woman had her youngest son, her two-year-old boy, safely strapped to her side. But when they rescued the woman out of the water, the boy belted to her side was already dead.

Didn't Sahro still have her life? Her legs and arms? Her eyes? She knew from the start that she'd be tested. Imam Torino had told her. Wasn't that what made a person strong? The *ichtabar*, the test? And wasn't the worst now over? Her mother and father dead. Ayaan dead. Dalmar gone.

Before getting on an air-conditioned express bus north—with one day left on her transit visa—she stopped at a stationer's store in the city. She still had her pocketknife and one pencil left. But now she purchased a new weapon: A place to put her words. A cover to conceal them in. Evidence and proof. A pen to fill those pages. A new notebook in which to hide.

21

The long day had finally come to a close on Blue Mountain. The rain had stopped and the twilight turned Wedgwood blue. Christopher went one last time to the Guest House to make sure Sahro was set for the night. Afterward he spoke with Brother Bruno in the dorms and promised the prior he'd consider holding a community vote concerning the woman's stay. Back in his study, he checked the canjeero mixture from early that morning. The batter was slightly bubbly now, the fermentation started. He'd leave the bowl covered overnight, then try to cook the canjeero before breakfast and bring it to Sahro as a surprise.

At twenty minutes after seven he slipped into the choir stall for Compline, the last liturgical office of the day. Twelve men sat on opposite sides of the choir stall. The candles were already lit on the altar. The abbot's aspergillum put in place, the ikon of Mary. Brother Anselm began with an unaccompanied voice:

O God, come to my assistance, O Lord, make haste to help me.

In winter it would already be dark at the monastery during Compline, but in spring the sun lingered longer on the mountain and the office became the hour of sunsets and birdsong at the end of the day. Compline came from the Latin word for "complete," and the office was a time for reflection and preparation for the coming night. In the Order's tradition it was also a daily practice of preparing for death and eternity.

The monks sang the plainchant hymn "Now in the Fading Light of Day." That evening they sang it straight, a capella, and not in folktale fashion as they did some nights, accompanied by Brother Luke on a classical guitar. When the fourth psalm began, Christopher tried to relax into the chant but found himself not ready; the chant was a train he couldn't catch; it had already left the station. Chanting was not like singing; you couldn't just leap into it. When you chanted, you followed the breath. When you sang, you followed the beat. One was contemplation in the moment; the other reflection on the future. You had to set yourself aside when you chanted, your ego and all your musical markers. You had to become a fish in a school and follow the drift and swell of the line. *Legato* was key—*lightness*. But Christopher was preoccupied with Sahro in the Guest House. And then another worry returned: his apples in the orchard—he hadn't checked on them all day.

They moved on to a reading and another psalm and soon the Salve Regina. Christopher looked over the choir in the dimming light. None of his fellow monks were young anymore. Their hairs had all turned gray or white and some were stooped or walked with canes. But when they sang, together, when they chanted, something green still came out of them, something still vital and young which always snuck up on Christopher and surprised him when he was least paying attention: the beautiful music they could still make together.

As a painter, he used to mix Mars yellow with Prussian blue to form a pigment that looked like frozen ivy, or fresh grass unexpectedly caught in a frost. Our lives pass through green on their way to blue, Kandinsky wrote. And blue leads to black. No, Christopher hadn't yet visited his apple trees in the orchard; perhaps in the morning he would.

IV

21

She moved through countries whose names she barely knew: Costa Rica. Nicaragua. Honduras. She traveled alone by truck, cab, minivan, on foot, in Kombis and school buses and even—once—a donkey cart. She tried to put the Darien Gap behind her, but she was always looking for Dalmar, asking anyone and everyone at each migrant stop or hostel, had anyone seen a man fitting his description? She couldn't not hope that he was still alive, somewhere on the road just a few steps ahead of her.

She dressed in baggy jeans, a loose shirt, and wore her hair hidden inside a feed cap, yet she still drew attention by her look, her body language and foreignness, things she couldn't hide. Men still grabbed and children shouted. She rarely responded; it was easier to say nothing, to be an enigma, to act deaf and dumb.

One morning in the capital Tegucigalpa she bought three razor blades for a few centavos from a vendor in the street. In the public bathroom at the bus station, she borrowed a hand mirror from the female attendant and locked the bathroom stall door behind. She ran the razor through her hair, close to her scalp, cutting one clump off at a time. She watched her hair fall to the bathroom floor, wavy and thick, as she had once before. The *wiilo*, the tomboy. Afterward, she took a torn T-shirt and wrapped her chest and dressed again and looked in the bathroom mirror, satisfied. When she walked out of the bathroom that day into the *centro comercial* in Tegucigalpa, she felt instantly invisible. Another black-skinned boy in a feed cap. She could have been Garifuna or Creole.

Another unknown body moving through the streets of Central America; most assumed she spoke Spanish.

—

She got used to hiding in plain sight, not speaking on the road, to the sounds of unknown words washing over her without comprehension or the desire to comprehend. She moved through the days with a single purpose, a dozen miles here and there, each night a bridge she had to cross till morning. Her needs made minimal. A pastelito or tamal from a roadside stand. She subsisted on whatever was easy to find. Rice and beans. An ear of roasted corn. A boiled egg. Water, begged or bought. Sometimes she ate nothing for days. Avoiding the interest of others became her goal. She learned to move like a shadow. Ungraspable. Pray in silence, make herself minute. Curled up the way insects did under rocks in the scrublands. Her shell of nonchalance. It was better to be mute, to say nothing, to volunteer nothing. She opened her mouth only to eat and pray.

In Guatemala she watched the other migrants and learned how to leap off a bus before a checkpoint or border crossing, how to hike a few hours and return to the road further on. She watched and listened and trusted no one.

By the time she reached the border of southern Mexico, she was mostly sinew and bones. She looked lean and haggard with her shaven head and clothes stiff with sweat and salt. Baggy trousers held up with a rope. She wore a button-down shirt and a blue vinyl jacket she'd picked up along the way. The blue Agar feed cap and bottle slung over a shoulder. The rougher she looked, the more she was left alone, protected by her filth, her reeking clothes. She no longer needed to worry about oiling her hair or braids. It was so much easier being a boy. Thin and sullen, dangerous looking, always traveling alone or with one or two other migrants. Always lowering her voice or not speaking at all and stepping away from the others and standing at a distance, pretending to pee, holding her imaginary penis, only to relieve herself later alone. If trouble came, she had her knife and now a razor too, tethered to a stick tucked inside her pants.

—

The afternoon she arrived at the Suchiate River she camped in the bushes along the riverbank outside the border town. She'd been studying the migrants ducking into the vegetation along the road near the wide gray river. On the other side of the Suchiate lay the State of Chiapas in Mexico, but the river was too swift to cross by foot. You had to find a ferryman to carry you across. Near the north end of town you could hire a man with a raft of wooden pallets strapped to inner tubes to pole you across for fifty quetzales, money Sahro could ill afford.

In the afternoon she wandered away from the crossing and found a place to rest along the riverbank among the yucca and scrub. It was winter in that part of the world, the *madre de cacao* trees in bloom, bright pink flowers scattered along the path. She was squatting behind a lantana relieving herself, when a small boy no older than five suddenly appeared out of the scrub. She shouted and gestured for him to go away, but he sat on his heels and watched her intently from a few meters away. He held a stick and had shining black eyes and raven hair and wore a faded red shirt and a leather thong around a small filthy neck. She cursed him in Spanish, then Somali, then flung a handful of dirt in his direction, but the boy didn't flinch. He was saying something to her in Spanish; his sneakers were reinforced with duct tape. She heard a man's voice calling from behind him, and she froze. She made her hand into a gun and pointed it at the boy. The man's voice came again. The boy turned and shouted.

"*Un momento, ya voy.*"

Sahro pulled up her pants and cursed beneath her breath. The boy looked at her with a conspiratorial grin and said something she didn't understand, then darted away.

An hour later she saw the boy again in his faded red shirt and black hair walking toward her with an old man along the river. Before she could cut into the bank to avoid them, the boy shouted and waved and ran in her direction, yelling something in his singsong voice. When he reached her he held open a white plastic bag.

"*Es para ti*," he said, out of breath, shaking the bag at her. "*Los encuentre en el pueblo.*"

He held the open bag beneath her face.

Sahro looked at the old man, then at the boy. Inside the bag lay a dozen ripe avocados.

She looked back at the old man, who stayed respectfully a few meters away; he had silver hair and short legs and he held a cluster of white plastic bags on a stick over one shoulder.

The boy was saying something to her in Spanish. She gave the old man a questioning look. To her surprise, he answered in English.

"He pick them for you," he said.

She looked down at the boy, who was smiling now, still holding open the bag of avocados.

The old man said something to the boy, then turned to Sahro and gestured to the area around the river.

"It's not a good place here." He frowned. "Police come. They take money. Here no good."

He shook a finger and said it was safer upriver a few kilometers away, where the river was wider and easier to cross and there were no police. They were heading there now, he said, to spend the night and cross in the morning when it was safest. He could join them if he wanted, he said and held up the plastic sacks and said they had plenty of food.

Sahro looked at the man and the boy; she had no reason to trust them. They were talking together fast in Spanish. Perhaps it was a ploy. The boy already knew her secret, and something about the old man's courtly manner indicated he did as well—despite his calling her "he."

The old man looked again at Sahro and shrugged.

"Okay then. Good luck. *Adiós.*"

"*Vamanos*," he said and waved to the boy and started walking toward the river, but the boy protested.

"*Olvidalo,*" the old man said, his back turned. "*Ella quiere estar sola.*"

The boy turned to Sahro one last time and said something, then dropped the bag of avocados on the ground.

She watched him walking away from behind, his red shirt, black hair, the river sparkling gold in the late sun. Swallows were dipping over the surface and making mournful sounds, and a sudden pang seized her. She shouted impulsively, "*Espera.*"

The boy in the red shirt turned, then the old man. She held up a hand for them to wait. She hurried back to the bushes and gathered her things, picked up the bag of avocados, and joined them on the riverbank.

—

They camped that night in a thin oak forest a few kilometers from the river. The boy climbed a tree and came down with two green rucksacks they'd hidden up in the branches. The old man unpacked food from the plastic bags. They were planning to leave at four the next morning; he knew the route, and she was welcome to join them, he said. But they could use her help crossing the river. The boy was too small, and the man couldn't carry both the boy and the packs alone. If she helped them across, he said, they'd be grateful. She could join them afterward or not. It was up to her.

They ate rice and beans off banana leaves as the sun went down. Avocados. Limes. Small, sweet bananas. The old man had bought fresh homemade tortillas in town, thick and crunchy, tasting of hominy and lye. They made no fire and finished their meal in twilight, and Sahro felt full and grateful.

The boy stared at her, stick in hand, and said something to the old man, who replied in Spanish.

"Where are his parents?" Sahro asked the man.

"His father . . ." The man made a vague gesture with his hand. "Who knows? His mother, she is in *el Norte*."

Sahro nodded. "You go there?" she asked.

"No. I just take him." He nodded to the boy, then said he'd been north many times in his life, always to work, but this was his last trip. He was too old now, and who would hire him, but he'd promised the boy's mother he'd bring him north.

Sahro asked when the boy saw his mother last.

The old man turned to the boy.

"*¿Cuando la próxima vez ha visto su madre?*"

The boy held up three fingers in the twilight.

"He was three years old."

And now?

"Seven," the boy said, in English.

It was growing dark. The boy said something, and the old man turned to Sahro.

"He asks where you're from."

"Far away," Sahro said.

"*Lejos*," the man said, turning to the boy.

"*¿Dónde?*" he asked.

Sahro took the stick from the boy's hand and stood. She drew a little map in the dirt by his feet. It was almost too dark to see, and the boy got down on all fours, and the old man leaned forward. She drew a North and South America and then a Europe and Africa across from them. Then she pointed to the side of Africa the farthest away.

"*Aqui*," she said, and tapped the stick in the dirt. "East Africa."

The boy repeated the words. The old man asked what country. Sahro said, "Somalia."

The boy looked up. She couldn't see his expression in the dusk. He repeated the name as if each syllable was a separate word: "So Mal Ee Ah."

"*Sí.*" She nodded.

Why had she come alone? the boy asked, and the old man interpreted. Sahro said she hadn't. She'd come with her cousin.

"*¿Que paso con su primo?*" the boy said, but the man didn't translate. Sahro turned to the boy and said in English: "He got lost."

Then she turned to the man and asked how to say the word "lost" in Spanish.

"*Perdido,*" he said. "*Se perdió.*"

She turned and said to the boy, "*Se perdió,*" and he frowned and nodded and asked nothing more.

—

They woke the next morning before the moon set. The old man roused Sahro from sleep and they made their way silently toward the river. The old man took the two packs and Sahro's bag and held them over his head. The boy climbed onto Sahro's back and she followed the man into the silver. The current moved around her legs, cold and steady, rising to her knees and thighs. She didn't mind the cold, the moonlight rippling on water. The boy's hands clutched her neck, his tiny fingers. She could feel his breath in her ear, the pebbles beneath her bare feet. The river hugged her hips, but the air was warm, and they had to keep quiet and unseen. They crossed without making a splash, and on the other side the boy climbed off her back and they slipped on shoes, took their packs, and no one said a word the whole time.

—

For five days they hiked together in the Sierra Madre. They'd leave before sunup and break in the middle of the day and continue in the late afternoon into evening. There were faster ways through Chiapas, through the town of Tapachula and north by freight train, but those routes were dangerous, controlled by gangs, and the old man preferred the mountains, where they were safe. One day they passed through pine forests and mountain mesophyll and bosques of *guayabo de charco*. Another through rocky chasms and gorges. They spent a night in a cloud forest on a coffee plantation, where they slept in a goat shed on a steep hillside and ate cabrito and rice with two workers and washed the meal down with strong black coffee sweetened with cane sugar. Some days (aside from the man and the boy) Sahro saw no one at all. She marveled at the beauty of the mountains, and there were times she wasn't afraid. At night the old man pointed out the *Estrella del Norte*—the North Star—and told her a story about the African slaves in America and a song they had sung about the star, how you had to follow it to freedom, the way its constellation formed a cup in the sky. She told him in Somalia the star was important too. They called it the *Hiddiga Qibladda* and it pointed to Mecca, so it was called the Prayer Star. Sahro had been sending her prayers in its direction her whole life.

One afternoon they hiked through a forest filled with fluttering orange and black butterflies, millions clinging to the trees. When the sun passed through their wings, they looked like panes of glass. The old man called them *mariposas monarca* and said they were overwintering in the forest there and would fly north in a few months to the *Estados Unidos*. They too were headed north.

Later that day they passed two White people in khaki shorts with enormous colorful backpacks and large binoculars hanging from their necks.

"Americans," the old man whispered to Sahro.

They said hello and stopped and took out their cell phones, but when they started snapping photos of Sahro and the boy, the old man raised a hand.

"No," he said. "No photographs please."

The Americans looked at one another and giggled and continued on their way.

—

They moved through the mountains, ten or fifteen miles each day. The old man knew which villages were safe and which to avoid. Sahro started writing again in her notebook. Thoughts and impressions. A letter she'd never send Ayaan. Spanish words. English words. She'd lost interest in language after the Darien Gap, in learning new words, in taking notes or writing anything down. She didn't care what others were saying and what things were called. But now in the Sierra Madre with the old man and the boy, she began jotting down the names of flowers and trees. The old man telling her *roble* for oak or *pino* for pine, the pink thistle he called *la reina de la india*. And each night the boy asked her questions about Africa.

"Are there giraffes in Somalia?"

"No," she said. "Not in Somalia."

"Are there lions?"

"*Sí*, there are lions."

"*Camellos*?" he asked.

"*Sí*, mucho camellos."

"*Tiburones*?"

"Who?"

"Sharks," the old man said and made his fingers into teeth.

"*Sí*," Sahro said. There were sharks everywhere. Even on land.

The boy looked shocked. Sahro made her fingers into teeth as well and feigned chomping at the boy's neck, to his great delight.

When he stopped laughing, he turned serious and asked where in el Norte she was going.

"Ohio," she said. "And you?"

The boy looked at the old man and the man said it was okay and the boy recited the numbers: "914 693 1459."

Sahro gave the old man a questioning look. He explained that the boy's mother lived near New York City, in a place called White Plains.

That she worked cleaning houses for rich people. The boy had to memorize her number in el Norte and couldn't write it down—anywhere—not the phone number nor the address nor the name of where he was going. If he was kidnapped by one of the gangs along the way, the first thing they'd ask and look for was a contact in the States, someone they could extort money from. It was best to have no destination, no one waiting on the other side. No contact. To memorize everything and trust no one.

Sahro looked at the boy, his eyes shining in the twilight. He repeated the phone number and shook his head and said:

No confiar en nadie.

—

For a week in the mountains they slept and ate on the move, and Sahro's hair started to grow in and she learned the boy's name—Oscar—but not the name of the old man. And on the seventh day they came out of the mountains and Sahro shaved her head again with a razor and wrapped her breasts. That day they hiked under enormous transmission towers in the rangeland around La Ventosa, the land flat and hot, a highway in the distance where trucks thundered in caloric waves. Anyone driving out there could see them walking, three figures in the heat haze beneath transmission lines. Where were they going? It was anyone's guess. Just another family of migrants heading north.

—

The migrant shelter in Ixtepec was packed to capacity, the compound run by a priest and hidden behind a green iron gate. Having been in the mountains so long, Sahro was amazed by the number of migrants. They'd seen few people in the mountains, and no immigrants, but here they were everywhere. Young men and boys and women. Salvadorans. Guatemalans. Hondurans. Hundreds in the plaza in town, at the freight yard, men and women sleeping on the train tracks with bags and water bottles. Children even younger than Oscar. They formed little gangs

unaccompanied by adults. It shocked and saddened Sahro, and for the
first time she wondered: Did anyone have a home anymore? Was everyone in the diaspora? Why were so many people on the road?

For a week she and the old man worked in the shelter's kitchen,
helping prepare meals, scrubbing the big aluminum cooking cauldrons,
chopping onions and garlic for beans. She stayed with Oscar and the old
man on the men's side of the shelter. They kept her secret; they covered
for her in the bathroom stalls. The priest's only conditions for staying
were no weapons in the shelter and everyone had to attend one religious
service a day—no papers or money required.

By then Sahro knew something of the *gaalo* religion, their strange
paintings and gaudy pictures of the prophet Issa—Jesus—and his mother,
Maryam. Throughout South and Central America, she saw illustrations
of him and his mother everywhere. Hanging on walls or in buses or
carved into stone. Statues on mountaintops, the thin, bearded prophet
with his arms outstretched or in agony tacked to the cross, nails in feet,
or his dead body in his mother Maryam's lap. Or sometimes it was
Maryam alone, pregnant or just after, nursing her little boy. In portraits
and necklaces, statues and keychains, her eyes were downcast or looking
up to the heavens. In Colombia, by the coast near Turbo, her skin was
coal black; in Guatemala she was reddish brown or gold. Sometimes
in Mexico she was pure white but other times copper- or cinnamon-
skinned or indigenous-looking, but no matter her skin color, her head
was always covered in a sky-blue scarf.

In the shelter at Ixtepec her statue stood in the center of the outdoor
space where the religious service was held. A galvanized roof covered
the outdoor area, and the ground was poured concrete. An old lemon
tree blossomed in the back. During the daily service they called *la Misa*,
Sahro would stand between Oscar and the old man and move her mouth
with the Spanish words, mimicking the others while having little or no
idea what was being said. The first time after the service, she lined up
with the others while the priest handed out bits of bread. Oscar tugged

her shirt and shook his head and explained in his broken English that not everyone was supposed to eat the bread the priest was handing out. She asked why, and he looked at the old man, but he couldn't explain either, and the old man stepped out of line and stood with her and Oscar did too and none of them took the bread that day but watched from the side.

The bread was not the only thing that mystified Sahro. In the back of the outdoor area, beside the lemon tree, two plywood closets stood back-to-back, an entrance on either side with a curtain in between. A person would enter on one side and stay for a few minutes, then come out a little later. Sahro thought at first it was a latrine, but when she peeked inside when no one was around, she saw no hole or plumbing, only a chair and a red curtain across a cut-out window between the closets. She was almost too shy to ask, yet when she did, the old man explained as best he could. The closet was a place, he said, where people went to tell the priest the bad things they'd done. If they apologized, the priest usually told them it was okay, but sometimes he gave them a fine. He called the closet and what took place in there *la Confesión*; the bad things they admitted, for which they were sometimes fined, were called *pecados*, or "sins."

From then on Sahro studied the closet with keen interest. She watched the priest step in one side while the others waited (sometimes an entire queue) to enter the other side one at a time. Some migrants looked downcast or sheepish, often with their hats in hand. Some stayed only for a minute or two inside the box, others longer. When they emerged they often looked different, she noticed. Relieved or refreshed or resigned. Sometimes a person walked out in tears. She wrote the words in her notebook. *Confession. Sin.* On her own—away from the others—she secretly prayed five times each day.

—

Ten days later, they were moving again, the old man, the boy, and Sahro; only this time they traveled with hundreds of others on the notorious freight trains called *la Bestia*. Sahro had learned the things she needed to know in advance; it was all the men ever talked about in the shelter. The quickest routes, the safest towns, which to avoid. How to jump onto a moving train. How to run alongside it first and grab hold of the ladder with your left hand. She learned this soon in action, again and again over the next few weeks. How to wait and match her running rhythm with that of the moving train, how to swing her inside foot up first (not her outside) and keep one eye on the wheels the entire time. She learned where the best place was to ride and to brace herself against the thrust of a starting train, the hard *tac-tac-tac* of the coupled cars jerking one after another to life. She endured the wind on top of the train, the terrible thirst after eleven hours in the sun. No shade. No shelter. Wind scalding her face and scorching her lips. One misstep—a hanging tree limb, a stumble in the night—she'd be cut in half by the wheels. The trains had a way of sucking falling bodies toward their centers. Rarely a person fell without losing at least a leg or arm—but usually their life. They called it *la Bestia* for a reason. Every journey, the beast claimed a victim or three.

One afternoon, after hours baking under the midday sun, she saw a little girl in a white dress stand up from where she'd been sitting at the edge of the boxcar. One minute the girl in the dress stood rubbing her eyes in the heat waves—the next she was gone. Sahro thought she was daydreaming from the sun. It happened so quickly. No sound or warning or scream. No one even seemed to notice at first. The shrieks came thirty seconds later, her family leaping up from their spot on the train. A mother holding a hand to her mouth. People pointing at something already far down the tracks.

Some nights the migrants formed watch teams with companions they could trust. Five or six together, waiting to fend off an imminent attack. They armed themselves with things they found along the tracks, a steel bar, a rock. A broken machete. A plank of wood. Sahro joined them too, razors on her stick. Hidden inside her baggy shirt and jeans, the men called her *el Flaquito*, not knowing her true gender.

—

One night north of Mexico City, they waited with hundreds of others at a rail station outside of some town. It was two or three in the morning, hot and steaming, and everyone lay spread out or sleeping on the tracks, the air ripe with piss and human feces. Sahro watched a man put his ear to the rail and lift a hand and shout (to anyone awake) *treinta minutos.* Twenty-five minutes later, two distant hoots echoed out of the the dark. The rails tingled and started singing. The crowd slowly stirred. Men and women, waking, slung packs, raised water bottles. They could barely rouse Oscar from his sweaty sleep. Then the headlights cut through the night. A bright beam swung over the crowd and caught everyone in its core. Sahro stood watching the chaos. Dozens of children shouting and jostling, hundreds of bodies surging toward the light.

The image stayed with her, the shadows and silhouettes, the arms and heads in the lights, the heat and the dozens of children. She thought of her own journey north as a child during the worst of the war, sent on the top of the truck, but who was waiting for these children up north and who could they trust along the way? She locked her fingers around Oscar's little hand. Yes, things had been bad back home in Somalia, but weren't they bad here as well, in this new continent, this country in North America?

She'd never pitied herself or thought her story exceptional or more tragic than anyone else's back home. Yet she'd believed—along with Dalmar, along with Ayaan—that living in Somalia, growing up in Xamar, had its own special danger and dysfunction and continual strife. But what of the place she found herself in now, the thousands of fleeing bodies she'd seen on the road? Maybe their experience wasn't so unique after all—she and Dalmar and Ayaan and the others who risked tahriib. The children on the tracks were all in transit too, everywhere she looked, with no adults to watch them. The hundreds of bodies rising off the tracks. They were all nomads now—not just she.

—

It took twelve days to reach Monterrey. Another eight to the top of Tamaulipas. She said goodbye to Oscar and the old man at a truck stop outside Ciudad Camargo, near the Texas border. She was going to cross without them, legally, and ask for asylum on the other side—that had always been the plan, Waardo's plan, Dalmar's plan, the whole nomadic network: the promise of asylum in the USA. Oscar and the old man had to travel the hard way, across the river and then a desert—and hopefully not be killed along the way.

They parted in the plaza of a Pemex station along the highway. Oscar wiped away a tear. Sahro hugged the boy briefly, felt his small ribs against hers—then had to pull away. She didn't want him to see her tears.

Afterward, she turned at the last minute and saw the old man help Oscar climb into the rear of a cattle truck and then pull himself in behind. They were continuing on to a place called Reynosa. The gold and red running lights of the truck glowed like gems in the purple twilight. She could see Oscar in the shadows behind the stock slats. One small arm appeared through the metal grates, waving. Sahro waved back but quickly turned aside. She put a hand to her mouth. She hadn't expected the desperate sobs, deep and uncontrollable now. But the night was drawing near and she had to pull herself together and find a place to safely sleep.

22

The summer Teddy Fletcher turned eighteen a team of scientists arrived on Blue Mountain to study a rare songbird that nested on the mountaintop each spring. The Bicknell's thrush wintered in isolated rain forests in the West Indies and migrated each May to the peaks of a handful of mountains in New England. Among the small, stunted conifers called krummholz, the secretive bird mated and fledged new offspring each year. Only a few breeding populations occurred in the world. One, as it happened, existed on the summit of Blue Mountain.

Teddy had been working weekends with his father at the monastery that year. As summer began and the biologists arrived, he helped the newcomers ferry equipment up the mountain and showed them where to find water and set up camp. He was awed by their radio telemetry and satellite equipment and volunteered to help in any way he could. There were five biologists in all, three graduate students and a married couple from North Carolina. In Teddy's circumscribed world, the scientists seemed incredibly worldly and glamorous, different from anyone he knew in Hart's Run. More than that, they listened to what he had to say and asked him questions and included him in conversations. As the mountain greened that year and high school let out, he spent more and more time on the mountain. Mornings, working around the monastery, afternoons helping the scientists up top.

He ended up attaching himself to a graduate student named Kate Walling, from Sarasota, Florida. Kate wore round glasses and hid a long chestnut ponytail inside the back of her shirt. She had calloused hands and a sunburnt face and was seven years Teddy's senior. She showed him how to set up mist nets and untangle the tiny feet of songbirds caught in the nylon, how to band the birds and rig a radio collar around a thrush and sample blood with a needle and pipette. For a large teen, Teddy was surprisingly nimble at banding (having handled small animals and fishing lures his whole life). Calm with a bird in hand. Unflappable. He knew a lot about the wildlife on the mountain, things he'd grown up with. Sparrows whose songs he could distinguish (but whose names he never knew), where the mast crops of beech and oak were thickest on the mountain, where the bears and porcupines denned. As a kid he'd fed venison to the resident ravens behind the monastery garage, had learned to call them in with a whistle. And that summer he showed Kate Walling his secret spots on the mountain: the waterfall, the cave, the place where herons roosted on top. Kate Walling, for her part, was impressed with the awkward young man, his unassuming knowledge and shyness, the curly red hair that fell in his eyes. She lent him a pair of binoculars and a field guide to Northeast birds. She called him her "fledgling" or sometimes simply "Red."

In the mornings Teddy worked alongside his father, mowing the monastery's fields, but each evening he'd drive to the summit in his car and help the biologists. By July, he and Kate Walling were spending every dusk together in a blind woven of birch bark and moss—recording bird sounds, jotting notes, picking ticks off each other's legs and necks. One evening, after dinner outside the camp kitchen, before Teddy climbed back into his car, Kate Walling took the sleeve of his flannel shirt and pulled him into her tent. It happened so seamlessly, with no drama or drawn-out effort on either one's part. She undressed by flashlight and he did too. She was frank and unceremonious and taught him what to do with his hands, where to put his mouth, how to hold her. Kate Walling, with her wool socks and hiking boots, her smell of armpits. She was generous and patient and Teddy was glad she'd acted on an impulse he'd never dare have the courage to. From that evening on, he spent almost every night in Kate Walling's tent, inside two nylon sleeping bags zipped together. Did his father know? How could he not? Though they never spoke about it when Teddy arrived at the garage for work the next morning, bleary-eyed and half asleep.

That summer Kate Walling told him about her field of study, the thrush family—the *Catharus* thrushes in particular. How they were all part of the family of famous singers: nightingales and fieldfares, the red-breasted robin. The hermit thrush and veery could sing two melodies at the same time. Teddy knew this intuitively, for he'd heard the song of the hermit thrush his whole life (but never identified its musical interval as "a minor third"). Kate Walling was studying the acoustics of the *Catharus* genus, doing her own graduate research into the species' vocalizations and songs. And watching Kate Walling's excitement while she explained things, sensing his own small tug of interest, Teddy felt a tiny window open in his world. She encouraged him to apply to college, to get a degree, to study forestry (he already knew so much, she said). He'd play with her long braid as she talked, the light from a candle stuck in an empty tuna tin flickering on her shoulders. She'd let him undo her hair and arrange it against her back. All of it sounded possible up there that summer with Kate Walling. College. Forestry. Vocalizations. Radio telemetry. Minor thirds.

"But who's going to pay?" he asked.

"A scholarship," she said.

"And who will write the application?"

"Me!" she yelled.

He listened and nodded, and they'd make love, and afterward he knew it would never happen, that something larger than age separated them. Teddy hadn't even bothered taking his SATs. He knew the only way out of the North Country was through the recruiter's office in Hart's Run. But he didn't tell this to Kate Walling, for he knew she'd disapprove.

—

In August the Bicknell's fledglings departed first. Somehow they knew where to go; Kate Walling said they were born with maps in their heads. The adults left around Labor Day, and then the biologists departed, and finally Kate Walling, who waved out the window of her Geo Metro as she drove away from the mountain her last day.

Senior year started for Teddy. He'd found a new confidence and began dating. First one girl, then another. The third became his fiancée. But he never stopped thinking of Kate Walling, even then, his senior year. He thought of her all the time. Kate in her socks in the tent, the long braid down her back, her armpits and calloused hands.

He hadn't expected to hear from her again. She'd left no address or phone number, and by then he and Karen Petit were spending all their time together. Yet sometime the following spring, a blue Aeropost arrived for him at the monastery and was passed on to Teddy through his father. It came with stamps from the Dominican Republic, where Kate Walling was studying the same birds, making new recordings of nonbreeding vocalizations on their winter grounds. "On one side of Hispaniola," she wrote, "they call the thrushes *Zerzoles* in Spanish. On the other side of the island, in Haiti, they're called *Grive solitaire*."

Teddy read the name out loud. *Grive solitaire*. It sounded to him like the saddest name in the world. He never wrote Kate Walling back. What was the point of disappointing her? Of telling her he hadn't applied to college or that he was already engaged? By then he'd found a quicker way out of the valley: the army. He'd already enlisted. He was due in Fort Benning for basic that coming June.

23

The night before Sahro crossed the border into Texas, she called Aunt Waardo from a pay phone in Ciudad Camargo. She'd finally reached the United States, she said with a little triumph in her voice. Aunt Waardo whooped and said alhamdulillah over and over again, and Uncle Cabdi Rashid came on speakerphone and shouted congratulations along with the younger cousins. For a moment, standing inside the cubicle at the phone center in the small Mexican border town, Sahro felt a sense of accomplishment and relief. Despite everything she'd lost, after all that struggle and time, she'd at least made it to America. A better future had to lie ahead.

In the morning she crossed the Rio Grande City Bridge, where a line of belching trucks idled on the asphalt in the dawn. Sahro picked her way alongside the semitrucks, the only person crossing that morning on the two-lane, steel-girded bridge. The customs agent seemed surprised to see her. He stepped out of his booth, brown-skinned, in aviator glasses, an olive uniform and hat, and said she wasn't at the right place for pedestrians. They had to cross elsewhere.

Where had she come from? he asked, suspiciously.

"Somalia," Sahro said.

Then she repeated the words she'd practiced for almost a year, first in Xamar with Aunt Waardo and Uncle Cabdi Rashid and then with Dalmar, and then to herself on many sleepless nights on the road.

"I am asking for asylum in the United States. I come because I fear for my life in Somalia."

The man scratched the back of his neck and stepped further out of the booth and studied her for a few seconds. Trucks were lining up behind her on the narrow bridge, the air already sticky at eight a.m. Sweat trickled down Sahro's armpits. The man said he couldn't give her asylum, that she was better off turning around and walking back over the bridge to Mexico where she'd be free to go where she wanted. If she insisted on asylum in the United States, he'd have to arrest her.

Sahro didn't understand. She squinted in the morning sun. She could feel the cool air-conditioning slipping from the inside of the guard's booth. Why would he arrest her? Hadn't she said the correct words?

She repeated them again, slower now, and the guard shook his head in what looked like disgust.

"Wait here," he said.

He stepped back into his booth, and she saw him pick up a phone.

She squatted on the concrete curb with her bag in the sun. Time passed. The trucks kept coming and going in clouds of diesel. Her head ached and she had no water left in her bottle.

An hour later, a black SUV arrived and a White man in a cowboy hat and boots stepped out. He exchanged words and papers with the border guard in the booth, then said something to Sahro in incomprehensible English. He pointed to her wrists and then—to her total surprise—he cinched them together in front of her with a plastic zip tie. She started to protest. The White man didn't say a word. He led her into the back seat of the SUV, set her bag beside her, and shut the door.

Sahro was flummoxed. Dehydrated. Confused. What was he doing? Where was he taking her? She started asking questions from the back seat, but the man couldn't hear through the plexiglass divider between the rear and front seats. They drove through ranchland on a four-lane highway. She sat back, fighting off tears, her rucksack beside her, the air-conditioning blasting through a vent. Outside, thunderheads towered over the ranchland. The only things moving out there were shiny new cars and trucks.

When she woke, rain pounded the roof. They were parked outside a concrete building, American flags out front. She was hungry and thirsty and chilled; a headache stabbed her eye. She said salat to herself the best she could. She hadn't drunk or eaten a thing all day.

The building inside was loud and cold, hard shiny floor, metal tables. She stood in the freezing room with dozens of others. Then they were loaded onto a bus with caged windows. Everyone looked as confused and tired as she, migrants clutching their one allowed bag, wrists cuffed. Brown and Black men and women, children and babies. They were driven onto a tarmac to a waiting plane. Where were they going? Someone said Mexico City; another, Tegucigalpa. They were being sent home, deported. A few people sobbed. Another man said, no, they were just flying to a different facility, someplace in the United States.

She was set in a window seat and told not to stand. A man from Sudan was put in the aisle seat. She recognized his features, a Dinka from the south. They shared a nod across the empty seat between them, and he told Sahro not to worry, the man on the bus was right. They were being transferred someplace else. He smiled, but she could see the worry in his eyes, the weariness, the resignation. Had he too come all the way from East Africa? From Juba or Khartoum? She sat back and closed her eyes. Her head hurt too much to ask.

They flew for several hours in the dark, Sahro half asleep, the future again out of her hands. "Surrender" was the English word for "Islam." Submit or surrender to God. She'd surrendered to the authorities, the police. Wasn't that what she was supposed to do?

She watched out the window the endless black below, the flaring patches of orange in the landscape, the flames of small cities and towns; then more black that went on for hours. Were they still in America? The land seemed to go on forever.

When she woke it was still dark, but the land below was filled with electric light, grids and angles, streets and highways, as far as the eye could see. How could one live in such a place? It seemed to Sahro they were turned upside down, that the constellations burned below, and the earth lay hidden in darkness above.

When the plane thumped down on the tarmac, no one was quite sure where they were. They taxied for almost an hour on an endless airstrip before being loaded into another bus with blacked-out windows. Sahro felt nauseated and sick. Nothing had passed her lips in twenty-four hours. They entered the bowels of an enormous warehouse and were separated by sex. She was processed, stripped, made to shower, then prodded and poked by a doctor, and given a nine-digit number, an alien ID, then handed an old pair of underwear and a tan jumpsuit, and mismatched sneakers without any laces. Only later, after she was shown to her section, assigned a bunk with a rough blanket, did Sahro at last learn where she was: inside a U.S. Immigration detention center in a place called Elizabeth, New Jersey, just two miles outside New York City.

—

Her first days in detention Sahro felt utterly deflated and numb, unable to grasp what had gone wrong: the handcuffs, the arrest, the flight, now prison. It wasn't at all what she'd expected upon reaching the United States. She'd never been told about this part—just as no one had said anything about the Darien Gap. They only spoke of the good things. Asylum. Democracy. TV, jobs, cars. Three taps in the kitchen (for orange juice, water, and milk). The first day they'd handed her some papers with a list of lawyers, the Somali consular numbers, an *Application for Asylum and for Withholding of Removal*, the pages largely incomprehensible. Questions she couldn't answer. What was her present nationality? Her mailing address in the United States? Her *I-94*, her *Travel Document Number*?

She bought a calling card using the last of her cash and waited in line for the pay phone. She called Fartumo and Ahmed in Ohio. Fartumo assured her she'd be okay. They'd find her a lawyer and call Aunt Waardo back home. They'd come up with a plan. Later, she tried to make out the forms with their questions. The enigmatic words: *Withholding of Removal. Torture Convention. Removal Hearing.* Questions about her parents and siblings and spouse. Had she family or friends who'd been threatened or mistreated? When and where and by whom? For what reason? She stared at the white boxes, the little spaces left for her answers. The boxes were so small, how could she fit anything of her life inside them?

It was summer in the northeast of the United States then, but Sahro could hardly tell. There were no windows in the warehouse and the fluorescent lights stayed on twenty-four hours a day. Hundreds of women slept in the center on thin mattresses on bunks, thirty in Sahro's section alone. Women from Bangladesh, Surinam, Moldova. From Haiti and Chad. From every imaginable country. Guards shouted them awake each night for lockdown. Head counts. They kept the warehouse so frigid, Sahro thought the word "ICE" on the guards' uniforms stood for the literal thing—*baraf*. Her bunkmate, Elena Ortiz, told her otherwise. ICE stood for Immigration Customs Enforcement, but it's no secret, she said that *they're trying to freeze us all out.*

She found a place to pray in the back of the TV room with a few other Muslim women. A cup of water for wudu; flattened cardboard boxes for mats. A Malaysian woman knew the direction of the qibla. The camaraderie gave Sahro comfort—saying salat together; the same holy words—even while the TV blared in the background or Sahro heard a White guardswoman say to another; "*Look at the fucking terrorists.*"

In normal times it took only a few weeks in detention before being screened by an asylum officer. But Sahro's timing, Elena Ortiz told her, was unfortunate. The whole system was swamped with thousands of new cases and not enough asylum officers or immigration judges to handle the influx. In other words, Sahro would have to wait in the warehouse with hundreds of others before her "credible fear" interview could even be scheduled. And that was only the first step (of many) of applying for asylum in the United States.

One day a Pakistani girl arrived. Shirin Kishani was small and delicate with dark curly hair and large eyes lined with kohl. She seemed to know the ins and outs of the asylum process better than most, even though she'd just arrived. She schooled Sahro on the applications and the odd English words. Fartumo and Ahmed had found a lawyer online and were wiring him money. Shirin Kishani warned her to watch out. A lot of them were fakes. She was better off finding a pro bono lawyer from an American sanctuary group.

—

Weeks passed in the warehouse. The air moved differently in the enormous vents, warm now instead of cold. Sahro started getting headaches, three or four a week. Everyone in the place got sick—from the cold, the rotting food, the stale air (fumes from the petrochemical plants next door, and the Newark International Airport). Sahro began to feel strangely anxious and untethered. The women joked with gallows humor; they'd gone from Guate*mala* to Gauta*peor*, Islama*bad* to Islama*worse*. Newcomers kept arriving, and the old ones left. Deported, sometimes voluntarily. All Sahro had to do was sign a piece of paper and she'd fly home for free—she'd been told repeatedly. How easy it was to leave. Only a signature and she could go. Wasn't she sick of the migraines? The lockdowns? The inmates screaming in the night? Of being cold all the time?

Her disillusionment came by degrees. When she was growing up, both in the scrublands and in Xamar, everyone knew America was the Father of Everything, the Boss of the World. America manufactured the bullets and tanks and bombs, but they also made the food. The bags of flour and rice they handed out at the camps and distribution centers. The tins of oil, the sugar, stamped with "USA" and the American flag. Even though they were the *gaalo*—nonbelievers, Christians—they shared the same two holy books, the Old and New Testament (even if they hadn't yet woken to the last and most holy, the Qur'an). Still, they worshipped the same prophets: Abraham and Isaac, Moses and Jacob, Noah and Jesus. And Americans, they said, sided with the widow and orphan, the unfortunate and the poor. Didn't they champion human rights around the world? She'd seen it again and again in their movies. Rambo and the Pale Rider. The White American savior helping the underdog. They were strong but fought for the weak. Unlike back home in Africa, where anything could be bought with a bribe and the law only served the powerful, in America people honored the law and were known to be fair and honest. At least that's what she'd grown up believing. But now in detention, seeing how things really worked, she wasn't so sure. Maybe America was just like every other place—self-serving, dishonest, a sham.

—

One night a new girl from Nepal was put in the bunk below. She was pretty and young and spoke no English and spent her days weeping in bed. What had befallen the girl from Kathmandu? Everyone tried to speak to her, to ask—which only made things worse. Everyone called her *la Llorona* or *Pobrecita*. At night Sahro could feel the metal bunk bed shake from the girl's sobs. She remained only a week in the warehouse before she disappeared. Deported. No one ever learned her real name.

Waardo wired money so Sahro could pay for the commissary and a phone card. And every few days she waited in line for the pay phone in the hall and called Columbus or Mogadishu and spoke with Waardo or Fartumo or Ahmed. They were still waiting on the lawyer, but there'd been some mix-up about money—who had sent it and when. Waardo said one thing; Fartumo another. Were the families disputing? Had something gone wrong? It wouldn't surprise Sahro. She blamed herself for losing Dalmar, for not going back and finding him; why shouldn't others too? Could she hear it in their voices, in things that weren't said?

Their disappointment? Their disapproval? Hadn't everyone she touched ended up dead? Perhaps she was a curse to them all. Perhaps they were better off without her. She asked God all the time, *why couldn't it have been me* and not Dalmar or Ayaan? And who'd blame the family if they were to cut her off now? What good had she ever done them?

She began having nightmares. She was always back in the jungle. Always being chased or on the verge of finding Dalmar, only to wake up shaking in cold sweat. Her headaches returned. She was afraid to fall asleep.

Sometime later that winter Shirin Kishani showed her the law library in the basement. A small cinder block room with metal shelves half-filled with books. The room was open only at certain hours, and she needed a pass to go there, but the books interested her: the red legal volumes, a big English dictionary, donated paperbacks, magazines. Novels in English and Spanish. Romances. Westerns. Murder mysteries, true crime. She wasn't allowed to take books back to her section, but at least she could sit on the cold floor and puzzle out the words of a Western with the dictionary.

One morning as she was rooting among the shelves, she pulled out a paperback with a familiar cover. A bright orange background. A black silhouette of a bird. She recognized the image instantly. The same cover of the book she'd "read" with Ayaan at the villa on Via Sanca. The same book!

She clutched it to her chest. She remembered the first time in the villa when Ayaan made her read the title. She opened the paperback now and brought it to her face. The pages smelled musty, the cover slightly torn, a USED sticker slapped on its spine. She read the title to herself. *I Know Why the Caged Bird Sings*. Then whispered the author's name: "Maya Angelou." What was the book doing here in the warehouse? Was it a talisman? A sign?

She opened the book and read the first line.

"What are you looking at me for?"

Then she quickly hid the book behind others. She didn't want anyone to take it away.

From the next day on, Sahro spent all the time she was allowed in the basement library. Now that her English was better, she was determined to finally read the book by the African American author, read it for its content and not just use it as a reservoir of unknown English words.

Armed with the library dictionary, she made lists of words and looked each up, parsed the paragraphs line by line, asked Shirin Kishani for help, enlisted other English speakers—a Nigerian woman named Inogenest, a girl from the Philippines. And soon Maya Angelou's autobiography began to come to life. Like Sahro, she—Marguerite, Maya—had been sent across a country as a child, shipped off with nothing but an address and a name pinned to her coat. Like Sahro, Maya had a tough and loving *ayeeyo* who taught her everything she knew. And reading about Maya's life in the basement of the warehouse, delving deeper into its pages each day, the English began to open for Sahro, like a flower unfurling its colors. She went among the pages now like a butterfly finding pollen in each fold of the book, between the paragraphs, words sticking to her on her way in and out of each sentence. Each time she left the library, she stashed the book in a secret place and returned upstairs to her section, but a piece of Maya Angelou remained with her throughout the day—a private place she could go to, separate from the uncertainty, the warehouse, the cold.

One morning a guard handed her a piece of paper. Her credible-fear interview was finally scheduled for the following week. Fartumo and Ahmed's lawyer never appeared. Just as Shirin Kishani had warned her: they'd been scammed. Sahro counted on her country of origin and her grasp of English helping her. Her life—and her family's—had been threatened for years. Surely everyone knew how unsafe Somalia was.

The morning of the interview, a woman guard ushered her from her section through one door and another and down a long hall with slanted windows. She hadn't seen daylight in months and found herself increasingly nervous in the hall, the cold sunshine strange on her skin. Another guard led her into a small room with a low ceiling and two video monitors, where a White man in an ICE uniform sat in a chair chewing gum. Sahro's throat felt dry; she needed to pee. A portrait of the American president hung on the wall, a flag on a pole. The ICE man glared at her and said nothing while chewing his gum. One of the video screens soon flashed on. An older Somali man in a tweed jacket appeared on the screen. He introduced himself as the court-assigned interpreter. To be in a room—even if just on video—with another Somali made Sahro's heart swell, but her initial excitement was soon dashed. They couldn't really talk; and the man seemed strangely formal and distant, so unlike the countrymen she knew. Yes, she could tell he was from Kismayo, but maybe it was something else. Maybe he wasn't supposed to be friendly? Perhaps that was part of his job. But it made Sahro suddenly nervous and self-conscious, as if she were being doubly judged.

The other video monitor flashed on. A White lady with yellow hair pulled into a tight bun appeared on the screen. She wore a navy blue suit and sat behind a big desk and looked too young to be a judge. The lady introduced herself as the asylum officer and set a pair of bifocals on a thin nose. She started immediately with questions. Names and dates. Aliases. Addresses and family members. She ruffled papers stiffly and looked up only occasionally from behind her spectacles. Who had threatened Sahro and when? Where did the events take place? She needed specifics. Dates and times. Corroborating details. Were there witnesses? Testimonies? Written accounts?

Sahro answered as best she could. When was her life *not* threatened? When was she *not* in danger? She told her about Ayaan, the bomb. The drought. Her parents. Her mother killed in the kitchen. The lady kept interrupting and asking unusual questions, trying to trip her up. Then she seemed to grow impatient with Sahro's English and kept checking her watch. In the end she stopped asking Sahro the questions and addressed only the interpreter. Sahro reverted back to Somali and let the man on the other screen translate for her.

It was over before she knew it. The blond lady thanked the interpreter, and her video monitor went black. The interpreter gave Sahro a formal goodbye but hardly looked into the camera—he must've known. The gum-chewing guard pushed himself out of the chair and muttered for Sahro to follow. It was all over, Sahro thought as she walked down the hall back through the locked doors and into the main facility. She didn't pass—she was sure of it. She hadn't convinced the lady officer of anything. A day later she learned she'd failed her credible-fear interview. She had thirty days to appeal before being sent back to Somalia.

Afterward, Sahro wondered what she could have said differently. How she might've explained herself better or been less anxious or woven a more compelling tale. Shirin Kishani told her not to worry. She could appeal. She could find a pro bono lawyer this time. It had happened to others. Maybe it was just the asylum officer—the lady; perhaps she was having a bad day, or maybe the interpreter had misrepresented Sahro. She couldn't give up hope.

But Sahro did give up hope. She blamed herself. She who prided herself on her storytelling skills, *Sheeko sheeko, sheeko xarir.* But she had no silk in English, and every word was a brick: heavy, angular, hard to get out of her mouth. Wasn't that the tragedy of exile? Loss of the mother tongue, loss of one's language. The salinity never the same again. Too much or not enough salt made the throat seize, the mouth choke. So it seemed to her in the warehouse, with the asylum officer: the words, not the thoughts, got in the way. She had no silk in English, only stones. Sandpaper. Ground glass. Every sentence made her bleed.

Back in the scrublands when she was growing up, her grandfather used to talk about a thing called *nuuro.* Nuuro was a substance that lay in the soil, that only the goats and camels could detect. Nuuro existed in some pastures and not in others, and the only way for humans to find its presence was to follow the animals and watch where they went. Sometimes a piece of land looked promising, filled with thorn bushes and scrub, but the goats remained undernourished or gave no milk or seemed uneasy there. That was a sign that nuuro was lacking in the soil. Yet in other places—drier, less appealing—the animals thrived. Often when an adult goat went wandering, she was actually looking for nuuro. Ever since Sahro's arrival in the United States, she wondered to herself if she'd come to a place lacking nuuro. Lush and green and promising on the exterior but missing an important element within. She hadn't shared this thought with anyone, not even Waardo or Shirin Kishani. But she'd noticed it the minute she crossed the border into Texas. Something fragile and cold in the air despite the hundred-degree heat. Something shapeless and desolate—the lack of people, the big-box stores. The yellow arches everywhere. Perhaps there was sterility in the soil? Or maybe the history of what had happened to the land after the Europeans came—what they did to the place and the people who lived there before. Or perhaps it was the language they brought with them? A language unrelated to the land, taken from an island in the Atlantic, as unmoored as its people? How could English encompass a landscape it never knew? Americans seemed to have everything, Sahro noticed, but not the most essential thing: a tongue of their own. A lineage. A root. A link to their ancestral home. Maybe that's why Americans always needed more?

—

One day a guard came to Sahro's section and shouted her name and number and said, "Visitor." No one had visited Sahro before in detention. She wasn't sure what to do. Shirin Kishani fluttered her hands at her and screamed: *Go!*

Sahro threw a scarf over her head and followed the guard. She had only fifteen minutes left, the guard said. She was already on the clock. They went through the locked doors and down the hall, but this time into a different, larger room where inmates sat in little boxes against a wall. The guard pointed her to a chair. Behind a pane of plexiglass sat a young African American woman with short, spikey curls and a denim jacket. Sahro sat, hesitantly, and the woman smiled and leaned forward and introduced herself through the metal mouthpiece. Her name was Angela Simms, she said. She was a volunteer with a group that visited asylum seekers in detention. Sahro had put her name on a list a few months back, and she'd come to say hello.

The woman flashed a smile. She wore long silver earrings and raspberry lipstick and looked older than Sahro but not too much. Sahro vaguely recalled Shirin Kishani urging her to sign up for something called "visitation," though she wasn't sure what "visitation" meant.

The woman sat with a big smile on her face. Sahro had no idea what to say.

Angela Simms did most of the talking that day. She lived in New York City, she said, and taught at a college named Hunter. She was thirty-two years old, had grown up in a place called Pittsburgh, and had been visiting detainees for the last year. She asked Sahro if she had any questions, but Sahro couldn't think of anything to ask just then. She sat staring at the woman—the shiny curls, the denim jacket, the raspberry lipstick—embarrassed by her own silence, but there was something sparkly in Angela's smile that reminded her a little of Ayaan. Later, when their time was up, the woman asked if Sahro wanted to see her the following week.

Sahro lowered her eyes and said, "Yes, please."

—

From that day on Angela Simms arrived each Friday. The guard fetched Sahro in the afternoon and she'd walk through the locked halls to the room with the cubicles and plexiglass, and Angela would already be sitting behind the glass. The big smile on her face, the hoop earrings.

Sometimes she asked Angela questions about her life, and sometimes Angela questioned her. Other times they just sat facing each other, saying little. Each week Angela wore something different. A maroon sweater or a ruffled collared shirt. Sometimes drop pearl earrings or a custard-yellow blouse, but always the raspberry lipstick. Sahro could always tell what the weather was like outside by what Angela wore. A light blouse or her jean jacket or a heavier one, or if it was raining outside, she'd see the dampness on Angela's hair or on her skin. And always near the end of her visit the guard would shout: *two minutes.* And Angela would put a hand to the plexiglass, and Sahro would put hers there too, and they'd mouth the word "salam" to one another.

Sahro asked Angela once about her religion. Was she a Christian?

"Technically," the woman said with a roll of her eyes.

Was she religious?

"No," the woman said emphatically. "Not religious but . . . *spiritual.*"

Sahro didn't understand the difference. A life without religion puzzled her. How could one even wake up each morning, let alone survive or grow old without *diin.* But she didn't press Angela Simms or ask what she meant by "spiritual." Westerners could be so sensitive, she learned, especially concerning God. They kept to other topics. Books.

Angela taught literature at her college and when she learned of Sahro's interest in reading, she started bringing books to her visitations each week. Thin paperbacks. Poetry mostly, none of which she was allowed to leave behind or give to Sahro—if she could, she said, she'd bring boxes! She had to share the texts during their twenty-minute visits. A poem here. An essay there. A short section of a book. One day she held a page to the plexiglass and asked Sahro to read the words. It was a xerox of a short poem on a page. She read the English and halfway through recognized the words and the poet. They mouthed the line together, on each side of the plexiglass: *i've been praying, and these are what my prayers look like—*

dear God
i come from two countries
one is thirsty
the other is on fire
both need water.

When they finished, Angela Simms was beaming; so was Sahro. Neither needed to name the poet, Warsan Shire, the British Somali woman: the poet laureate of London.

—

One Friday Angela arrived with another person, a woman around Angela's age. She wore a charcoal suit and carried a briefcase and had cropped black hair. Norysell Massanet was an immigration lawyer; Angela had found her through a friend. Norysell had looked through Sahro's case and found reason to believe she could help with her appeal. She'd take on Sahro's case—pro bono—under the condition that Sahro tell her the absolute truth and agree to meet with a psychiatrist for a trauma report.

Sahro didn't know what a "trauma report" was, but she looked through the glass at Angela, who was pumping her fist and mouthing the word "yes." Sahro hardly needed the encouragement; it's what Shirin Kishani had been urging her for months.

— .

By the time Sahro passed her second credible-fear interview, she'd been inside the detention center for eighteen months. She consulted with the family. They came up with a plan. Even though she had family in Columbus, Ohio, it was better she wait for her trial in New York City. Yes, she'd be away from her family and friends—and she'd need a place to stay—but the pool of judges was more sympathetic in New York than in Ohio. Her chances for asylum were therefore better there. Angela Simms, meanwhile, had offered to house her and act as her local sponsor.

The family would pay what was needed. Pending her "240 proceedings," Sahro would be let out of the warehouse under the condition she wear an electronic tracking device (which she'd have to pay for) and stay confined to a certain prescribed area and check in once a day with an ICE officer by phone.

After she'd waited so long in detention, everything happened so fast. It made Sahro's head spin: the new credible-fear interview, the application for parole, the bond and release; and then there was the day she stepped out of the warehouse, unsteady on her feet. Angela had brought her new sneakers (with actual shoelaces) and this itself seemed a minor miracle. The sneakers, the laces, the sunlight; the shiny blue Audi, the Uber, waiting for them in the parking lot, driven by a young man from Accra. It was October and chilly and the towers of Lower Manhattan thrust into a cobalt sky. Everything seemed too bright to Sahro, too fast, too high, too swift. She'd been locked up so long, she didn't know what daylight looked like anymore. Trucks thundered past, inches away. Enormous overpasses zigzagged overhead. They crossed a monstrous bridge. Sahro felt it all in her stomach. They raced underground into a tunnel, and when they emerged on the other side, they were surrounded by sidewalks and gray streets and glass buildings that mirrored the car and shot into the air. Sahro had to shut her eyes and say the dua for travel; it made her dizzy to watch. Angela put a hand on her shoulder and covered her mouth not to laugh.

"Poor thing," she said. "You'll get used to it; you just need a little time."

How much time she'd be given, Sahro didn't know that day sailing up Sixth Avenue in Lower Manhattan. It was the end of October 2016, a slant of autumn light in the air. Two weeks later the country she'd come to would elect a new president named Trump, and that would change everything—including the judge who was finally assigned Sahro's case. The one Angela Simms called the "total bastard" and Norysell Massanet called the "two-percent judge." The one who would deny her asylum—if she stayed in the city and did not run.

V

24

Sahro rose early the next morning and readied herself for Fajr, morning prayer. She scrubbed her hands and face and washed her feet and performed salat in the corner by the bed. She checked her phone after. Five messages had arrived in the night from Fartumo and Ahmed and Aunt Waardo, and the contact from the sanctuary group, the man named Hassan. He'd be coming tomorrow to pick her up at the monastery. That was the plan. He hoped to arrive by early afternoon. She should be packed and ready to leave immediately. She texted everyone back and thanked them before stepping into the hall.

That morning the sun was bright in the kitchen, the Guest House warm. The abbot had left breakfast on a tray covered with a tea towel on the table. She removed the towel and found the rolled, spongy pancakes on a ceramic plate. Canjeero! Or at least something that looked like them, a little damp but still warm on the plate. Were they really canjeero? A bottle of amber syrup stood by the plate, a dish with pats of butter. Had the abbot cooked the cakes? She broke into a small smile, then pinched a piece of the bread between two fingers and brought it her mouth. It wasn't bad at all.

She ate the breakfast outside on the porch, sitting in the sun at a little wooden table. The sweet, dark syrup on the canjeero, the melted butter, washed down with cups of sweet black tea she poured from a thermos he'd left.

Afterward, sated, she sat in the sunlight and listened to the birds. The leaves on the trees looked brighter that morning, larger, more luminescent. Lime green. The same color that came to the Hawd after the first rains. The gentle fuzz on the thorn trees that meant new life. New milk. Here too on the mountain, in the north—the same thing.

She stood and stepped off the porch and wandered under the trees. The grass was damp and chilly on her bare feet. A mass of bright yellow flowers nodded next to a stone wall. She didn't know their names but recognized them from the blue vase in the kitchen; neither did she know the names of the slender trees with the white bark that looked like bleached paper. She walked among them now, curious about what they were called. Perhaps it was the spring air or the silence or the smell of woodsmoke. Or maybe seeing the sky the other night, the unfiltered moon. But for the first time she almost believed what the abbot had told her when they first met. That she was safe at the monastery on Blue Mountain. Inside the "enclosure." She didn't have to worry about anyone coming to take her away.

She turned a corner into a little alley of shaped hedges. At the end of the cul-de-sac stood a painted statue and a bench. She recognized Maryam right away, the holy woman the Christians called "Mary." She sat on the marble bench and gazed up at her painted features, her white dress and powder-blue robe, her outstretched arms and downcast face. The ruffles of her robes around her body looked like a scallop's shell. Sahro used to love hearing stories about Maryam in dugsi. How she was raised inside a room in a temple all by herself and looked after by the caretaker, Zechariah; how sometimes he'd enter her room and find fresh fruit out of season. Mangoes and melons and guavas. When he asked the young girl where the fruit came from, she replied: *Allah provides all.*

There were other stories she recalled from dugsi about Maryam. How the Angel Jibriil came and told her she was pregnant, even though she'd never been with a man. How she gave birth to her baby under a date palm, and the labor was long and hard and she shook the trunk of the palm tree so that dates rained down to feed her. But the most memorable thing Sahro learned about Maryam was how she had to leave her home and family as a young woman, had to travel to a foreign land to give birth to her son, the prophet Issa, Jesus. And even then their lives were in danger.

Sahro sat on the marble bench and looked at the statue. She listened to the birds flitting in the trees. The grass smelled good and moist, the air scented with unseen flowers. A warm breeze lifted the silk of her scarf. She looked up at Mary's face, the sad blue eyes, the same face she'd seen all over South and Central America. Her sky-blue robe and white headscarf (the same colors as the Somali flag). What was it about Maryam the *gaalo* loved so much? She couldn't quite understand. If they didn't like Muslim women wearing headscarves, why did they pray to one from Palestine who always wore a hijab?

25

Just then Father Christopher made his way toward the apple orchard. He'd missed the early offices that morning but finally caught up on his sleep. He was dressed in work clothes and carried a rake and ladder. He was finally getting around to checking on his trees. It was his first visit to the orchard since the storm.

When he reached the rise, his shoulders relaxed. In the warmth of the morning he saw the slopes carpeted in white blossoms, the apples in bloom. He slowed his pace and meandered down the rows, the air sweet with odor. They'd all survived the freeze. The white row cover still hung over the dozen Northern Spy saplings. They looked a little derelict and forlorn, the fabric torn. He stood the ladder against one and climbed and tore off the row cover, revealing the pink buds. Like all the others in the orchard, his Northern Spy saplings had survived just fine.

He searched the ground for evidence of the moose—bitten apple branches. Scat, but found nothing. For an hour he stayed in the orchard. He cleared storm debris. Carried downed branches, piled them in the rows, raked around the base of trees. Afterward, on his way back up the hill, he heard an alarming sound. The throaty murmur of a two-stroke engine. An all-terrain vehicle. Probably a turkey hunter, he first thought, until he reached the rise and saw below a man in a black uniform standing on the foot pegs of a quad. Christopher dropped the ladder. His pulse quickened. He hurried down the dirt lane. What the *hell* was a police officer doing so close to the cloister?

By the time he reached the rider, the man had parked his ATV beside the back of the cloister and was unstrapping his helmet. He wore mirrored sunglasses and an all-black uniform—field jacket, vest, chaps, riding boots.

"Blessings," Christopher hailed him, catching his breath.

"Good morning, sir." The officer thrust a gloved hand in Christopher's direction. Christopher leaned on his rake and eyed the man's belt loaded with pouches and cuff cases, keys, radio. Flashlight. Zip ties. Glock.

"How may I help you?" Christopher asked, still a bit winded.

The man withdrew his outstretched hand and leaned across his quad and cut the engine; the morning turned silent again.

He introduced himself as Agent Fusco with Immigration and Customs Enforcement and said he'd tried calling earlier but hadn't gotten through.

"Tried calling?" Christopher asked.

"The monastery," the man said. "Someone named Fletcher. Haven't heard back, so decided to take a trip up here."

The man pressed his lips together. He was clean-shaven and muscled, younger than Christopher first thought, his eyes hidden behind his shades. The front of his jacket bore the letters ICE.

"I'll get right to the point," the man said. "We've received a report from the state police regarding a vehicle left on the river road. The plate and VIN numbers match a vehicle being investigated in an immigration crime. That's why I'm here. I assume you know about the matter."

"What matter?" Christopher asked.

"The vehicle. A red Honda Civic. 2010."

"No," Christopher said. He didn't know about the car.

"You haven't seen anyone or anything unusual up here?"

Christopher looked around and made a face.

"No individuals you haven't seen before," the man prompted.

Christopher shook his head.

The officer let out a small brittle laugh. He pulled the Velcro strap from the wrist of his right glove and yanked it off, finger by finger. Then did the other. The quad's engine ticked in the cool air. The man clipped his gloves to a ring on his belt and removed his glasses. He looked beyond Christopher toward the cloister. His eyes were a surprising pale gray.

"Nice outfit you have here, sir," the man said.

"Thank you, Officer Fusco. We're truly blessed."

"Agent," the man corrected.

"Excuse me, *Agent* Fusco."

They stood for a moment not speaking. The agent peered off in the direction of the orchard. Christopher rested both hands on the handle of the rake.

"Agent Fusco?" Christopher finally spoke. "Do you have any idea what we do up here?"

The man looked at him and shrugged.

"You're a monastery. You're monks," he said.

"*Contemplative* monks," Christopher corrected him. "Which means the monastery and the land is closed to the public and no one is supposed to enter the enclosure. I'm sure you saw the signs riding up here?"

"Yes, sir," the man conceded. He'd seen the signs.

"'Monastic Enclosure'? 'No Trespassing'?" Christopher said.

The agent nodded dismissively. He stepped back to his quad and opened the side pouch of a saddle bag, pulled out a metal folder, and walked back to Christopher and handed him a piece of paper.

"We're looking for this woman," he said, tapping the page with a finger. "Have you seen her?"

Christopher looked at the color-copied photograph. Sahro seemed younger, thinner, her hair cropped short, hollow cheeks, empty stare.

"No," Christopher said. "I don't recognize this person." He handed the page back to the man.

"She's wanted by Immigration and Customs Enforcement," the agent explained. "She's an illegal alien from a country on the United States'

Foreign Terrorist Organizations list. She's broken the law, her in-house detention, and destroyed government property. She's a fugitive who might be dangerous. We've received a report she's here at the monastery."

Christopher looked around, surprised, heat rising to his face.

"Here?" he asked with alarm.

"Yes, sir."

Christopher shook his head. He put a hand to his mouth.

"You must be mistaken," he muttered and looked around again. He tried to control his breathing. He set his mouth into the shape of a saucer. Tongue touching his upper palate behind the teeth. A pose he'd learned years ago at the Zen monastery. The smile of the Buddha. It helped him relax.

"I'm sorry, Agent Fusco. I wish I could assist you better, but I can't."

"Can't or won't?" the agent asked.

Christoper kept smiling. The agent's mouth twisted a little at the corner.

Christopher rested the rake against his body and looked at the sky. The morning had turned lovely. A lapis sky. Big cumulus clouds. Not too cool or too hot. Tree swallows twittered high above the monastery lawn. They'd finally returned for the summer.

"One thing I can tell you, sir," the agent said. "We know two women arrived in the Honda but only one left. Can you explain that to me, Father?"

Christopher shrugged.

"It sounds like a mystery," he said.

"No sir. Not a mystery, but a crime."

"I'm sorry, Agent Fusco." Christopher folded his hands in front of him, his smile genuine now. "We traffic only in mysteries up here at the monastery. I trust you can find your way out of the enclosure without assistance?"

"You don't mind if I take a look around, Father, do you?" the agent asked and swirled a finger in the air.

"I mind very much," Christopher replied. "And the other monks will too. I hope you'll choose to respect our enclosure and not disturb our peace."

The agent shrugged and nodded noncommittally. He set his shades back on his face and climbed onto the quad.

"As you wish, Father," he said with a hint of sarcasm. He was already putting on his gloves.

"We will pray for you and your missing fugitive," Christopher said, and he gave a little bow.

The man nodded and snapped the strap of his helmet beneath his chin.

"I'll be seeing you around, Father," he said with an eyebrow raised.

He started the engine and kicked his ATV into gear. Christopher watched him slowly drive away, taking his time, at a quarter pace, making no secret of his scanning the roadside and the grounds. He mounted the hill and disappeared into the woods, and the murmur of his quad faded. When he was completely out of sight, Christopher let out a long, terrible breath and stood on the road, alone. His whole body was trembling.

26

He thought of going directly to the Guest House but was afraid the agent might follow. He turned instead to the cloister, checking behind him every few seconds to listen and look. He took the back staircase to the second floor and headed into his study, and once there, he poured himself a glass of water in the bathroom and drank. His hands shook slightly. He filled the glass again and drank some more.

How did the man know Sahro was there? Who had informed ICE— could it be Teddy Fletcher or Brother Bruno? Would the prior go that far, bucking the community for his own sense of morality? No. Christopher dismissed the thought. Bruno wouldn't call outside the cloister. He needed to talk to Teddy Fletcher; the agent had left the man a message. But first he had to see if Sahro was okay.

—

He knocked on the Guest House door, but no one replied. He knocked again, louder, and opened the door and called her name. The front room was empty, the kitchen too. He started to panic, then found her sitting at the table out back on the porch in Edward's red check coat. She was penning something in her notebook, canary scarf on head. She sensed something wrong right away.

"What is it?" she asked.

He didn't speak at first. He paced the stone porch and caught his breath. He wasn't sure how to tell her. There was no gentle way.

"We just had a visit," he said, "from Immigration and Customs Enforcement."

Sahro put down her notebook and pen. The life seemed to drain from her face.

"He's gone now," Christopher hastened to add. "He came by himself on a four-wheeler, over by the cloister but . . ." He looked around. "We should probably go inside."

"Yes," Sahro said and gathered her things quickly and stood, and they both hurried into the house and closed the door.

She stood by the kitchen table breathing hard, wrapping her scarf tighter around her neck. Christopher gestured to the chair, and she put her book down and sat while he paced the room.

"I just don't understand how they know," he said, rubbing the back of his scalp. "I can't figure it out."

"The electronic monitor," Sahro said.

Christopher stopped pacing.

"What's that?"

"I had one before I came here," she said, and pointed to her leg.

He looked at her, uncomprehending, and she told him about the GPS monitor she'd had to wear and how she'd cut it off in New York City before she came north.

"Maybe ICE somehow followed me here," she said. "Through the car or the skies. They have many ways of seeing."

She lowered her eyes and fell silent. Christopher started pacing again.

"I'm sorry," she said weakly.

"No," Christopher protested, "don't be sorry. The important thing is, you're safe here. He can't come back. Legally, they can't enter any of the buildings. That's the law."

Sahro glanced at him quickly from under her scarf and looked away.

"It's my fault they come here. I bring you trouble."

"No," Christopher said again and walked around the table and pulled out a chair and sat. He looked across the table. She was chewing the inside of her mouth, preoccupied. She looked on the verge of tears. Then suddenly she peered out the window as if checking that no one was there. In all her time in the Guest House Christopher had never seen her scared. Wary, yes. Reserved, yes. Fierce even, but never frightened the way she looked now, under her scarf—and it broke his heart to see her reduced to fear and not be able to do anything about it.

He stood and started pacing again. He said they'd come up with a plan, that the monks would protect her. They'd make her sanctuary formal, go public if need be; there was nothing ICE could do. Then he spoke about sanctuary and legal precedents and things he'd read. He cited examples of ancient Rome, and the universal belief in "the contagion of holiness," how a person could always seek protection in a church or synagogue or mosque (or any sacred place), where they became automatically invested with the sacredness of the place and made immune from removal. He paced and spouted, then looked at Sahro and saw she wasn't listening. He stopped talking and sat again.

Sahro said nothing for a long time. Neither did he. The daffodils he'd placed the other day on the table had already turned to tissue paper. Sahro leaned forward and set her elbows delicately on the table and rested her chin on her fists. She thanked Christopher for everything he'd done and his offer of sanctuary, yet there was no point in her staying any longer. Even if he could guarantee her sanctuary, what good would it do? For how long could she stay? No—she shook her head—she had to leave as soon as possible. That was the only way—life in danger knows only running. Her contact was supposed to arrive the next day, but even that was too late now. She'd text him and make other plans. She apologized again for bringing Christopher trouble. It seemed she was still being tested, she said, and explained to him about *ichtabar*, the concept of being tested. Allah had not finished with her yet. In Somalia, she said, they had a saying. If one good thing happened to you, a bad one would inevitably follow. This was the bad.

She gave him a rueful smile and looked out the window. Christopher gazed at her across the table. She was lost in her thoughts again, unapproachable. How incomprehensible her life seemed just then to Christopher. Separateness was the source of the world's evil—but it lived here too, inside the monastery, in his own Guest House. She, a fugitive. An African. A refugee. He a White man, American, in robes. His was a protected body; hers was in constant jeopardy. The full weight of their asymmetry appeared to him in a flash. How could he deny it? The heartbreaking gulf. Just the other day he'd told her the monastery was a "refuge," a "sanctuary," a place where people came for "asylum." How hollow his words seemed now. How make-believe the whole idea of an enclosure, a magical circle, a safe space. Maybe such places existed for men like himself, but what about people like her? No, he'd been wrong again, unable to see beyond his own story. What good was a sanctuary if it only allowed in the few and excluded everyone else? There were no safe places in the world, no sanctuaries, unless you held the power and the land—especially the land. He thought of this now honestly, without deceiving himself. The only safe place in the world lay inside a story or in the pages of a book.

The sound of bells echoed from outside the window. Two tolls from the church tower. The ten-minute warning before prayers. He'd already missed the midday meal and now he'd miss the Office of Sext.

"I'll take you," Christopher said.

"When?"

"Right away."

"You have a car?"

"Yes," he said. "The monastery has a car."

She leaned back against the chair and chewed her lip then looked up again.

"I will text the contact and see what he says. Where to go. Where to meet him."

Christopher nodded. The bell banged again, strangely. There were only supposed to be two tolls.

Sahro looked up.

"Your *azaan*?" she asked.

He gave her a funny look.

"Your call to prayer," she said.

"Yes." He forced a smile. "My azaan."

"Mine too," she said. "This is Zuhr. Midday prayer."

"Sext," Christopher said.

"I know," she said, smiling. "We have the same prayer time."

Christopher stood and said he'd be back in an hour or so. Sahro said she'd be waiting. She'd pack her bag.

27

A day before his first deployment to Afghanistan, Teddy Fletcher bused home from Fort Drum to say goodbye to his family. It was August and hot and he visited his fiancée and mother and sister in Hart's Run. His father wasn't living at home anymore, so Teddy drove his mother's Malibu to Blue Mountain to say goodbye to his father at work. He stood outside the tool shop and garage in the hot sun that day while his father changed the oil on a tractor and complained about everything from Teddy's mother to the heat and the monks. When it came time to say goodbye, all his father could muster was a sweaty handshake and a grumble about Teddy keeping safe and not doing anything too heroic "fighting someone else's war." Normally Teddy wouldn't have taken the bait, but he was fresh from training and watching videos from 9/11 and he blew up unexpectedly at his father. He wasn't *fighting someone else's fucking war*, he said. He was fighting *their* damn war and doing it overseas so the war didn't come home to the United States.

He elbowed sweat from his face. His father looked stricken.

"Just take care of yourself," Ted Sr. muttered and crawled under the tractor.

Teddy felt remorse immediately. His father was probably just concerned for his safety, yet it pissed him off nonetheless what people said. Particularly about the Army. Everyone dumped on the infantry, and he'd grown to love his platoon.

Before Teddy climbed back into the Malibu, Brother Christopher arrived on foot and out of breath. He'd heard Teddy was deploying overseas and he'd wanted to catch him before he left.

The monk handed him a small gift—something from all the brothers, he said—a silver pendant on a chain. Saint Michael was technically not a saint, Christopher explained, but an archangel, the protector of warriors. Who knew, Christopher shrugged, handing him the holy medal, perhaps it would help him overseas.

Teddy thanked him, then both he and the monk turned toward his father, but Ted Sr. still lay beneath the Kubota, only his legs sticking out.

Christopher winked at Teddy.

"Don't worry," he said. "We'll make sure the old man doesn't get into any trouble while you're away."

—

Teddy had all but forgotten about that afternoon and the Saint Michael medallion until, years later, back east, he was rooting around in the Malibu in his mother's—now his sister's—backyard. The car had sat stored under wraps since his mother stopped driving. The mice had built nests in the seats and eaten through the brake lines—all of which Teddy would have to replace. He was searching in the glove box for the old registration when he found the silver chain and pendant behind the owner's manual and some papers and loose pens. He must have shoved the Saint Michael there years earlier and forgotten about it in the aftermath of saying goodbye to his father. He held the medal in his hand now and wondered: would it have made any difference had he taken the thing with him overseas? He wasn't the least bit religious (let alone Catholic), but he hung the pendant on the stem of the rearview mirror. He was planning to repair the car. By then, Teddy figured, he could use all the help he could find.

28

Sometimes Christopher prayed for clarity, other times for obscurity. Sometimes he prayed to find himself and other times to lose himself or become lost. The state he was able to enter during prayer depended on so many factors but mostly on grace. He could pray earnestly with every ounce of compunction and nothing might happen. Or he might come to prayer half-hearted and distracted and find bliss. The rewards were not his reasons for praying, but he couldn't deny their inducements. You prayed for the pollen and sometimes ended up as well with nectar. Beauty is the mouth of a labyrinth, said Simone Weil: God was always waiting at its center to eat you up.

Christopher's sister Ana, the biologist, once told him that all his praying and prayers, his chanting in church, was probably just an evolutionary form of self-soothing. Other mammals, she argued, did the same things. Cats purred when under stress—not just when content. There'd been studies, she said. Hard science. They purred at a frequency that helped heal their tissue and bones (a frequency between 25 and 100 hertz). Their purring was a kind of pranayama or yogic breathing. Chanting, Ana said, was probably the exact same thing.

Christopher had laughed when she told him about the purring (and when she added: *You were always such a big pussy*). He'd kept that image in his head. The big cat purring. The waves washing in and out. The right frequency. The right hertz. What if chanting *was* "just" self-soothing? Didn't the sound of purring help heal whoever else was around?

"Not," Ana said, "if you're the mouse."

—

He arrived in church just as Sext was about to begin, slipping into his seat in the choir stall. Brother Luke began the office. *O God, come to my assistance. O Lord, make haste to help me*—and the rest joined in.

He sat in the choir stall, distracted. Halfway through the second psalm he saw a sparkle in the altar window, something silver and hovering outside the glass. He stepped into the aisle, and the hair rose on his wrists. He'd never seen a drone before but recognized it immediately: the two upright props, the antennae, the lens below. He stepped out into the aisle and walked toward the altar. One by one, the other monks stopped singing. The drone hovered now clearly in view of them all, ten feet above the ground. Christopher drew near the window. The other monks approached from behind—all except Father Teilhard, who kept singing in the stall, his earpiece turned down.

Christopher stared at the hovering instrument, the baleful camera angled toward them. Before any of the monks could say a word, the drone sped into sky.

—

At the Guest House, Sahro sat by the kitchen window texting Aunt Waardo, when something silverly caught her eye over the lawn. The flying object was too large and slow to be a bird. She dashed down the hall into the bedroom, closed the door, and lay flat beneath the bed.

—

The unmanned aerial vehicle lifted majestically above the Guest House and cloister, above the apple orchard and access road, above all the monastery lands and beyond. It bore no external markings, no way of identifying who or what operated it remotely from near or far. It flew with a bird's-eye view, with impunity, over all the acreage and surrounding land, mastering all within its range. Wingless, minatory, it circled the mountain's summit, the communication towers, the old fire station; it saw through its camera all the way east to New Hampshire and west to New York and north into Canada over all the native lands.

—

Teddy Fletcher was just making lunch at that hour inside his small apartment above the monastery garage. Two pork chops sizzled on the stovetop burner. The morning had been so pleasant, he'd opened all the windows and doors and stood now in his underwear at the stove. He turned the chops with a fork, when Cora started barking frantically outside the window. He knew all her barks and what each meant, and this one said: *alarm*. He left the stove and stepped to the window. The drone hovered a few meters below. It was surveilling the interior of the open garage downstairs. The color rose to Teddy's face.

"What the *fuck*," he muttered.

He crossed the room and grabbed the shotgun where he'd left it against the wall, then opened his ammo bag and took a few shells. On the way toward the window, he slid shells into the Browning and cycled one into the chamber and loaded the third. The drone had moved a few meters lower. He didn't have a clear shot. He leaned against the window frame anyhow and lifted the muzzle and fired.

The drone jerked; its camera spun. He pumped another shell into the chamber, but before he could pull the trigger, the drone disappeared in the sky.

29

After Christopher left the church, he met briefly with the monks—
avoiding Brother Bruno—and hurried back to his study. By the time he
got there, Teddy Fletcher was already entering the hallway with Cora.
The dog ran to greet him and Christopher patted her distractedly on
the head.

Before he could say a word, Teddy asked, "Did you see it?"

"In the church," Christopher said. "During office. Right in the
altar window."

"*Shit*," Teddy said, shaking his head.

Cora darted into the abbot's study and the men followed. Christopher walked to the window and pulled the curtain aside and peered out.

"What do you know about this Agent Fusco?" Christopher asked
and looked straight at Teddy. "He said he left you a message."

Teddy nodded and said yes, he did the day before.

"And?"

"I didn't call him back," Teddy said. "I wanted to talk to you first."

"You waited a full day to tell me?" Christopher asked, one eyebrow
raised. He dropped the curtain, then waved a hand in the air and walked
toward his desk.

"I know," Christopher said. "I told you to take the day off."

"It's not that." Teddy shook his head. "I thought I'd buy you
some time."

Christopher looked at Teddy and dropped into his chair. Teddy
took the seat opposite.

"I'm sorry," Christopher said. "I just don't understand how the man found out."

Teddy set his cap on his knee. Cora sniffed around the room. Teddy pursed his lips.

"Could have been any number of ways," Teddy speculated. "Anyone else know she's here? Any of the brothers?"

"Every one of them," Christopher said. "I told them all yesterday."

Teddy scratched the bottom of his beard and made a little face.

"No." Christopher shook his head. "I don't think any of them said a word."

Christopher picked up a rosary lying on his desk and began absently fingering beads.

"ICE might have tracked their vehicle," Teddy conjectured. "Or maybe CBP or the state police. Any one of them."

"They're looking for her," Christopher said. "Immigration and Customs Enforcement. Homeland Security."

"Do you know why?" Teddy asked.

Christopher shrugged.

"The man said something about breaking detention. Government property. An ankle monitor . . . Who knows?"

Teddy nodded thoughtfully, and the two men sat a moment in silence. Cora came over to Christopher and laid her chin on his lap.

"What are you going to do?" Teddy finally asked.

Christopher set the rosary down on his desk and patted the dog. He said he was going to drive her to the border. He didn't see what else he could do.

"*You?*" Teddy asked, with evident surprise.

"Why not?" Christopher asked.

"No disrespect, sir . . ." Teddy said. He scratched the back of his neck and leaned forward in his chair. "But you won't make it very far. Not if you go the front way. If that agent went to the trouble of sending up a surveillance drone, ICE probably has eyes all over the place."

"Which means?" Christopher asked.

"Surveillance," Teddy said. "Other kinds. They'll be watching points of egress. Trailheads. Access road, the tollhouse. You can't travel any of those ways."

Christopher picked up his rosary again.

"You'd be surprised," Teddy continued, "at the assets they've got at their fingertips. The technology they can see and hear with."

"You sound just like Sahro," Christopher said.

"Who?"

"Sahro, the woman. She said a similar thing."

"Smart woman," Teddy replied.

Christopher looked at him across the desk.

"So what do you suggest?" he asked.

"In general?"

"Yes, in general."

Teddy sat back in his chair and toyed with the brim of his cap.

"Well," he said. "If it were up to me and I was still in the service, I'd have to turn her in."

He bit his lip and looked at Christopher, who stopped fingering his beads.

"But . . . ?" Christopher prompted.

"But . . ." Teddy said and pursed his lips. ". . . Different situation. Different time. You're the superior. Chain of command. I'm at your service. I'll do what you ask."

He looked at Christopher now with the smallest glint in his eye.

"So you'll help us?" Christopher asked.

Teddy didn't answer but set his cap on his head. Christopher stood and started pacing behind his desk. He asked Teddy how they could get the woman off the mountain. The only way, Teddy said, was on foot, the back way through the orchard and over Pruddy Mountain and down to Lost Lake.

"And then what?" Christopher asked.

"Someone else would have to pick her up there."

"At Lost Lake?"

"Yes sir." Teddy nodded.

"Why wouldn't they be looking over there?" Christopher asked.

"They might." Teddy shrugged. "You can't rule anything out."

But, he said, he doubted that they had the will or manpower to post someone so far away for what sounded like an immigration infraction. They were probably more interested in people coming *into* the country than out.

"Unless, of course," Teddy ventured, "the woman's done something really awful, something she's not telling you about."

Teddy looked up at Christopher, who stopped pacing. Christopher let the question hang in the air. What awful thing could Sahro have possibly done? Aside from cutting off her ankle monitor—what else hadn't she told him?

Christopher dismissed the thought. He slipped his rosary into the pocket of his tunic.

There was one other question he had for Teddy Fletcher Jr., the groundskeeper, the veteran.

"When do we go?"

30

They decided to wait until nightfall. It was better to travel by dark. They'd leave in the morning right after Vigils. Christopher would accompany Sahro over the mountain and down to Lost Lake. And Teddy would pick them up there sometime after sunrise. At a slow pace, the hike to the other side would take around four hours. Christopher would bring food and water. Sahro should bring water too. Meanwhile, Sahro would spend the night in the cloister. It was no longer safe to leave her alone in the Guest House. Christopher would sneak her in during Vespers. Brother Bruno would no doubt object—if he found out. But that was the least of Christopher's worries.

Sahro, meanwhile, made plans in the Guest House. She texted the contact—Hassan—with the new plan. He wrote back later with a new address at the border, a time and place they'd meet. She wrote to Fartumo and Ahmed and apprised them too of the plan.

The abbot arrived at the Guest House just as Sahro was finishing Maghrib, her evening prayers. Her bag was already packed and by the door. Before they left for the cloister, Christopher disappeared into the bedroom and returned with a monk's habit draped over one arm.

He held out the cream-colored tunic, the slate-colored scapular, and told Sahro to put it on. The habit had belonged to Father Edward, the dead abbot. It was safer for her to wear it now. If anyone saw her, they'd think she was just another monk.

—

She slept on and off that night. The room the abbot called a "cell" sat in an older part of the monastery attached to the basement, with a high window looking out on the ground floor. A narrow bed and mattress. A smell of mothballs. A cinder block wall. Another crucifix on another wall. She woke to bells in the dark. The sound of murmuring overhead. A humming in the pipes. She got up and prayed in the dark, then dressed and climbed into the heavy wool tunic—it smelled of aftershave.

Outside, the morning was moonless, a touch of cold in the air. She walked into the meadow behind the cloister where they'd agreed to meet. The heavens sparkled overhead, the sky so thick with stars, it reminded her of the Hawd. She stood under the vault of stars and searched for ones she knew. The Sky Camel, the Prayer Star, the Trench. She found the Morning Star glittering in the west. Venus, they called it in English; it was the same planet as the Evening Star. In the Hawd they called it *waxaro xidh-xidh*, or the "the gatherer of the goats," for when it appeared at dusk, the star always indicated the time to gather up the goats and shut them safely into their protective pen for the night.

She looked at the Morning Star now, twinkling over Blue Mountain. She recalled the story her grandfather used to tell, how sometimes the star went away for six nights and other times for sixty days. When it came back from its six-night journey, it asked the question: *How did you spend your nights?* But when it left for the longer duration, it asked a different question upon its return: *What have you lost while I was away?*

The whole time Sahro was in New York City and in detention she hadn't seen the night sky. The last time she saw the Morning Star was from the top of a train in Mexico, among dozens of others trying to keep warm in the dark, unable to enjoy the sky overhead. *What have you lost while I was away?* Many things too hard to mention, too numerous to number. She'd almost forgotten what the night sky looked like, the depths of darkness, the stars. *What have you lost while I was away?* The confidence in a country, the idea of asylum, replaced by something else, a core of sadness, a grief borne inside her body. A map of uncertainty and pain. *What have you lost while I was away?* All her running had affected her brain, the lawyer told her; it's why it hurt in her head, her heart, in her liver, why she felt tired all the time. That was a life of running, or maybe a life with no home.

When she looked up again, the Morning Star—the gatherer of the goats—had lost some of its shine. Perhaps it too was leaving now for its long journey, the sixty days away, its own hegira. Maybe during that time, it would travel all the way home to Somalia.

31

She saw the abbot's figure walking toward her in the dark, a flash of his tunic, a cap on his head. She slung her pack over her shoulder, and they met in the middle of the field.

"Good morning," he said. "Did you sleep?"

"Little," she said.

"Me too."

He asked if she had everything she needed.

"Yes." She nodded and lifted a plastic bottle filled with water.

"Good," he said, and they began walking through wet grass. They went in the direction of the Morning Star and reached a dirt road in the dark, and soon they entered a gallery of trees the abbot called an orchard. They walked under rows of small saplings, the air sweetly scented with blooms. Branches silhouetted against the stars, the white blossoms above looked like snow.

Sahro didn't know the word "orchard," and the abbot explained it's a place where fruit trees grow.

"What fruit?" she asked.

"Apples," he said.

"Do you have apples in Somalia?" he asked.

"No," she said. They had dozens of different types of fruit but no apples.

They came to the end of the orchard and entered the woods, and for nearly an hour they descended into a steep ravine. Sahro followed the abbot's pale tunic in the dark, grabbing limbs of trees for balance.

A memory of a different forest flashed in her head. The Darien Gap. But how different this forest felt, cold and silent and empty, tree trunks spaced far apart like columns holding up the sky. For some reason she trusted the man in the tunic, the abbot with his glasses and shaved head and face that often flushed red. She'd been wary of him the first day in the Guest House but quickly came to feel at ease alone with him. There was something gentle and quiet about him that reminded her a little of Imam Torino back home in the Hawd. She'd noticed too a certain odor whenever he was around, a familiar fragrance, so out of context, she couldn't place it at first. The second time he came to the Guest House, the morning when it rained, she smelled the *foox* on his tunic. Frankincense! That was the smell! Aunt Waardo's burning incense. Sahro was too shy to ask why—or how—the smell had traveled all the way from the Horn of Africa to Vermont. Did the abbot even know that frankincense came from Somalia?

They reached the bottom of a ravine. Birds were starting to wake in the trees, branches visible, night slowly lifting from the forest. They crossed a swift-running brook and began immediately to climb. Even in the half-light, Christopher knew the way—though he hadn't been along that path in years. He rarely got into the forest much anymore, and never this early in the morning. He'd almost forgotten the joy of heading out into the hushed woods. Life in the cloister became so busy, sometimes he forgot the forest *and* the trees, the great sink of green ringed around them, whose consciousness he barely acknowledged. In the old days he used to walk in the woods all the time. Father Edward had been a great believer in walking meditation. *Solvitur ambulando,* his favorite expression. He often spoke of their life as a pilgrimage and migration, their monastic journey into the unknown, the spiritual desert, each called like Abraham into a foreign country. Walking was a good way to replicate the lifelong pilgrimage of the soul by putting one foot in front of another. Was it any wonder that other religions embraced walking meditation? The Buddhists and Hindus, the circumambulation of the Eastern Church, the great Muslim hajj to Mecca? Years ago, all the able-bodied monks of Blue Mountain went on an all-day annual hike in early spring. They called the daylong hike the "Long Walk" (in the tradition of the Carthusians). Sometimes they trekked down the mountain to the river road or headed north to the neighboring valley. Once in a while they took the route that Christopher was taking Sahro on now, down the ravine and over Pruddy Mountain to Lost Lake. They always brought a picnic and ate peanut butter sandwiches along the way, and in the afternoon they'd hike the old road to Ebenville and circle around to the river road. By the time they made it back to Blue Mountain, they'd climb the last two miles in twilight and arrive at the cloister completely knackered, ready for Compline and bed. They were all so much younger then, Christopher thought. Their hips, their knees in better shape. He hadn't done a "Long Walk" in almost a decade. He doubted most of the monks could make it today—himself included. He had to remember even now: *pace yourself.*

—

By sunrise they reached a granite outcrop halfway up Pruddy Mountain. The sun, lifting across the valley, sent spears of misty light through birch and pine. Christopher was perspiring. He turned to Sahro and suggested they rest awhile and refuel. Sahro looked a little winded herself, bent over and catching her breath. Christopher had almost forgot how ill she'd been just days before.

They found a spot in the sun on the edge of the outcrop with a view of the valley below. Sahro shook off her rucksack. Christopher wiped sweat from his face and opened his pack and removed a thermos and two mugs. The night before he'd made tea for the following morning, a surprise for Sahro. Tea made the Somali way, sweet and spiced and milky. He'd found the recipe online for *shaah cadeys* and all the ingredients in the refectory kitchen: sugar, tea, milk, cinnamon, and even the cardamom pods.

He unscrewed the thermos cap now and carefully poured out two mugs and capped the thermos again. He handed a mug to Sahro. Steam swirled in the morning sun. He lifted his mug and waited and watched her taste.

When she turned, she had a knowing smile on her face.

"How is it?" he asked.

Her eyes widened.

"You make Somali tea?"

"I did." He nodded and blushed a little.

"Is it good?" he asked.

"Very good," she said. " . . . I can't believe . . ." She looked at him a moment, then looked away and sipped her tea some more.

Christopher tried to hide his grin. They sat in silence and sipped their tea, listening to the sound of birds rising from the valley, a caw of a raven high overhead.

Sahro broke the silence first. She talked about her grandmother making shaah cadeys, with fresh goat milk and ground spice, the smell of smoke from the fire that flavored the milk—that was the best part.

Christopher asked what food she missed the most.

Oh, she said, listing them off one by one.

"Sambusas. Suugo suqaar. Goat milk. Camel milk. Camel meat."

"Camel meat?" Christopher asked.

"Yes. The hump. Kurus is the best part."

Christopher made a face and Sahro laughed.

"You should try sometime," she said.

"I will."

"You make a promise?"

Christopher chuckled but made no reply. He removed from his pack a tea towel and set it on the outcrop between them, then set out food from inside a Tupperware container. Slices of buttered bread. Squares of cheese, four hard-boiled eggs. Apples. Dates. Dried figs.

"Is there something you say before eating, a prayer?" he asked.

"Yes," Sahro said. "Always there is, but inside." She tapped her head. "To yourself."

"We say grace out loud," Christopher said.

Sahro lowered her mug. Then Christopher bowed his head.

"Father of us all," he began, "this meal is a sign of Your love for us. Bless us and bless our food and our journey and Sahro's deliverance. And help us to give You glory every day through Jesus Christ, our Lord. Amen."

He looked up, then added, "And let us celebrate the shared source of our one God, the Father, Allah."

Sahro kept her eyes downcast, then uttered the word *amin* beneath her breath.

Christopher looked up and handed her some bread. She took it and thanked him and they ate and drank watching the sun light up the valley.

The slopes that time of year had already turned pale green, but the summits were still winter brown, the trees up top not yet in leaf. The colors were so radiant Christopher often thought of painting them. The pigments he'd use. A cadmium yellow and burnt sienna and sap green. The sky cerulean blue.

After a while Sahro put down her bread.

"May I ask a question?" she said.

"Please," Christopher said. "Of course."

"Why do you choose," she asked, "to be a monk?"

Christopher put down the hard-boiled egg he was peeling.

"That's a long story," he said.

"Yes, but aren't the best ones long?" she asked.

They both laughed; then she gave him a serious look.

"Here in America where you can do anything, it is a strange job . . . no?"

"Being a monk?"

"Yes," she said.

Christopher nodded and said yes, it was strange. "Not normal at all. Not many choose to become monks, to live life in community, single, celibate."

He looked at her with a rueful smile.

"But don't you want children?" she asked. "A wife. Grandchildren. A family?"

He set his egg down on the cloth and wiped his hands. Then he told Sahro he did have a family, that they surrounded him all the time inside the cloister. That just because they didn't look like a "normal" family, it didn't mean they weren't one or cared for each other the same way, with the same love and connection; that his family had old people and young ones and it generated new life in the already living.

He stopped and looked at her listening face. He thought of saying more, of telling her what he'd often told his sister, that just because monks were celibate didn't mean they didn't love all the time—in every sense of the word. For love was the reason he'd come to the cloister in the first place. An overwhelming love that couldn't be contained inside a singular relationship or nuclear family but overspread the boundaries of convention. How many times had he attempted, along with Father Edward, to untangle C. S. Lewis's "four loves"—*storge, philia, eros, agape*—pulling apart each strand until the taxonomy fell into meaningless pieces?

Christopher lifted his egg once more and asked Sahro instead about herself. Did *she* want children, a husband, a family?

She seemed taken aback by the question and lowered her eyes and sat a moment holding her mug in both hands.

Yes, she said, looking at him. Of course she wanted all those things. But not until she was safe in a place where she could have them. She'd seen how difficult it was to have children, or to be a child, back home in Somalia, in the city and in the country, with all its insecurity and war, and she didn't want to have children in those conditions, worrying constantly about where to find food or where to sleep or if a bomb or soldier might come to kill them. No, she said. She would wait until she was someplace safe, wherever that might be. Then, maybe, she could think about those things, but not before.

Christopher said that made sense, and Sahro lifted her mug and drank and they ate for a while, some bread and cheese and dates.

"I have another question," Sahro said, apologetically, removing a date pit from her mouth.

"Yes?" Christopher waited.

Sahro put the pit down and leaned forward and asked about the little box, the closet, she'd seen in the Catholic migrant shelter in Mexico. Is it true that people go into the box, she asked, to tell the priest their secrets or the bad things they'd done? Could he explain how the box worked?

"The confessional?" Christopher asked.

"Yes!" Sahro brightened and explained how she'd seen people lining up to go inside but didn't understand exactly how it worked, and no one could quite explain it to her at the time.

Christopher set down his mug and leaned back on his arms.

Confession, he said, was one of the holy things—the sacraments—of his church. That it always happened privately between two people, the priest and the "penitent." He didn't go into great detail about the absolution of sins or the "seal of confession," which guaranteed confidentiality, but he did tell her it was a good way for people to say things they wouldn't otherwise, that the confessional was a safe place where people's words and deeds were protected, no matter how bad the thing they'd done.

"Even if they did a crime?"

"Yes," Christopher said. "Even a crime. Technically the confession is between only two people—and God."

Sahro nodded but looked perplexed.

"In Islam," she said, "we do confession directly to Allah, for He is merciful and all-forgiving. Why not just confess with Him? Why say these things to another person?"

Christopher leaned forward and hooked his knees in his elbows.

"It's true," he said, "that God or Allah is merciful and forgiving, and true as well that the most important thing is to confess to Him. But," he added, ". . . there is a big difference between communicating silently to God inside your head and having to say something out loud to another human. Without being forced to articulate the difficult or humiliating thing out loud, those very things tend to stay bottled up inside, no matter how many times you tell Allah. Sharing your secrets with Him changes nothing—for He already knows your secrets! But saying a shameful or traumatic thing out loud in front of a caring witness—that forces the secret into the open and helps a human heal. Helps them to feel regret or compunction or relief—whatever the case may be. It gets the thing out of their system. Does that make sense?"

Sahro gave him a skeptical look.

"Is the confession always about a bad thing the person does?" she asked.

"Not at all." Christopher waved a hand.

"Sometimes people just need to talk. Confession is a way of unloading things, getting them off your chest. Fears. Insecurities. Pettiness. The priest, or confessor, can also just give counsel or advice. In the monastery, each monk has his own confessor with whom he shares his doubts or problems. Often monks listen to the confession of a fellow monk too. One gets to talk, the other listens, and then the roles reverse."

"Does it always happen inside the box?"

"No." Christopher shook his head. "Confession can happen anywhere. Father Edward was my confessor, and I was his. We used to always give and take our confessions while walking."

"So, this confession . . ." Sahro said, searchingly. "It is like telling stories about things you did or think or about your life. Like *shaah and sheeko.*"

"What's that?" Christopher asked.

"Tea and stories. It's what Somali people do. Women in the afternoon, they share tea and stories. Some confessions. Some gossiping. The bad things. The good things. Always with tea. Always stories, like we do right now!" she said.

"*Sheeko* means story?" Christopher asked.

"Yes." Sahro nodded.

"*Shaah and sheeko*," Christopher repeated. "I like that."

He uncapped his water bottle and drank.

"So," Sahro asked directly, "who do you do the confessions with now?"

"No one," Christopher admitted. He hadn't chosen a new confessor yet, he said, not since the old abbot died.

He put his bottle down and Sahro said nothing and Christopher checked his wristwatch. The sun was rising higher in the sky.

"We should probably go," he said.

Yes, Sahro agreed, handing Christopher back his mug and thanking him; they'd rested long enough.

—

They started again through the forest, silently now. Sahro took the lead, through a grove of white birches, their trembling leaves translucent green. After a little while she said, in Somalia they have a saying: There are three kinds of people to stay away from while traveling on a long journey. The person who eats everything, the person who is afraid of everything, and the person who doesn't know how to tell a story.

She turned and looked back at Christopher, his forehead white and gleaming without its hood. He made a face and said he hoped she didn't think he was one of those types.

"No." Sahro shook her head. She just wanted to make sure he didn't think *she* was one, so she would tell him a story just to make sure.

"A sheeko?" Christopher asked.

"Yes," she smiled. "Maybe a confession too."

"I'm ready," he said.

"So many years ago," she started, while walking, "there was a girl named Faay Geedi who lived in the Hawd, the scrublands, with a husband who was a camel herder. One day the husband met a stranger who asked him to fight. The husband must prove he is brave, so he says okay, we fight. But right away the stranger killed her husband, tore off his clothes, and ate him. For the stranger was not really a man but what we call Qori-ismaris—a Hyena-Man."

She looked back to see if Christopher was following.

"Go on," he said.

"The Hyena-Man," she continued, "returned to Faay Geedi, dressed now as the husband and looking just like him. She didn't notice anything strange, other than he had no appetite for her food, for hyenas don't like human food. He said to Faay Geedi, 'Tomorrow we'll go to visit my family's village.' And Faay Geedi said, 'You'll have to ask first for my parents' permission.'

"So, in the morning they went and the Hyena-Man asked Faay Geedi's parents' permission. And they both said, 'Go, take our daughter.' And with that they loaded up Faay Geedi's favorite camel, Bayla, with lots of gifts for his family—dried meat, spices, and jars of ghee—and the couple set off with Faay Geedi riding on top of Bayla. But when they got far from the camp and no one was around, the Hyena-Man said to Faay Geedi, 'Woman. Get off the camel and let me ride on top. I am tired.'

"Faay Geedi was shocked! Men don't ride camels, only children or women do. But maybe her husband was sick, Faay Geedi thought. So she let him ride while she led Bayla as if she were the man. Yet not five minutes later, Bayla let out a horrible scream.

"'Bayla, my sweet camel, what is wrong?' Faay Geedi asked.

"The Hyena-Man, chewing a mouthful of camel hump, said, 'Bayla doesn't like the sound of your noisy bracelets; take them off and she'll calm down.'

"Faay Geedi listened to the Hyena-Man and took off her bracelets. But five minutes later the camel screamed again.

"'Bayla, my sweet camel, what is wrong?' Faay Geedi asked.

"The Hyena-Man, chewing another mouthful of meat, said: 'The noise of your sandals is too loud. Take them off and Bayla will get calm.'

"Faay Geedi removed her sandals, but a third time, Bayla cried even louder. And when the husband told her to take off her dress because it was making too much noise, Faay Geedi already knew something was wrong. That the husband was not the real husband but a Qori-ismaris, a Hyena-Man. So she said to the man sweetly, 'Husband, I am tired now. Come down from Bayla and let me ride for a few minutes, then I'll take the rope again.'

"The Hyena-Man said, 'I'll come down only if you promise not to look under the blanket covering Bayla's hump. There is a surprise for you I'm saving for when we reach my family's village.'

"Faay Geedi promised she wouldn't, but once on top of Bayla she peeked under the blanket and saw the bloody hump, the flesh all bitten and torn, and knew she had to save Bayla's life and her own.

"'Husband, sweetheart,' she said from the top of the camel, 'when I was last in this part of the scrub I left some dried meat and a milking vessel hanging in those shade trees. Take us there so we can pick them up as more gifts for your parents.'

"The Hyena-Man did as Faay Geedi asked. Maybe there was some extra meat to bring to his friends? He led Bayla to the trees, and the moment they got under the branches, Faay Geedi grabbed the jars of ghee and leapt off Bayla's back and climbed into the high branches where the Hyena-Man couldn't reach her.

"Then she shouted at the Qori-ismaris: 'I know who you are, and you'd better go back to your cave or I swear by Allah, I will kill you and roast you in a fire.'

"The Hyena-Man laughed the way hyenas laugh, and right in front of her he changed back into a hyena and threw his head back and called to all his hyena friends and cousins to come feast on a she-camel and a girl.

"What could Faay Geedi do? She sang out to the birds in the sky a song for them to come and help her.

"First a big crow came and Faay Geedi said, 'If you go to my family and tell them the trouble I'm in, I'll give you some ghee for your feathers.'

"The big crow agreed but asked for the ghee first. And when she gave him a jar, he flew off without looking back. An eagle arrived next. He too promised to help but wanted the ghee first; when Faay Geedi gave him some from another jar, he took it in his beak and flew off too without helping.

"Finally a tiny sparrow arrived and when Faay Geedi asked the little bird to help in exchange for some ghee, the sparrow flew straight to the parents to alert them to her trouble."

Sahro paused and stopped walking. They were nearing the top of Pruddy Mountain now, the sun hot and risen above the trees. Christopher stopped behind her, perspiring in the sunlight. He waited, catching his breath, then asked, "Well? What happened next?"

Sahro began walking again, slower now, with Christopher by her side.

"So the little sparrow first went to Faay Geedi's brother and sang him a song about his sister, stuck in the shade tree surrounded by hungry hyenas. But the brother was busy watering his camels and didn't like the song, so he threw a rock at the sparrow and broke her wing. Next the sparrow flew—as best she could—to Faay Geedi's mother's hut and sang the same song about her daughter stuck in the shade tree surrounded by hungry hyenas.

"The mother was busy cooking soor by the fire and found the sparrow's song annoying so she threw a flaming stick at her and burned the bird's other wing.

"So the little gray sparrow dragged herself last to Faay Geedi's uncle's hut and sang the same song, but this time the uncle ran outside and called the rest of the family. 'We must go immediately,' he said. 'Faay Geedi is in danger.'

"So the family rushed to the scrubland following the injured sparrow and arrived just in time to chase away all the hyenas. And they were happy, because Bayla and Faay Geedi were still alive. But Faay Geedi was not pleased, especially when she saw the sparrow with the burned wing on one side and the broken wing on the other.

"First Faay's father stepped forward and said, 'Dear daughter, you are safe now, alhamdulillah. Come down and let's go home.'

"Faay Geedi shook her head. 'Why should I come home,' she asked, 'to a father who lets a hyena take his only daughter away?'

"Her mother stepped forward next. 'Come, Faay,' she said. 'Don't be ridiculous. You're safe now, alhamdulillah. Climb down and come home.'

"Faay Geedi shook her head. 'Why should I come home,' she asked, 'to a mother who doesn't listen when her daughter asks for help or when someone comes to ask for her?'

"The mother stepped back, ashamed. Next Faay Geedi's brother tried, but she scolded him too. Then Faay Geedi's uncle stepped under the tree and asked Faay to reconsider the mistakes her family had made, to let the past go and make peace now. And as Faay Geedi sat deciding whether to stay there or go home, the branch she sat on broke and she crashed to the ground. She was only slightly injured, though. Just two fingers broke on her left hand. It was a sign from Allah, she decided, to return home with her family. The only harm was to Bayla's hump and Faay Geedi's two broken fingers, which stayed broken the rest of her life."

Sahro stopped again and shook off her knapsack and pulled a water bottle from her pack. They'd reached the pass over Pruddy Mountain and stood under towering pines. She elbowed sweat from her forehead and took a long drink from the bottle. Christopher thanked her for the story and took off his own pack and removed his bottle too; and they both removed their habits and rested in the shade of the pines.

The morning had grown warm, but a finger of cool hovered at the top of the mountain. Sahro sat in a T-shirt and jeans and headscarf, Christopher in trousers and a button-down damp with sweat.

"You're a good storyteller," Christopher observed.

"Thank you," Sahro said.

"You must be even better in Somali."

She took a pull from her bottle and didn't answer. Christopher removed a bag of raisins and nuts from his pack and held the bag open to Sahro. She looked at the bag and picked out a few raisins.

"Do you know what you'll do," Christopher asked, "once you're settled in Canada?"

"If . . ." she said.

"If," Christopher repeated.

"Inshallah." Sahro shrugged. "Maybe I tell stories."

"Really?"

She waved a hand and shook her head.

"Who knows," she said. "I just hope they will let me in. That's all that matters. The asylum—whatever else, that is extra."

She fell silent and they passed the bag of nuts and raisins back and forth and sipped water from their bottles. It was nearing eight o'clock now, and the cool was welcoming at the higher elevation, the dry smell of pine needles. The sound of chickadees in the trees.

"And what if they don't let you stay?" Christopher ventured.

Sahro said nothing for a long time. She sat picking raisins from her palm, eating them one by one. She wasn't sure what she'd do if she had to go back, she said. She heard things were a little safer in Mogadishu at the moment, though that could change so quickly. As for herself, she'd do whatever was best for the family, for her little cousins. Whatever Allah had in store. She really had no idea. But if she did go back, she said, she'd have more things broken than just two fingers.

She looked at Christopher with a wan smile, and his heart broke a little for her bravery, her strength, her faith. He looked down at his hands. All he could do was listen, accompany, be present, walk with. *"To contemplate what cannot be contemplated (the affliction of another), without running away"*—he remembered that quote now from Simone Weil—*"and to contemplate the desirable without approaching—that is what is beautiful."*

—

They finished the nuts and raisins. Christopher felt suddenly sleepy on the bed of pines. He'd hardly slept the night before. Maybe he could just shut his eyes for a minute, he mused out loud, and leaned back against the trunk and closed his eyes. Not five minutes had passed when he was shaken awake by a low, thudding sound. Something pulsing in the sky. Sahro was already pulling on the tunic and flipping the hood over her head. Christopher scrambled to his feet and threw on his tunic too. The thudding grew louder and violent. The forest floor shook. The blades of a helicopter, then the shriek of an engine, passed high overhead. And just as quickly, the sound faded as the helicopter sped east.

Christopher's legs felt shaky. Sahro's face looked drained. A passing helicopter anywhere near Blue Mountain was unusual, but why today? Could it be just a coincidence? Christopher didn't want to wait and find out. They lifted their packs and started moving right away, a new urgency in their steps. It was mostly downhill from there, into the hardwoods again, the birches and beeches, the ash and oak. And after some time had passed, and neither of them had spoken, Christopher announced he had a story to tell. Not a real *sheeko* like Sahro's, but something he wanted to share. He looked back and saw she was preoccupied, eyes on the ground, but he started anyhow.

He told her about working in the apple orchard as a young monk when he first came to Blue Mountain, about learning the names of the different varieties of apples. One in particular, he said, was his favorite, not because it tasted good and kept well and made nice apple cider or pies (all of which was true) but because of the story attached to its name. The apple was called the Northern Spy.

He looked back to see if Sahro was listening. Her face was hidden beneath her hood, yet he continued anyhow.

There was a legend, he said, that the Northern Spy apple got its name from a real man who lived in the north of the United States before the time of America's Civil War. The man, he said, was an abolitionist, which meant he fought for the emancipation—the freedom—of the African descendants who'd been enslaved in the American South. It was believed that this man, this "Northern Spy," helped runaway slaves who'd escaped their captivity, Black men and women and children—sometimes whole families—who were fleeing north on the network known as the Underground Railroad. The man called the Northern Spy hunted down and sometimes killed the mercenary slave catchers who came north to try to recapture former slaves—or sometimes any Black person they could find. Christopher had first read about the legendary Northern Spy in a fruit-tree catalog, and he'd since tried to confirm the story. Yet in his mind, the connection between the abolitionist hero and the apple made perfect sense. The Northern Spy apple originated in Upstate New York and northern New England in an area people sometimes called the "North Country." The variety grew particularly well up there in the same place where—not coincidentally—the Underground Railroad had thrived, along a route from Albany, New York, west to Syracuse and Rochester, New York, and from Albany north through Vermont to the Canada border. Every farmer or townsperson along those routes back then would have been familiar with the apple that came to be known as the Northern Spy—they'd likely have a tree or two growing in their own backyard—just as, presumably, they'd be aware of the Underground Railroad, or at least know of its nearby existence.

For Christopher, though, the apple evoked something else. And he told Sahro now that the Northern Spy variety was the best producer in the monastery's orchard, well-suited for the mountain soil and early frosts. He always planted a few new Northern Spy saplings in the orchard each spring and pruned the older ones, and there were few things he enjoyed more than pruning trees on an April morning, shaping the crowns with shears and loppers in a foggy dawn when the trees looked, at least to him, like figures rising—arms outstretched—from the muddy earth. In his mind, the shapes of the trees, the history of the apple's name, and the presence of the nearby Underground Railroad all seemed to converge around the same idea of going underground, of running away, of hiding and keeping silent, rising only at the right hour when the conditions were ripe.

He glanced back at Sahro. She'd stopped walking, thumbs hooked around the straps of her knapsack. She lifted her face from under the hood.

"Fuge, late, tace," she said unsmilingly.

"Yes." Christopher brightened. "Exactly."

She started walking again, head down, and caught up to Christopher. Then he told her how the coldest hours and darkest days often led to the sweetest apples, how trees needed the frost and the freeze to come into bud, to make the fruit. That hardship and despair and going underground—both physically and emotionally—had the ability, with God's help, to produce the opposite in a person. That just as love connected people, so did grief.

He caught himself preaching but continued on, whether Sahro was listening or not. He let himself ramble about pruning. How pruning apple trees was all about seeing what wasn't yet there, envisioning the shape and future of something still growing. He was still learning how to prune. It would probably take the rest of his life to learn. He had only one time a year to practice—springtime—and the results of his pruning wouldn't be visible for years to come. Shaping trees was all about time and patience; it reminded him of painting—looking and doing and stepping away and looking again, and how with a few well-placed strokes—a thinning cut here, a heading cut there—you let in more light or carved a new space that didn't exist before. It was all about sharing the light and letting things grow. The key was to follow the fall of the sunlight as it made its way through the limbs. To predict what would end up in the light, and what in dark.

He looked back. Sahro had fallen several steps behind. He could tell she wasn't listening anymore, though he had so much more to say on the subject: Photosynthesis and Saint Francis. The forty-four leaves it took to make one apple. All that sunlight—all that love—for just *one single fruit.*

At last he stopped talking. He shut his mouth. Silence was always the better option—sometimes he had to remind himself. They were nearing the slope down to Lost Lake, and he was nervous about the rendezvous; that's why he'd rambled so much. He waited for Sahro to catch up and they walked together side by side now in silence.

After five minutes Sahro looked at him from under her hood and yellow scarf.

"Is it true," she asked, "about this man, this Northern Spy? Did he really kill slave catchers and help the runaway Africans?"

Christopher didn't answer right away. They could see the azure lake below. He let out a sigh and said he wasn't sure how much of the Northern Spy legend was true and how much was made up. He could never verify it. "But," he asked, "does it matter one way or another if a story is fiction or real?"

32

Early that morning, Teddy Fletcher had boiled a pot of water in his studio apartment above the monastery garage. With a pack of disposable Bics and a new can of Barbasol, he stood at the bathroom sink and lathered his face and razored the hard red hairs off his chin and cheeks, beneath his nose, along his neck. It took a long time, and all dozen razors, to shave off his entire beard. Afterward, blotting nicks of blood, he lowered his washcloth and hardly recognized his pale hairless face. Ever since he'd come back east, he'd let the red beard grow in; it was one of the benefits of leaving active duty. For a brief moment that morning, staring into the bathroom mirror, he saw his younger self reflected back, the one before Barmal Province and Walter Reed and tramadol. In a flash he saw the face of the Teddy Fletcher who hadn't yet fought overseas and was still whole. For some reason, looking into the mirror, he thought of Kate Walling again and their time together that summer. Maybe it was time to finally contact her on Facebook or on the web—try to write her a message. Yes, it was years ago, but how hard could it be to find a biologist named Kate Walling who studied the acoustics of the Bicknell's thrush?

33

Sahro and Christopher came out of the woods and onto a sandy path along the shore of Lost Lake. Red-winged blackbirds trilled in the reeds. The lake sparkled opal blue. Christopher led the way. They wore their hoods over their heads. Two monks out for a stroll along the lake. Sahro could hear the slip of water by the shore, smell the sour aquatic odor of mud in the air. She had the strange sensation they'd already crossed into a different time zone and place, the shore shadowed with conifers, the air darker, more dense with pine.

They passed an empty pebbled beach, a boarded-up lifeguard station. Christopher assured her the place was closed; it didn't open until later that spring. They were going to meet the driver a mile's walk away at the entrance to the park.

They rested a moment at an empty picnic bench in the sun. Christopher removed his pack and water bottle. Sahro checked her phone. She had no service. Christopher looked at his watch; it was not yet ten, but Sahro was anxious to pray. She didn't want to miss Zuhr if they were in the car by then—who knew where she'd be in two hours?—and she'd felt unsettled since the helicopter that morning. She needed to be alone. She shook off her pack and took out her water bottle and asked Christopher to watch while she went off to pray. Was that okay?

"Of course," Christopher said. He'd keep watch.

She walked away from the empty beach. He watched her from behind, the tunic and scapular, her hood up as she disappeared into the empty picnic area under the pines. He took out his own water and drank what little remained.

He sat by the lake, and thought of her praying—her prostrating and kneeling and invoking Allah and doing so in Father Edward's old habit. He wondered what Edward would think. The combination of the Qur'an and the sacramental cloth. The metaphors all mixed and jumbled. He imagined Edward—the converted Jew—would be fiendishly pleased; yet everything he knew about his old friend and mentor, his novice master and confessor, had abruptly changed the last week of the old man's life.

Most monks of Blue Mountain, if they were lucky, died peacefully inside the comfort of the cloister, prayed and watched over by their brothers during their passing. The death vigil and prayers could be—and often were—a profound experience, one they'd waited their whole life for; one Christopher had witnessed again and again, the slow slipping of life, the candles and chants, both life-affirming *and* death-affirming; and, most important to the monks, it confirmed their solemn vows, taken decades earlier, that their own "death to the world" had readied them for the larger prize that came later. *It's easier to die in the evening if you've already died in the morning,* they liked to say in the monastery. Death in life was a victory. Death at the end of life: a promotion. For his whole monastic career, Father Edward said, he was looking forward to his promotion.

And yet the last seventy-two hours of Edward's life had been a kind of hell for both him and Christopher. The community had honored Edward's wish to die alone in "his hermitage" and not in a hospital or with the aid of a resident hospice nurse—they compromised and accepted the hospice nurse's drugs. But as Edward neared death and could no longer get out of bed, something changed in his whole being. His calm energy vanished, his humor. He struck out in bed and became violent. He cursed and raved about his "*Fifty years of darkness.*" His "*wasted life.*" "*The fucking sham, the monastery.*" Christopher knew—intellectually—Edward's agitation was part of his death throes, something happening in his body. When his pain began to look unbearable, Christopher dropped morphine into Edward's mouth from the bottle the hospice nurse had left. At that point he should have called for help, for backup from one of the brothers, who would've been happy to take on some of the burden (Edward was *their* abbot too). But Christopher thought at the time he was protecting the rest, keeping the others away from Edward's profanities and curses. In the final moments, when Edward was striking out at unseen ghosts and violently flailing in bed— his skin cold and clammy, death already arriving—Christopher slipped him the other drug the hospice nurse had left—Haldol—and that seemed to help. His convulsions immediately quieted; he murmured softly, his mouth a rictus of pain. But the damage was already done. The days of struggle, the eleventh-hour heresies wounded Christopher. He sat on the edge of the bed and wept, defeated, exhausted. There'd been no comfort in the prayers, or death vigil, none of the triumph and beauty Edward had expected of his own death, his "promotion." There was only confusion and pain.

For some reason Christopher thought about those last hours just then, as he sat in the midmorning sun beside Lost Lake. He heard a swoop of air overhead and looked up. A great blue heron was passing low over the lake. When he turned, he saw Sahro stepping out of the woods in Edward's old tunic, and something lifted in him, a long darkness. He watched her walking toward him. A radiance seemed to surround the young woman in the habit—the canary headscarf, the walnut skin— though from the distance, she could be anyone dressed in a monk's habit, stepping into sun.

34

Sahro saw the blue Malibu first near the lake entrance. When a White man in a visor cap stepped out of the car, she stopped short, but the abbot continued and went straight up to the large pale man and shook his hand. Then he waved Sahro over. She didn't recognize the man from the other night, the groundskeeper who'd saved them in the storm. Without his beard he looked younger, stranger, a bit ghostly.

The abbot introduced them.

"You probably don't remember," he said, turning to Sahro. "You met the other night."

Sahro lowered her eyes. The groundskeeper squinted into the sunlight with a strained smile. He started to reach out a hand but stopped, then shoved both his hands into his back pockets and made an awkward bow.

Sahro thanked him for rescuing her in the storm.

"*Mahadsanid*," she said. "I am grateful to you. God bless you and your family."

The man blushed and looked at the ground, then back up at the abbot. "Are you ready?" he asked.

"Yes," Christopher said, and the three climbed into the car.

———

Teddy knew most of the back roads to the border from his youth. He used to drive them with his friends on Saturday nights his senior year to drink in Quebec. He hadn't driven those roads in years but the abbot had given him coordinates on a map—degrees and minutes—where someone was supposed to meet them. He'd looked up the spot on the computer the night before and plugged the coordinates into his phone.

He sat in the driver's seat now with his window half-open, both hands on the wheel. The abbot rested in the passenger seat and the young woman in back. Earlier, he did a double take when he first saw the woman in the monk's outfit, her dark face beneath the hood, her guarded look; but once the abbot introduced them, she brightened, and for the first time he saw the foreign woman smile.

He gripped the wheel now feeling awake and calm. He'd swallowed half an Ativan earlier and drunk a thermos of coffee, and the combination kept him sharp. Keyed and alert without the nerves. Not unlike the way he'd felt on better days in Barmal Province on patrol. The tiniest part of him still missed those days, the radio static, the adrenaline rush, those moments of stark clarity after enemy contact, when the world divided cleanly between life and death, each moment lived exactly on that edge. The feeling could be addicting, *was* addicting—but his injury had stopped all that.

He scanned the road ahead, aware of his responsibility for the delicate cargo in his care. Hadn't he gotten everyone into this situation in the first place, picking the women up in the storm? What else was he to do? You helped people in a storm. Whoever they were. That was in the blood, a North Country ethic. Even his father, he'd like to think, would've done the same—and been proud.

—

Sahro checked her phone again in the back seat. Still no service. She was growing more anxious by the minute. The border couldn't be far, and she wanted to send a last text, tell them she was near. But maybe her phone was somehow being monitored? She hugged her pack to her chest and watched the meadows outside.

Birds on wires. A farmhouse with laundry flapping on a line, yellow flowers dotting the lawn. So much open space, she thought. So much land, She couldn't understand why they wouldn't let people in, why everyone she knew in detention couldn't stay. It wasn't for lack of room; America was so full of room. Just as in Texas, here too—in Vermont—stretched long parcels of unpopulated land. Aside from the abbot and the driver, she hadn't seen one other person the whole day.

—

Christopher watched the same fields pass, the sunlight warm in the front seat on his face. He was tired from the morning's hike but too tense to relax. Like Sahro, he didn't recognize the roads or the names on the signs. How little he knew of the world of his nearest neighbors, only an hour outside the cloister. What did he know of those even closer, sitting alongside him? The groundskeeper behind the wheel, the young woman in the back? Each seemed a separate sphere that refused to overlap, that stayed within its skin, each consciousness made strange to the other, despite their forced intimacy and physical nearness. Even at times like this, it was only the smallest section of themselves, a grudging sliver, that conjoined.

He rested one hand on his pack and fingered his rosary with the other. He recited the Litany of the Blessed Virgin Mary. He found himself—oddly—saying the Litany in times of distress, unconsciously intoning the names he could mostly remember: *Mother Most Pure. Mystical Rose. Tower of David.* Something about the list or the sound or the syllables calmed him. *Refuge of Sinners. Health of the Sick.* He'd learned the Litany on long afternoons one winter decades ago when he stayed with the Camaldolese in Ohio. Six bearded men lived in their own lauras, which circled a central church where they met in a room each afternoon to chant the Litany. *Mother Most Admirable. Mother Most Pure.* There was something touching and a little pathetic about their yearning song, but once the Litany got into Christopher's head, he found it strangely moving and hard to get out. *Mother of Justice. Cause of Our Joy.*

He chanted it now to himself, one eye on the road, the other on Teddy Fletcher. His newly shaven face, pasty cheeks, thin lips pressed tightly together. A face he hadn't seen in years. Then the sun caught the chain wrapped around the rearview mirror; Christopher hadn't noticed it until then. He leaned forward and took the silver pendant in hand. The memory came back. The Saint Michael. He looked over at Teddy, who turned to him and nodded, and they caught one another's eyes—and looked away. Christopher dropped the chain, and neither said a word.

—

Five minutes later, a blue light flashed ahead on the road. A strobe. All of their eyes reacted as one. Christopher's stomach rose to his throat. Red flares stood in the road. Lights flashed from a squad car. Sahro flattened in the back seat and hid under the habit. A trooper with a traffic vest stood on the center line. Two cars were pulled to the side, the right lane closed. Teddy slowed the Malibu. There was no turning around. Christopher started to speak, but Teddy stopped him.

"Don't—" Teddy said. "Don't say a thing."

He braked and rolled his window completely open, stopped and and leaned his head out of the car.

—

Sahro breathed the dua for deliverance to herself beneath the habit. She lay as still as she could, head pressed to the vinyl. She could hear the hacksaw of English words. A man's voice. Then another. And then they were moving again, slowly, and she heard the abbot say weakly, "Thanks be to God," and he turned around and said, "Sahro, it's okay."

She sat up slowly from the seat and peered out the window. The thing at the side of the road didn't register right away. The animal emerged as if from the depths of Sahro's fevered dreams: the camel with a hump on its head. The moose lay flat, splayed on her side. Her enormous thin flank unmoving on the pavement.

It was only an animal dying in the road.

35

There were several ways to cross into Canada from Northern Vermont, both legal and illegal. Beecher Falls, Derby Line, Richford, Highgate Springs among the legal. Among the illegal, the most popular place was Roxham Road over in New York State. Since the American election the previous fall, people fleeing to Canada traveled that way. They took a twenty-minute taxi ride from Plattsburgh, New York—at greatly inflated rates—to the town of Champlain. At the wooded end of Roxham Road, they carried their luggage across a ditch into Canada. Arrested, then assisted, by the Royal Canadian Mounted Police, they were driven to a processing center to claim asylum. If their papers were in order and they posed no risk, they were often handed a one-way bus ticket to Montreal, where they'd wait for a hearing on their refugee status. Often, they stayed in the YMCA in downtown Montreal on Stanley Street.

—

Sahro wasn't going to Roxham Road that morning, and neither to Highgate Springs or Derby Line. The address the sanctuary people had given her were coordinates in the middle of nowhere. Sahro knew no one in Montreal and no one knew her. The family didn't want her to end up there alone, awaiting an unknown fate once again. So the plan was for someone—the man named Hassan—to pick her up across the border and drive her to Toronto, into the arms of Fartumo and Ahmed from Ohio, who'd traveled to their friend's apartment on Dixon Road. There, in the safety of a Somali family, surrounded by familiar faces and sounds, Sahro would finally be welcomed to North America. And once safely rested, after a few days, Ahmed and Fartumo would take her to the IRCC on Victoria Street to make her asylum claim. She wouldn't be alone anymore. The hard part was getting her out of Vermont without being arrested.

—

It was almost noon now, and they were nearing the spot, north of the town of Troy. Teddy kept checking the coordinates on his phone and glancing in the rearview mirror. They drove through open hay fields, along a meandering brook, the signs now both in French and English. The road narrowed and dipped into a wooded ravine and Teddy abruptly pulled over and parked beside a small bridge.

"We're here," he said and shut the ignition.

Christopher and Sahro looked around. They were tucked in a small ravine, among a copse of quaking aspen, open country on either side.

"It's one thousand feet over there." Teddy looked at his phone and pointed through the aspens.

Sahro nodded to the field on the other side.

"That way?" she asked.

"According to the numbers," Teddy said, then scanned the road and said they probably should get moving. CBP had cameras everywhere.

It all happened so quickly. Sahro swung on her pack. Teddy offered to cross, but Christopher said no, to stay by the car. He and Sahro scrambled into the aspens and leapt across a small stream then walked out into the bottom of a big meadow plush with new alfalfa. At the top of the field, where the slope met the horizon, a silver car sat parked and silhouetted against sky. A man emerged from the driver's seat. He was tall and Black and lifted a hand in the air.

Sahro waved back, then turned to Christopher and smiled nervously. She set down her pack and started to remove the habit, but Christopher stopped her.

"Keep it," he said. "It's better you have it."

She looked at him in confusion a moment. Her eyes were shining. Then she lifted her pack again.

"How do you say 'safe travels' in Somali?" he asked.

"*Nabad-geylo*," she said.

He repeated the words gamely. Then she took his hand a moment in hers.

"Abbaye," she said. "Thank you."

She reached her arms around him and hugged him bashfully for a second and let go. Then she was hurrying up the hill, half running, not looking back. Christopher watched the whole time, the cream-colored habit flapping, the green grass, the milk-blue sky.

When Sahro reached the man, she turned once and waved, and Christopher waved back.

Then he watched her climb into the car befored it raced away.

—

Later that afternoon back on Blue Mountain, Christopher entered the Guest House. He checked the cold woodstove and stripped the sheets from the bed. He put away the washed cups in the kitchen and wiped the counter and stove. On the table by the window, the little bottle of maple syrup stood in the afternoon sun, its amber glowing inside. He sat at the table and picked up the bottle and wept.

—

Around that same hour, speeding west on Ontario 401, Sahro watched out the window the unknown landscape blur past. She drifted in and out of sleep and fell into a recurring dream:

She is sitting on an airplane filled with passengers. Some of them she knows. The girl from Nepal, *la Llorona*. Shirin Kishani from detention and Elena Ortiz, the little boy Oscar. Dozens more who wave across the aisles to one another. Dalmar sits in the seat to her left, Ayaan on the other side; they are clutching each other's hand in Sahro's lap. The three of them lean together toward the window, press their faces as close as possible to the plexiglass, trying to see what's left of the world below.

On this flight the passengers wear no handcuffs, and no guards patrol the aisles. They're free to get up and walk where they want. But no one seems to know exactly where they're heading, or who is piloting the plane, or if they'll ever get to see land again. They are miles above the planet now, Venus setting in the west. The light leaving the earth. Down there, all they can see is an earth on fire. The world is slowly burning below.

NOTES

Page 13   "the water is safer than the land" from "Home" by Warsan
           Shire.

Page 117   "My solitude is not my own . . ." from *Conjectures of a Guilty
           Bystander* by Thomas Merton.

Page 144   "emotional response to light" from *Landscape into Art* by
           Kenneth Clark.

Page 145   "Here are your waters and watering place . . ." from "Directive"
           by Robert Frost.

Page 204   "dear God / i come from two countries . . ." from "What They
           Did Yesterday Afternoon" by Warsan Shire.

Page 248   "To contemplate what cannot be contemplated . . ." from *The
           First and Last Notebooks* by Simone Weil.

AFTERWORD

Every story grows from a communal matrix, fed by multiple springs. Three nearby communities inspired *North*. All three are neighbors: monks, Vermont veterans, and Somali refugees. Without the wisdom and contribution that came from each, there'd be no story, no book.

I live in Vermont next door to a Carthusian monastery (the Charterhouse of the Transfiguration) and hear their vesper bells each evening on the mountain. Another monastery, New Skete, makes its home twenty miles down the road across the border in New York State. A few miles farther live the nuns of St. Mary's-on-the-Hill in Greenwich, New York. The men and women who reside in these places arrived in the North Country for the same reason I moved to Vermont decades ago: for sanctuary, or at least the idea of it, an idea I wanted to explore in this novel.

People who fled Somalia started arriving in Vermont in 2003. They were Somali Bantu at first, but soon ethnic Somalis joined as well. In the years since, some 1,500 Somali men, women, and children arrived in the state, most settling in the Burlington and Winooski areas. They were resettled by a small nonprofit in Colchester, Vermont, called the Vermont Refugee Resettlement Program, subsequently named USCRI Vermont (a field office of the nongovernmental organization the U.S. Committee for Refugees and Immigrants). Since 1989, USCRI Vermont has helped more than 8,000 refugees displaced by violence, persecution, or war—people who have come from Africa, Asia, and Eastern Europe, from countries such as Bosnia, Bhutan, Iraq, Congo, Burma, Syria, and Sudan, to name a few.

I started visiting Burlington and the USCRI office during the Obama administration, when the global refugee crisis became unignorable. The work USCRI Vermont was doing, with a small budget and staff, was nothing less than heroic. Through staff members I was slowly introduced to the Somali community in Vermont. They were men and women raising families, working jobs, going to school, keeping shop, paying rent. Their spirit and intuition, insight and encouragement, challenged and inspired. In their stories I found faint echoes of my own family history. My grandmother didn't become an American citizen until my father was almost an adult; Somalis (like Jews), live in a global diaspora, exiled and often scapegoated; they settle in cities because they're the only places they can afford and find jobs.

In attempting to write this fiction, I was always painfully aware of trespass and the cycle of harm perpetuated by White writers pretending to speak for, or somehow represent, people of color. I make no claims here: there already exists a vibrant, international community of Somali writers whose work gives voice to a globally diverse, multivalent, and ever-expanding literary community—from the novels of Nuruddin Farah, Nadifa Mohamed, and Ubah Cristina Ali Farah to the haunting stories of Diriye Osman, the lyrics of Ladan Osman, and the celebrated poetry of Warsan Shire; the list goes on (for a fuller one, see the resource section at the end). Somali life and literature are too varied and complex (with their own class, racial, and ethnic divisions) to claim any singular experience or representation.

Novels are always attempts to cross borders, the border between one consciousness and another, the writer's and the readers', mine and yours. The question always is: *who gets to cross whose borders?* Who has the passport and why? Power is always at play, and White American writers have historically owned the passports, the visas, the point of views (the whole real estate). I wrote this book in—and against—the White settler literary tradition in which I was raised, knowing I could never see enough, know enough, experience enough, beyond my own blind spots and ignorance. Beyond my own body. My aim was not to extract from, but ally *with*. To give an offering, an accompaniment. I'm not sure I succeeded. Perhaps just failed a little less.

A set of Vermonters who grew up here and have family roots in the state going back several generations informed this book as well. Unlike the rest of us "flatlanders," who come from elsewhere, many "native" Vermonters have limited job and economic opportunities in the small, rural state. Often in the past, to get an education or pay the bills—or simply out of a sense of patriotism—they joined the army or national guard. Many of them, post-9/11, found themselves fighting in wars overseas. For such a small state, Vermont paid a heavy price for the wars in Afghanistan and Iraq. More soldiers from Vermont died in those places per capita than from any other state in the country. Is their sanctuary any less vital?

When I began this novel in 2012, I imagined it taking place in a near-dystopic future, when Americans would turn their backs on refugees and close the country's borders. What I didn't know back then was how quickly that future would arrive (it already had).

During the Trump years I met Fardusa Abdalla Abdo and her family, who lived in Winooski, Vermont. Fardusa generously opened her home and heart to a stranger, and over several months—then years—she and her son, Mohammed, acting as translator, shared Fardusa's story with me and Laurie Stavrand, community partnership coordinator for USCRI Vermont. Their story was one of incredible family strength and character and perseverance against colossal odds. Fardusa fled Somalia as a teen and lived as a refugee in Yemen while single-handedly raising six children, two with disabilities. After years of hardship, setbacks, and delays—and then the outbreak of war in Yemen—Fardusa resettled her family in Vermont in 2013. After seven years living there, she passed her citizenship test and was naturalized at a ceremony in St. Albans. I was privileged to be a witness that early October morning outside the Department of Homeland Security in St. Albans. Donald Trump was still president, but there was Fardusa, smiling under the October sun, surrounded by some of her children. She was sworn in outside the building, in the parking lot, across the street from a cornfield, wearing her hijab and waving a small American flag.

One other group of people needs acknowledgment, those who've lived here long before any Europeans or Africans: the Abenaki and Mohawk Nations, whose land we occupy today. Their presence—and absence—always raises the question: at whose cost does sanctuary come? Can one group's sanctuary not mean another's annihilation?

—

I'm indebted to the Minneapolis author and playwright Ahmed Ismail Yusuf, who lent the earliest solidarity and support. Raised as a nomad in Somalia, Ahmed's understanding of Somali storytelling, culture, and language is encyclopedic. He tirelessly offered knowledge, humor, and wisdom. (He read an early draft of *North* on a flight to Mogadishu, his first trip back since 1984; he wanted to make sure the manuscript *would see the motherland and back*—hopefully, he joked, "she will recognize the capital.") Thanks to Ahmed for his breadth of kindness and to Cawo M. Abdi for introducing us. Thanks also to Abdihamid A. Muhamed and Shadir Mohammed, vice president of the Somali Bantu Association of Vermont, for sharing their knowledge and the stories of their own resettlement. Thanks to Isra Kassim for doing the same. Thanks also to Fartumo Kusow, Marian Hassan, and Masiti Mohammed for their initial exchanges.

The Charterhouse of the Transfiguration in Arlington, Vermont, served as source and inspiration, yet my sincerest gratitude goes to the monks of New Skete Monastery in Cambridge, New York. Brother Christopher Savage provided continual ballast and insight, as did the examples of other community friends, particularly Brother Ambrose and members of the Battenkill Chorale—Brother Stavros and Brother Mark and Father Luke.

I spent several weeks at Saint Joseph's Abbey in Spencer, Massachusetts, as a retreatant and am grateful to their guest house and guest masters. The many conversations and ongoing dialogue with the brilliant Father Simeon Leiva (OCSO) shaped my understanding of contemporary monastic life, as did exchanges with other Trappists at Spencer—Father James and Father Luke, among others. Thanks as well to the hospitality of Father Basil at the Holy Family Hermitage in Bloomingdale, Ohio, and the staff at Zen Mountain Monastery in Mount Tremper, New York. And to Sister Mary Elizabeth of St. Mary on-the-Hill.

The Harvard Program in Refugee Trauma, which I attended in 2019, helped me better understand the psychological effects of displacement and possible strategies of repair. Many thanks to the work and vision of its founding director, Richard Mollica, and to the staff: Eugene Augusterfer, Omar Bah, Anna Dethridge, Taiwo Lateef Sheikh, Theoni Stathopoulou, and Jerry Streets. Special thanks to the constant probing and support of "Group E" (Amy, Anna, Brinda, Elizabeth, Minal, Eszter, Heidi, Marielena, Pamela, Laura, and Will). Joanne Ahola, MD, at Physicians for Human Rights continues to be a lodestar for her work with asylum seekers, as does Ariel Shidlo. Thanks to Michelle Jenness and the Association of Africans Living in Vermont; Kristen Rengo, Mary Lou Hardwich Leavitt, Luke Stavrand, John Killacky, and Carmela Franklin and the American Academy in Rome.

Thanks also to the military insights of my neighbors Kevin Dunican Jr., Julie Robertson, John Bushee, and others deployed overseas. Thanks to Kristi Ericson (USMC) for her feedback, and Staff Sargent Daley of the Army Recruiting Station in Saratoga Springs, New York.

I'm grateful to readers Andre Alexis, Suzanne Gardinier, Catherine Bush, Peter Cameron, Nancy Zafris, Steve Hubbell, Joanna Ruocco, Jim Krusoe, Bernadette Murphy, and—above all—Uwem Akpan, fellow traveler. Thanks also to Chris Abani, Lisa Dickey, Stanley Hadsell, Maurice Sendak, Isabel and Stuart Kessler, Betsy Lerner, Michael

Jacobs, and Tracy Carns. And to Pat Towers—gatherer, sorceress, presiding muse.

It's fair to say *North* would not have been published (at least in its current form) if not for the intervention of Laurie Stavrand, community partnership coordinator for USCRI Vermont. Laurie had the honesty and wisdom to know what was wrong with the book and offered an avenue for mending what was broken. Neither could it have been written without the knowledge of Abdirashid Hussein, senior case manager of USCRI Vermont and expert on immigration and asylum. Abdirashid is a touchstone and leader in the Somali community in Vermont. He navigates many worlds, local and global, with quiet intuition and grace. He offered critical consultation and advice on every aspect of Sahro's journey. He and Laurie carried this work to the finish.

The following books provided indispensable information: *En el Camino: México, la Ruta de los Migrantes Que No Importan* by Edu Ponces, Toni Arnau, and Eduardo Soteras; *The Beast* by Óscar Martínez; *Folktales from Somalia* by Axmed Cartan Xannge; *The Terminology and Practice of Somali Weather Lore, Astronomy, and Astrology* by Muusa H. I. Galaal; *Call Me American* by Abdi Nor Iftin; and *Teaching My Mother How to Give Birth* by Warsan Shire. (See bibliography for more.)

Finally to Dona Ann McAdams, steadfast love. The eyes behind all these words.

All royalties from the North American sales of *North* will be donated to the Vermont office of the U.S. Committee for Refugees and Immigrants in Colchester, Vermont.

SELECTED BIBLIOGRAPHY

Abdi, Cawo M. *Elusive Jannah: The Somali Diaspora and a Borderless Muslim Identity*. Minneapolis: University of Minnesota Press, 2015.

Abdullahi, Mohamed Diriye. *Culture and Customs of Somalia*. Santa Barbara: Greenwood Publishing Group, 2001.

Akou, Heather Marie. *The Politics of Dress in Somali Culture*. Bloomington: Indiana University Press, 2011.

Alter, Robert, trans. *The Book of Psalms: A Translation with Commentary*. New York: W. W. Norton & Company, 2009.

Angelou, Maya. *I Know Why the Caged Bird Sings*. New York: Random House, 1969.

Armstrong, Karen. *The History of God: The 4,000-Year Quest of Judaism, Christianity and Islam*. New York: Ballantine Books, 1994.

Arnau, Toni, Edu Ponces, and Eduardo Soteras. *En El Camina: Mexico, La Ruta de los Migrantes Que No Importan*. Blume, 2011.

Ash, J. S. and J. E. Miskell. *Birds of Somalia: Their habitat, Status and Distribution*. Nairobi: Ornithological Sub-Committee, EANHS, 1983.

Bigelow, Martha H. *Mogadishu on the Mississippi: Language, Racialized Identity, and Education in a New Land*. Hoboken: Wiley-Blackwell, 2010.

Bonhoeffer, Dietrich. *Psalms, The Prayer Book of the Bible*. Minneapolis: Fortress Press, 1974.

Browning, Frank. *Apples*. New York: North Point Press, 1998.

Casey, Michael. *The Art of Winning Souls, Pastoral Care for Novices*. Kalamazoo, MI: Cistercian Publications, 2012.

———. *Fully Human, Fully Divine: An Interactive Christology*. Liguori, MO: Liguori Publications, 2004.

———. *Strangers to the City: Reflections on the Beliefs and Values of the Rule of Saint Benedict*. Orleans, MA: Paraclete Press, 2005.

Cassian, John. *The Conferences*. Translated by Colm Luibheid. Mahwah, NJ: Paulist Press, 1985.

Catozzella, Giuseppe. *Don't Tell Me You're Afraid*. New York: Penguin Press, 2016.

Clark, Kenneth. *Landscape into Art*. New York: Harper & Row, 1976.

Clark, Robert. *Dark Waters: Art, Disaster, and Redemption in Florence*. New York: Anchor, 2009.

The Cloud of Unknowing and *The Book of Privy Counseling*. Edited by William Johnston. New York: Image, 1996.

Chu-Cong, Joseph. *The Contemplative Experience: Erotic Love and Spiritual Union*. Chestnut Ridge, NY: Crossroad Publishing, 1999.

Cruz, Rosayra Pablo and Julie Schwietert Collazo. *The Book of Rosy: A Mother's Story of Separation at the Border*. New York: HarperOne, 2020.

Cummings, Charles. *Monastic Practices*. Kalamazoo, MI: Cistercian Publications, 1986.

Dōgen. *Moon in a Dewdrop: Writings of Zen Master Dōgen*. Translated by Kazuaki Tanahashi. New York: North Point Press, 1995.

Fanon, Frantz. *The Wretched of the Earth*. New York: Grove Press, 2005.

Farah, Nuruddin. *Yesterday, Tomorrow: Voices from the Somali Diaspora*. London: Cassell, 2000.

Foner, Eric. *Gateway to Freedom: The Hidden History of the Underground Railroad*. New York: W. W. Norton & Company, 2016.

Fortis, Paolo. *Kuna Art and Shamanism: An Ethnographic Approach*. Austin: University of Texas Press, 2013.

Fry, Timothy, ed., *The Rule of Benedict in English*. Collegeville, MN: Liturgical Press, 1981.

Galaal, Mussa H. I. *The Terminology and Practice of Somali Weather Lore, Astronomy, and Astrology*. Somalia: printed by the author, 1968.

Hadith of Bukhari. 4 vols. London: Forgotten Books, 2008.

Herrera, Heraclio, Valerio Nuez, and Jorge Ventocilla. *Plants and Animals in the Life of the Kuna*. Translated by Elizabeth King. Austin: University of Texas Press, 2010.

Hough, Mazie, Kimberly Huisman, Kristin Langellier, and Carol Nordstrom, eds., *Somalis in Maine: Crossing Cultural Currents*. Berkeley: North Atlantic Books, 2011.

Humfrey, Peter, ed., *The Cambridge Companion to Giovanni Bellini*. Cambridge: Cambridge University Press, 2008.

Iftin, Abdi Nor. *Call Me American*. New York: Knopf, 2018.

An Islamic Book of Constellations. Oxford: Bodleian Library, 1965.

James, William. *The Varieties of Religious Experience*. London: Forgotten Books, 2015.

Kandinsky, Wassily. *Concerning the Spiritual in Art*. Translated by M. T. H. Sadler. Dover Publications, 1977.

Kavanaugh, Kieran, and Otilio Rodriguez, trans., *The Collected Works of St. John of the Cross*. Washington, DC: ICS Publications, 2010.

King, Max, Beth Loffreda, and Claudia Rankine, eds., *The Racial Imaginary: Writers on Race in the Life of the Mind*. Fence Books, 2015.

Kisly, Lorraine, ed., *Christian Teachings on the Practice of Prayer: From the Early Church to the Present*. Toronto: New Seeds, 2006.

Kossmann, Fr. Benedict. *Sounds of Silence: A Monk's Journey*. Self-published, AuthorHouse, 2005.

Lacarriere, Jacques. *Men Possessed by God: The Story of the Desert Monks of Ancient Christendom*. New York: Doubleday, 1964.

Leiva-Merikakis, Erasmo. *Love's Sacred Order: The Four Loves Revisited*. San Francisco: Ignatius Press, 2000.

Leroux-Dhuys, Jean-Francois. *Cistercian Abbeys: History and Architecture*. Potsdam: H.F. Ullmann Publishing, 2008.

Levine, Adele. *Run, Don't Walk: The Curious and Courageous Life Inside Walter Reed Army Medical Center*. New York: Avery, 2015.

Lewis, C. S. *The Four Loves*. New York: Harcourt Brace and Co., 1960.

Lewis, David, trans., *The Life of Saint Teresa of Avila by Herself*. Digireads. com, 2019.

Lockhart, Robin Bruce. *Halfway to Heaven: The Hidden Life of the Carthusians*. Kalamazoo, MI: Cistercian Publications, 1999.

Loori, John Daido. *The Eight Gates of Zen: A Program of Zen Training*. Boulder: Shambhala Publications, 2002.

Martinez, Oscar. *The Beast: Riding the Rails and Dodging Narcos on the Migrant Trail*. Translated by Daniela Maria Ugaz and John Washington. New York: Verso, 2014.

Meiss, Millard. *Giovanni Bellini's St. Francis in the Frick Collection*. Princeton: Princeton University Press, 1964.

Morrison, Toni. *Playing in the Dark: Whiteness and the Literary Imagination*. New York: Vintage, 1993.

Maguire, Nancy Klein. *An Infinity of Little Hours: Five Young Men and their Trial of Faith*. New York: PublicAffairs, 2007.

McGinn, Bernard, ed., *The Essential Writings of Christian Mysticism*. New York: Random House Modern Library Classics, 2006.

Merton, Thomas. *A Book of Hours*. Notre Dame, IN: Ave Maria Press, 2007.

———. *The Asian Journal of Thomas Merton*. New York: New Directions, 1975.

———. *Conjectures of a Guilty Bystander*. New York: Image, 1968.

———. *Contemplative Prayer*. New York: Image, 1971.

———. *In the Valley of Wormwood: Cistercian Blessed and Saints of the Golden Age*. Kalamazoo, MI: Cistercian Publications, 2013.

———. *New Seeds of Contemplation*. New York: New Directions, 2007.

———. *Praying the Psalms*. Eastford, CT: Martino Fine Books, 2014.

———. *Seasons of Celebration: Medications on the Cycle of Liturgical Feasts*. New York: Farrar, Straus & Giroux, 1965.

———. *The Seven Story Mountain*. Boston: Mariner Books, 1999.

———. *The Silent Life of the Carthusians*. Sandgate, VT: Charterhouse of the Transfiguration, 2011.

———. *Thoughts in Solitude*. New York: Farrar, Straus & Giroux, 1999.

Mollica, Richard. *Healing Invisible Wounds: Paths to Hope and Recovery in a Violent World*. Nashville: Vanderbilt University Press, 2008.

Order of the Cistercians of the Strict Observance. Constitutions and statutes of the monks and nuns. https://ocso.org/resources/law/constitutions-and-statutes/.

Perata, David D. *The Orchards of Perseverance, Conversations with Trappist Monks About God, Their lives, and the World*. Ruthven, IA: St. Therese's Press, 2000.

Parnell, Sean. *Outlaw Platoon: Heroes, Renegades, Infidels, and the Brotherhood of War in Afghanistan*. New York: William Morrow, 2012.

Pennington, M. *A Place Apart: Monastic Prayer and Practice for Everyone*. Liguori, MO: Liguori Publications, 1998.

Phillips, Michael. *The Apple Grower: A Guide for the Organic Orchardist*. Hartford, VT: Chelsea Green Publishing, 2005.

Palmer, G.E.H., Philip Sherrard, and Bishop Kallistos Ware, trans., *Philokalia; the Eastern Christian Spiritual Texts*. Nashville: SkyLight Paths, 2006.

Rankine, Claudia. *Citizen: An American Lyric*. Minneapolis: Graywolf Press, 2014.

Rawlence, Ben. *City of Thorns: Nine Live in the World's Largest Refugee Camp*. New York: Picador, 2016.

Row, Jess. *White Flights: Race, Fiction, and the American Imagination*. Minneapolis: Graywolf Press, 2019.

Sheikh, Fazal. *Ramadan Moon*. Self-published, 2001.

Shire, Warsan. *Teaching My Mother How to Give Birth*. London: Flipped Eye Publishing, 2011.

Steiner, George. *Real Presences*. Chicago: University of Chicago Press, 1990.

Ward, Benedicta. *The Desert Fathers: Sayings of the Early Christian Monks*. New York: Penguin Classics, 2003.

Wood, Trish. *What Was Asked of Us: An Oral History of the Iraq War by the Soldiers Who Fought It*. New York: Little, Brown and Company, 2006.

Weil, Simone. *Gravity and Grace*. London: Routledge, 2002.

———. *The First and Last Notebooks*. New York: Oxford University Press, 1970.

———. *Waiting for God*. New York: Harper Perennial Modern Classics, 2009.

Xaange, Axmed Cartan. *Sheekoxariirooyin soomaaliyeed* [Folktales from Somalia]. Somalia/Uppsala: Somali Academy of Sciences and Arts, with Scandinavian Institute of African Studies, 2003.

Yusuf, Ahmed Ismail. *Somalis in Minnesota*. St. Paul: Minnesota Historical Society Press, 2012.

———. *The Lion's Binding Oath and Other Stories*. New York: Catalyst Press, 2018.

FURTHER READING BY
SOMALI WRITERS AND POETS

FICTION

Ali, Hanna. *The Story of Us*. London: Market FiftyFour, 2019.

Ega, Abdi Latif. *Guban*. Self-published, CreateSpace, 2012.

Farah, Cristina Ali. *Little Mother*. Bloomington: Indiana University Press, 2011.

Farah, Nuruddin. *Crossbones*. New York: Arcade Publishing, 2012.

———. *From a Crooked Rib*. New York: Riverhead Books, 2006.

———. *Gifts*. New York: Arcade Publishing, 2012.

———. *Hiding in Plain Sight*. New York: Riverhead Books, 2015.

———. *Knots*. New York: Riverhead Books, 2008.

———. *Links*. New York: Riverhead Books, 2005.

———. *Maps*. New York: Arcade Publishing, 2016.

———. *North of Dawn*. New York: Riverhead Books, 2018.

———. *Secrets*. New York: Arcade Publishing, 2016.

Gaildon, Mahmood. *The Yibir of Las Burgabo*. Trenton, NJ: Red Sea Press, 2005.

Kusow, Fartumo. *Tale of a Boon's Wife*. Toronto: Second Story Press, 2017.

———. *The Youth of God*. Toronto: Mawenzi House/TSAR Publishers, 2019.

Maxamuud, Yasmeen. *Nomad Diaries*. Self-published: CreateSpace, 2011.

Mohamed, Nadifa. *The Fortune Men*. London: Viking, 2021.

———. *The Orchard of Lost Souls*. New York: Farrar, Straus and Giroux, 2014.

——— *Black Mamba Boy*. New York: Farrar, Straus and Giroux, 2010.

Osman, Diriye. *Fairytales for Lost Children*. London: Team Angelica, 2018.

———. *We Once Belonged to the Sea*. London: Team Angelica, 2018.

Osman, Ladan. *Exiles of Eden*. Minneapolis: Coffee House Press, 2019.

———. *The Kitchen-Dweller's Testimony*. Lincoln: University of Nebraska Press, 2015.

Santur, Hassan Ghedi. *Something Remains*. Toronto: Dundurn Press, 2010.

Waberi, Abdourahman A. *Passage of Tears*. Translated by David Ball and Nicole Ball. Kolkata: Seagull Books, 2018.

————. *Transit*. Translated by David Ball and Nicole Ball. Bloomington: Indiana University Press, 2012.

————. *In the United States of Africa*. Translated by David Ball and Nicole Ball. Lincoln: University of Nebraska Press, 2009.

————. *Harvest of Skulls*. Translated by Dominic Thomas. Bloomington: Indiana University Press, 2017.

NONFICTION AND JOURNALS

Ahmed, Ali Jimale. *The Invention of Somalia*. Trenton, NJ: Red Sea Press, 1995.

Bildhaan: An International Journal of Somali Studies. Saint Paul, MN: Macalester College.

POETRY

Ahmed, Ali Jimale. *Diaspora Blues*. Trenton, NJ: Red Sea Press, 2005.

Ahmed, Ali Jimale. *Fear Is a Cow*. Trenton, NJ: Red Sea Press, 2002.

Shire, Warsan. *Bless the Daughter Raised by a Voice in Her Head*. London: Random House, 2022.

————. *Her Blue Body*. Manchester, UK: Flipped Eye Publishing, 2015.

IN SOMALI LANGUAGE

Afrax, Maxamed Daahir

Axmed, Ibraahin Yuusuf "Hawd"

Cige, Cabdillaahi Cawed

Hadrawi

Xasan, Maxamed Baashe Xaaji. *Afka Hooyo Waa Hodan*. Somalia: Garanuug Limited, 2020.